Praise for Recognize Fascism

"These are voices we need to be hearing now, a powerful chapter in the F&SF tradition of speculative resistance, 'realists of a larger reality' as LeGuin put it, whose word-art nurtures freedom and the seeds of change."

—Ada Palmer, Astounding Award winner
and Hugo Award finalist

"'Fascist' is so often an epithet that we sometimes forget that it is also a descriptor, a label that can and must be accurately applied if we are to avoid reliving history's greatest horrors. *Recognize Fascism* isn't just a collection of fiction: it's training data for knowing when it's time to take to the streets."

—Cory Doctorow, award-winning author of
Little Brother and *Radicalized*

"These stories are passionate, heartbreaking, and important. Also, occasionally very funny!"

—Naomi Kritzer, award-winning author of
Catfishing on CatNet

"[T]his timely anthology… will no doubt resonate with politically minded readers."

—Publishers Weekly

RECOGNIZE FASCISM

A SCIENCE FICTION AND FANTASY ANTHOLOGY

Edited by Crystal M. Huff

World Weaver Press

RECOGNIZE FASCISM

"Introduction" Copyright © 2020 by Crystal M. Huff
"A Disease of Time and Temporal Distortion" Copyright © 2020 by Jennifer Shelby
"The Scale of Defiance" Copyright © 2020 by Nina Niskanen
"May Your Government Be the Center of a Smelly Dung Sandwich" Copyright © 2020 by
Justin Short
"The Company Store" Copyright © 2020 by Kiya Nicoll
"Scholar Miaka's Brief Summary of Memories Imbued in Memory Object Exhibit Item
132.NW.1" Copyright © 2020 by Jaymee Goh
"Just an Old Grouch" Copyright © 2020 by Laura Jane Swanson
"A Brilliant Light, An Unreachable Dawn" Copyright © 2020 by Phoebe Barton
"Octobers/October" Copyright © 2020 by Leonardo Espinoza Benavides
"That Time I Got Demon Doxxed While Smuggling Contraband to the Red States"
Copyright © 2020 by Luna Corbden
"Go Dancing to Your Gods" Copyright © 2020 by Blake Jessop
"Brooklyn" Copyright © 2020 by Jonathan Shipley
"Sacred Chords" Copyright © 2020 by Alexei Collier
"The Three Magi" Copyright © 2020 by Lucie Lukačovičová
"The Body Politic" Copyright © 2020 by Octavia Cade
"In Her Eye's Mind" Copyright © 2020 by Selene dePackh
"What Eyes Can See" Copyright © 2020 by Lauren Ring
"We All Know the Melody" Copyright © 2020 by Brandon O'Brien
"Chicken Time" Copyright © 2020 by Hal Y. Zhang
"Notes on the Supply of Raw Material in the Bodies Market" Copyright © 2020 by Rodrigo
Juri
"The Sisterhood of the Eagle Lion" Copyright © 2020 by Sam J. Miller
"The Turnip Golem" Copyright © 2020 by Dianne M. Williams
"Today is the First Day of the Rest of Your Life" Copyright © 2020 by Meridel Newton

Published by World Weaver Press, LLC
Albuquerque, NM
www.WorldWeaverPress.com

Cover Artwork by Geneva Bowers.

*

First edition: October 2020
ISBN-13: 978-1-7340545-0-7

Also available as an ebook

RECOGNIZE FASCISM

CONTENTS

ACKNOWLEDGMENTS

This book was conceived in friendships, born via a shift in publisher (with many thanks to all parties involved!), raised in the midst of Black Lives Matter protests, and will hopefully reach you with all the growth and possibilities we've managed to invoke on these pages.

I owe many thanks, but the height of gratitude goes out to Ken Liu, Esther Wakefield, Suzanne Palmer, Kay Holt, Sarena Ulibarri, and of course, my sweetheart, Steve Huff.

INTRODUCTION

Crystal M. Huff

After co-editing *Resist Fascism* in 2018 with Kay Holt and Bart Leib at Crossed Genres, we decided to embark upon this follow-up anthology, *Recognize Fascism*, last year. Working on this second book, I've frequently struggled with Impostor Syndrome (essentially, a persistent feeling of fraudulence, despite evidence to the contrary), but particularly so when Crossed Genres closed and I became the sole editor of the project. Could I truly manage this by myself? In my other professional life, I facilitate trainings to combat Impostor Syndrome; struggling like this while working on the book seemed like my worlds were colliding in a particularly ironic fashion.

It's not only that this is my first solo editing project to be published, not only that I started this book with very different expectations of how the project would go, not only that I suddenly found myself needing a new publisher in the middle of the effort. It's also that I have doubts about my knowledge of politics and history. When faced with fascism, can I recognize it? Do I know enough about politics to thoroughly engage with the theme of *Recognize Fascism* at a high level? Do I know what I'm doing, in essence?

One of the things that fascism does, however, is exactly this.

1

Fascists foster uncertainty in order to undermine the ground you stand on when you declare, "This is fascist." It's akin to developing a political Impostor Syndrome, until you are second-guessing yourself at each turn. Fascism evades and evolves, such that you can't exactly pinpoint it. It is a moving target. It gaslights. If you are unclear about what it is and can't put your finger on it, pushing back against it is so much more difficult! Fascists then weaponize this confusion to secure your acquiescence.

To be quite frank, I feel that *Recognize Fascism* is published during an even more urgent political moment than when it was conceived, a mere eighteen months ago. It almost makes sense that the development of this book therefore included particular challenges— the gap between reality and speculative fiction situations narrowed dramatically in this time!

For example, Leonardo Espinoza Benavides' story, "Octobers/October," includes the use (and subsequent ban) of bandanas while protesting. In October of 2019, during a high point of citizen protests against the Chilean government in Santiago, there was a period when bandanas were common in order to protect from tear gas exposure. Next, the government restricted bandana and mask usage, in order to improve facial recognition. Facial covering became a political point of contention in Chile, with far-left and far-right groups labeling the other side as fascist. Leo's story in this book deviates from the real world in several obvious ways, but mask-wearing rhetoric is one place where reality shifted more and more toward the fiction already written. It shouldn't surprise me that mask-wearing has become a global point of political contention, and yet. It does.

Laura Jane Swanson's story, "Just An Old Grouch," was originally set in a different Midwest-sounding location, intended to be the name of a generic town. When that town was suddenly in the news due to a high-profile sexual assault, we decided to change it. One goal in the story is to highlight the effects of gaslighting and manipulation (including the effects on survivors of sexual harassment), but the intent is to do so without unduly triggering readers who may have experienced sexual assault or sexual harassment, themselves. We worried that the original town's name would have an enduring painful association for readers who are survivors.

Capitalism in Luna Corbden's "That Time I Got Demon Doxxed While Smuggling Contraband to the Red States" is something we talked about a fair bit, prior to publication. Capitalism and fascism have had a complex interaction, historically speaking, but it's a relationship that has only increased in convolution during the modern era. Suffice to say, I learned a lot from my conversations with the author about some corporate activities I hadn't seen on my news feed. With so many companies enabling fascism on an international scale, it's hard to even evaluate which are the worst offenders in the corporate world.

For all that it is a farcical piece, global events with regard to online censorship have run uncomfortably close to some aspects of "Chicken Time" by Hal Y. Zhang. I had some enlightening discussions with the author and with my spouse about how technology can be used to suppress text messages. Initial censorship of messages would likely be achieved via "Mechanical Turk" (data analysis by humans in order to be deployed on a large scale by computers). It might take thousands of person-hours of effort to be able to train a computer program for censorship at scale, using keywords, but this is well within the capacity of any nation. The idea of this process being utilized in China to censor references to President Xi and Winnie the Pooh is simultaneously sobering and... well, sobering.

While editing "The Company Store" by Kiya Nicoll, the author and I made the editorial choice to capitalize Black and not capitalize white when referring to race. This is something I've been doing in my own writing for some time; Black people, Black voices, and Black culture could benefit from more focus and attention paid to them, to put it mildly. This choice also happens to have been ratified by the recently-published guidelines of the Associated Press. It's my hope that more organizations will follow suit. Race wasn't the focus of Kiya's story, but the systemic oppression inherent in all-white corporate leadership is important to address in examining fascism.

Several authors included phrases in their story in a language other than English, which I particularly encouraged for stories in translation. We chose not to italicize non-English words unless the italics were used for emphasis, in an attempt not to exoticize the languages. (Many thanks to Daniel José Older for his activism on this topic.) There is nuance to this issue, however—if we had a story translated from Chinese, Korean, or Japanese, for example, we might have made a different decision. Those languages aren't natively written in the Roman alphabet, so to present the words in italics can be a refusal to normalize colonization. (Thanks be to Ken Liu for educating me on this aspect of translation.)

All of the above is also to say: The authors and I have grappled with each piece in this book, in one way or another. You might also struggle with reading them, and I want you to know, that's part of the point.

In the hope it's helpful to readers, each of the stories in this book includes one or more content notes at the beginning. By doing this, we offer those with traumatic experiences the option to emotionally prepare for what's ahead, or to decide not to read a story. We know this may mean some stories are not seen by all who read this book. Our first priority, however, is an attempt to do no harm.

Content notes can be considered a broader schema than trigger warnings. They serve as warnings for topics, it's true, but not only topics that trigger distress. A reader trying to remain sober may wish to avoid stories that mention alcohol, for example, but that may not distress them so much as impact their resolve. Out of caution, for this reason, we have attempted to include a content note even if a topic is only briefly touched upon within a story.

The content notes used in this anthology are as follows:

- Ableism
- Ageism
- Alcohol
- Anxiety
- Body Dysphoria
- Body Horror
- Bullying
- Child Grooming
- Death of Child
- Death
- Dissociation
- Drugs
- Gore
- Guns
- Homelessness
- Homophobia
- Illness
- Indentured Servitude
- Manipulation
- Pedophilia
- Physical Assault
- Police
- Prison
- Racism
- Sexism
- Slavery
- Suicide
- Terrorism
- Transphobia
- Violence
- War
- Weapons
- Xenophobia

We replicate this list here, as well as include the applicable content note(s) at the top of each story, in order to make the information more easily accessible for those who need it. Hopefully, through this list, a reader will also be able to tell if their particular concern is annotated. If you are someone who prefers to be prepared for any of the above topics, I hope these content notes are helpful. If you are concerned with a topic that is not in the list above, please do feel empowered to contact me, and I will do my best to answer any questions.

೫

I don't know what will happen once we send this book out into the world. I have angsted over this introduction for the past few months, if I'm being honest with you, while watching the planet light itself on fire. In that time, we have raised enough money not only to publish this book and bring it to you, but to send copies of *Recognize Fascism* to each sitting member of the US Congress, the Supreme Court, and leaders of government where several of the authors live. While I'm proud of that fundraising accomplishment, it has also brought on a major flare-up of Impostor Syndrome.

As when dealing with my Impostor Syndrome on other topics, I try to bolster my confidence with what I know is possible. Fiction can, and has, changed the shape and outlook of the world. The fact that 894 people supported the initial crowdfunding campaign to make *Recognize Fascism* into a reality gives me courage. It's my hope that each reader is ready to examine fascism on a global and local level.

Once you recognize fascism, what do you feel able to do about it?

A DISEASE OF TIME AND TEMPORAL DISTORTION

Jennifer Shelby

Content Notes: Ableism, Death, Guns, Manipulation, Sexism, Violence

Red moon dust swirled in the soft lunar winds of the market where Revekah kept a tent. Timelines flashed by, dulling her sense of place. They'd calm soon. Time disease wrought its best havoc in the early morning, her defenses dulled from dreaming.

She opened the flaps, and the red tent where she practised her trade filled with shadows to match the moon Kiturnia. The red reminded Revekah of old passions, while the dim light and heavy shadow served to hide her illness. Inside her tent sat a table covered with scarlet cloth, and in its center, a ball of crystal glimmered in the gloom.

Revekah chanced upon this timeline early in her career. Temporal smuggling was good money and better adventure, but the life also created armies of enemies and false friends playing allies. This timeline, Revekah had set aside as sacrosanct. When her enemies outnumbered her friends, she hid her family here. They never forgave her for it, but they flourished, hidden and safe. She checked on them from time to time, always from a distance, respecting their wish to never see her again. It gave her comfort to spend her final years in the same timeline as the grandchildren she'd never meet, on a moon in orbit around the planet Jiterra, which they called home.

Revekah took up fortune-telling when she retired from smuggling. There was decent coin to be made and the diaphanous costumes suited her, flowing from her aged body like the timelines she once explored. Her temporal twitches, common to her advanced stage time disease, added to the mystery of the fortunes she told.

The flaps of her tent slapped in the wind as she pulled them back, nodding to her fellow vendors. There were two other fortune tellers in the markets: an Andromedan to her left who told fortunes with cards and runes; a dark, hooded Kiturnian monk across from her who read palms; and Revekah, a human who employed a crystal ball to divert her patron's attention from the temporal travel device embedded in her palm. She smoothed the purple satin gloves she wore to conceal the device, sensing a twitch coming on. It began as a ringing in her ears, followed by a muffling sensation in her auditory canals, and then a quick twitch to the past or future.

A screen flickered to life near the ceiling of Kiturnia's shuttle station. She knew the place well, though it was difficult to tell what year she'd traveled to.

A young male smiled out from the screen—handsome by Kiturnian standards, skin of deepest red, a human physique, and black hair coiffed into a tall pompadour. "We need to stop Enhancing natural life," the man explained to his interviewer. His name appeared in a blue strip overlaid beneath the collar of his expensive shirt: Colonel Edtrist Chitin.

"But surely you agree that these medical Enhancements are saving lives," the unnamed interviewer said.

"Are they? For how long? By meshing technology with organic life, we are creating hybrid cyborgs capable of surpassing an organic being's abilities—but ultimately, they are machines. Programmable, *corruptible*. What's to keep our enemies from hacking into these cyborgs and turning them against us? We need to focus our military forces inward, not outward!"

An approving murmur passed through the crowds waiting at the terminal. Revekah's body tingled with horror. Why were they agreeing with that nonsense?

A mother standing near Revekah pulled her child close, quickly hiding the child's Enhanced arm inside the sleeve of an overlarge coat. The mother's eyes were frightened, her body language growing as twitchy and jagged as Revekah's.

"We need to put aside our differences as species and focus on the real threat: the technological invasion of organic life," the Colonel spewed on.

Revekah clenched her fists. She knew fascism when she saw it.

The camera switched to a shocked reporter with ocular Enhancements sitting at her desk in the newsroom. "And there you have Colonel Chitin's most recent press conference."

An un-Enhanced reporter turned to the first. "How do you feel about Chitin's bid for Solar System Leadership, as someone with Enhancements, Samara?"

Revekah twitched again; an anchor fitted into her temporal device returned her to her tent. Without the anchor she could never be certain what timeline she twitched to, lost in the maze of her Temporal Distortion. Pulling an old-fashioned pencil and notebook from her pocket, she made quick notes of the details she'd witnessed. Her fingers trembled with fury as she laid out a familiar set of temporal equations to estimate how far into the future she'd twitched. Five solar years, plus or minus one.

She set the pencil down by her crystal ball, quivering with rage. This timeline was supposed to be peaceful. Instead, she'd dropped her family off in a pre-fascist generation about to make war against medical Enhancements. Dark dread pooling in her gut predicted that the Colonel would win his election bid.

Her original research into this timeline had taken her fifty years ahead. Any more than that and the calculations grew risky, percentages of likelihood unstable and unreliable. That research was forty-some years ago, now.

The tent fluttered as a young Kiturnian tri-gender sat down at her table.

"Fortunes told for five credits," Revekah told them.

The patron nodded and transferred the credits. A giddy energy rolled off of their shoulders and shivered against the canvas walls. "I'm Estay. I'm mating with my boyfriend solmorrow. Can you tell me if our union will be a fulfilling one?"

Revekah nodded and whirled her hands in a practised show of grace over her crystal ball. A twitch caught her, negating the need for Revekah to use her temporal device.

Estay, dressed in the military grey of Kiturnia, stood at the top of a tall, sleek structure. Chitin's image, older now, smiled down from projections onto low hanging clouds. At the bottom of the stairs lay a male Kiturnian, his Enhanced leg sparking as blood pooled around fried circuits. With a disgusted sneer, Estay tossed their mating band down atop the lifeless body.

Revekah twitched back to her tent, staring again into her patron's eager eyes. Revekah shook her head. "This union will only bring despair and death."

Estay's expression fell, the giddy joy bleeding from their energy. "Are you sure?"

"I am certain. He is not your true mate."

Tears poured from Estay's eyes as they stumbled to rise from their seat and run from the tent.

Revekah willed herself calm. A lifetime of temporal travel made her wary of coincidences. Her twitches were coming in clusters, a sign of her fast-approaching end. Time, for once, was not on her side. Every temporal leap, twitch or not, exacerbated the disease to which she'd watched too many friends fall prey.

The memories pulled her into another twitch, this time into her past. Safeguards built into her temporal device protected the universe from paradox, automatically slipping Revekah inside her former self when the timelines crossed.

In this moment, Hal, her old smuggling partner, sat across from her, dying in his ship. Time disease only affected illegal temporal Travelers, so those suffering from the disease monitored and recorded their condition outside of traditional medical circles. In the end, each Traveler made their own study of the disease, sharing what they gleaned with each other when they could.

"We have the coordinates. I could take the ship and meet you there, try to rescue you," she told him.

Hal shook his head. "It's too risky, too dangerous, and I'll just twitch back again a moment later. I'm tired, Rev. Let me go."

She nodded, wanting nothing more than to hold his hand but knowing it was too dangerous. His heart beat arrhythmically; the medical monitor beeped its warning. This was how time disease signaled one final twitch. Another heartbeat, and Hal would twitch back to the dawn of time and meet his end.

A handful of temporal Travelers had journeyed there to save their friends, finding countless frozen corpses floating in space as the first stars kindled. There was a brief moment to search before the force of the Big Bang sent the searchers spiraling home again, shot through time and space with a force too great for mortal flesh. The scant few who survived the trip gasped terrible warnings before succumbing to their wounds.

Hal twitched, once, twice, before his body disappeared forever. Revekah sighed; another good Traveler gone. Working in pairs, Travelers rarely died young, for their partners could just go back and rescue them. Thus, too, they seldom got caught in their highly illegal profession. Time had one kind of rigidity, the past as well as the future: temporal Travelers could only affect timelines outside of their own. Timelines they had no business messing with, according to galactic policing agencies.

Eventually time disease caught up with them, a long term effect of temporal distortion on the brain. Hal had called it "a deterioration of our temporal existence." In a moment of philosophy or poetry, he expounded, "That's why we end up at the beginning of time. I think it will be beautiful to see it all begin. Don't you?"

Revekah wasn't so sure, but everyone had to die of something. These sols, she wondered if she'd see Hal again before exposure to deep space killed her. She hoped so.

She twitched back to the tent, her heart beating fast. A young human male sat across from her. He looked like an asset she'd had on a job once, Paul Stark. It bothered her that she didn't remember him coming into the tent and sitting across from her.

"Fortunes told for five credits."

His brow creased. "I just paid you?"

She ignored the slip and carried on. "How can I help you?"

"My grandmother read my tea leaves once when I was a child. She said my future was dark. It's always bothered me. Can you tell me more?"

Revekah's fingers danced along her crystal ball. No convenient twitching this time. She pressed the button of her temporal device, her will steering its direction. Soon she sat behind the grimy window of a second story, looking down upon an alley. Not-Paul was there, some seven years older, with three others. Their faces were twisted with menace, kicking a male Kiturnian with a neural Enhancer as he curled up on the cobbles. Not-Paul's boot connected with the man's Enhancements. The man's eyes rolled back as a blue bolt of an electric arc zapped through his tech. A cheer rose up from the men; tendrils of black smoke coiled from their victim's brain. Not-Paul high-fived his cohorts and they ran off, a soft trail of blood dribbling from their shoes.

The horror twitched her back to face the man's younger self.

"Well?" he asked, eager. "I'm not a bad person, am I? I mean, I try not to be. I certainly don't want to be a bad person, but my Gran…

she never looked at me the same after those tea leaves. She saw something bad."

Revekah nodded. She had options and experience, she could fight this. It would be exhausting, but such work was worth it.

"You will protect the weak and the innocent."

She hardly said the words before she pressed her temporal device again, checking to see if her words had any impact. She watched him kill the Enhanced man a second time before carefully returning to her tent in the moment before she'd spoken.

Time for a different tactic. Maybe something less abstract, more literal, would work better. "Someone with Enhancements will save the lives of your children from a terrible death. Perhaps this is the darkness your grandmother spoke of."

Revekah flashed forward to check her work. Instead of the alley, she stood in an unfamiliar market, watching Not-Paul push a stroller, a happy expression on his face. It worked. She could do this.

When she returned, Not-Paul smiled at her, joy glowing through his skin. "Thank you. That means so much to me." He tipped her an extra credit and left.

Revekah tapped the credit with her index finger. She was old and tired, but she had fight left in her yet. Her notebook and pencil found their way to the table again as she listed off options for what she could do to change the future. Killing the Colonel, of course, though Revekah didn't consider herself a murderer or assassin. Could she suggest to Chitin that someone Enhanced saves his children, too?

"Knock, knock," said a smug, familiar voice at the door of her tent.

Her breath stilled as she recognized Colonel Chitin. No, not Colonel, too young yet, but Chitin the same. Coincidences like this did not happen. Their timelines were crossing by design of another temporal Traveler, she was sure of it. She knew the patterns.

"Fortunes told for five credits," she squawked, her voice unruly.

He sent her a disarming smile topped by calculating eyes and sat down across from her. Did she imagine the light dimming as he entered? "Madame fortune teller, can you believe this is the second time I've had my fortune told today?" His smile did not falter.

Revekah's skin grew cold. "What answers do you seek? I will tell you all you need to know for five credits."

"Oh, I've no intention of paying you. That's not why I'm here." He stood again, black hair falling onto his brow in a way his admirers must have adored, and gestured across the market to the hooded palm reader's tent.

Revekah followed his gesture, meeting the Monk's eyes. He bowed to her and held up his left hand. The familiar black bulk a temporal device flashed from his palm. She'd long wondered if the Monk was a Traveler like her. But why had he sent the monster to her tent?

"The Monk has read my palm. I have great aspirations for the future of this solar system, you see."

As did Revekah.

"It would seem as though you, despite being a diseased old woman, stand in the way of these goals." He laughed through his nose and cracked his knuckles, staring into Revekah's eyes.

She held his gaze, reading the thrill it gave him to threaten an old woman, the joy and rush of power to manipulate another person, how it must turn him on to gaslight anyone and everyone. Today was becoming one hell of a day.

Chitin pulled a blaster from his belt, leveling it over the table at her sternum.

Revekah shrugged. "You can go ahead and try."

Chitin's brow furrowed briefly before he recovered himself and fired.

Nothing happened.

"Lost its charge, did it? Funny thing, that. If I'm actually meant to affect your future, you can't alter it by killing me now. Sorry, kid, your future's locked in."

Chitin's face reddened with fury. "What are you talking about?"

"Basic time laws. You can't alter your own timeline. Now, if you smuggled me into another timeline, you'd have a chance. Do you happen to have a temporal device on you? No? I thought not. Murder's easy enough to cover up, but getting caught with an illegal device, that could ruin your political aspirations, couldn't it?"

His lip pulled into a sneer. "How do you know about that?"

"What's your problem with Enhanced people, anyway? Oh yes, I've seen your future. I've seen what you do. The lives you ruin."

His sneer smoothed into a placid peace. "So I do succeed."

"Oh, yes, your fascist regime comes to pass. Congratulations, you're Hitler the fifth. Or whichever. Your names aren't worth remembering."

Chitin laid his blaster on the table and leaned back in his chair, smugness oozing from his pores like the slime of a Kiturnian moon snail. "My mother lost her accounting job to a Ferf with a neural Enhancement which made it an organic supercomputer. It was just her and us, a brood of nine. She couldn't find another position or compete in her field anymore. Fed us kids with charity credits and shame. It wasn't right. Galactic law decreed machines couldn't replace natural life without the creation of new positions for the displaced naturals. So machines infiltrated natural life instead. Becoming part of us to take what they were denied."

"You think the machines acted with intent? That's a wild conspiracy. Enhancements are saving lives! Neural Enhancements repair traumatic brain injuries, replace lost limbs and malfunctioning organs. They're miracles for those who need them."

Chitin slammed his fist on the table. "Of course I see that. It's what makes their plan so insidious, they come to us promising they'll save us, save our children. With positions in every sector of government and industry, they're perfectly poised for the uprising."

"Who is this 'they' you're talking about?"

"Inorganic tech. Meshing with our brains, they've gained sentience. Their consciousness has been awakened."

Nothing of Chitin's theory reflected reality, not in any of the thousands of timelines Revekah knew. "And your mother?"

"She martyred herself after doctors forced an Enhanced heart upon her. No way was she willing to be a pawn in their bid for control of the universe."

Revekah nodded. Of course. Villains never thought themselves evil, did they?

"What are you doing here, this late in your life? You should have it easy now, not be stuck out here peddling futures. You're a pure, organic life form—you deserve better!" His smile could charm a Vastolian venom hawk from its nest.

Revekah exhaled slowly, stealing herself against him. "That's a tricky poison you're selling, Chitin, but I've seen enough of this old universe to blame no one but myself for where I've ended up."

"Join me." He leaned over the table, eyes glistening. "You can tell me which of my followers are faithful to the cause, point me toward the quickest route to our salvation. I will make you powerful!"

"Time laws, remember?" Revekah shook her head, uncomfortable with even the breath of hesitation she felt from one moment to the next. "I've already betrayed you."

He shrugged. "Keep your enemies close. You've already told me I succeed." He clasped his hands behind his head. "It's liberating, to know you'll succeed before you begin. I think I'll accelerate my plans. Start recruitment."

Revekah felt the twitch coming and braced herself. A moment later she stood in the center of a massive rally. Thousands of people cheered around her as Chitin, twenty years older, spat into a microphone. "Last week a known Enhanced gave birth to a litter of robots! Fortunately, the nurse was faithful to our cause—a hero! He reported the illegal medical assistance given to the woman at her birth and we wiped out the infestation before they could destroy our city. We have closed this medical clinic for good. Let this be a lesson to the foolish doctors who refuse loyalty to pure, organic life! Helping the Enhanced is treason! Unnatural! From today on, anyone caught offering medical help to the Enhanced will be charged with treason and sentenced to death."

The crowd cheered with a dark, feverish energy which vibrated through the stands and snarled at Revekah's feet.

Chitin raised his hand to silence the crowd, and soldiers marched out a terrified Andromedan. They could be anyone, though Revekah supposed they must be a doctor. Another gesture of Chitin's hand, and his soldiers aimed blasters at the Andromedan.

She closed her eyes to what came next. Were her grandchildren somewhere in the stands? Were there any good people left who hadn't succumbed to Chitin's twisted logic? What happened to Not-Paul and his baby—were they safe?

The button for her temporal device burned in her palm. Her heart beat a strange rhythm. She tried to breathe normally, Hal's face flashing through her mind. Increasingly close twitches, followed by arrhythmic palpitations: the final signs of time disease. Oh no, not now. She needed more time to save her family's timeline from this monster.

Revekah lifted her head and focussed on Chitin and his stage, a plan developing in her mind. She hadn't been a smuggler all her life for nothing. A smile flirted on her lips as she pressed her temporal device, willing herself back to her tent to face young Chitin.

"I think I'll start recruiting in high schools," he was saying, too caught up in his plans to have noticed her twitch.

"No," said Revekah, reaching over the table to take his hand.

He sneered, gripping her hand painfully tight. He intended to break her fingers, Revekah supposed. Have at it, son. She didn't need them anymore. Her vision blurred, blood pumping too fast through her erratic heart.

"You can't stop me." Chitin guffawed, snapping the bones of her left index finger. The pain didn't make it far beyond the pressure on her chest. "It's already happened. You can't stop it."

Revekah laughed, a wild, free thing that escaped from her lungs and filled the tent. Death was here; she could feel it in the signal of one final twitch. "Do you recall what I said? I'm not from this timeline, fool. I can change everything." She grabbed his other hand as the world swirled around them and unravelled back to the beginning of time.

Chitin's expression turned to shock at his sudden exposure to outer space. Revekah exhaled, pushing him away, unwilling to die holding hands with a monster.

Her gaze met Hal's, their years apart meaningless. Hal blinked once, a small smile lurking on his freezing face, as everything exploded and the universe began anew.

***

Jennifer Shelby hunts for stories in the beetled undergrowth of fairy-infested forests. She fishes for them in the dark space between the stars. This story, and many others, are a part of her ongoing catch-and-release program. If you'd like to learn more, you can visit her website at jennifershelby.blog or on twitter @jenniferdshelby

THE SCALE OF DEFIANCE

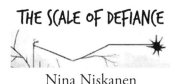

Nina Niskanen

Content Notes: *Anxiety, Racism*

In the city of Väinölä, as a result of an almost-forgotten spell gone wrong, the citizens become smaller and larger according to their mood. Leena sat on the subway, barely 15 hands high, trying to keep the teenagers kissing each other next to her from completely invading her space. She would not go any smaller, partly because she did not want to force that on herself, but also because she had once before tried to be doll-sized on the subway, and that had been enough for her to last the remainder of her life. Instead, she pressed herself into the wall. The teens brought to mind the first, tentative time she held the hand of the woman she would later marry. These teenagers seemed to expand to fill all available space, which matched her own memories. She did not want to take away from their happiness by making them stop.

Her size fell just slightly from the regret of never having been so open, and the dark-haired, dark-eyed boy turned to her with a sheepish grin.

"Sorry," he said, the Northern accent burrowing into his words.

His shaggy black hair fell in strands around and over his face, and his smile was exactly the kind to melt a thousand hearts. Both he and the girl wore the latest fashion of a long shirt that reached their hips, coupled with loose trousers whose waist strings got lost in the mess of other strings decorating the waistline.

Leena shook her head to let him know that it was all right. She still felt like she didn't matter, but at least he had made the effort. His girlfriend leaned her head against his shoulder, her red hair tumbling down his back, and the two of them entwined their hands and talked in low voices, still larger than they'd been when they boarded the subway. Leena turned her head away with a grin. Even if they were inconvenient, even if it rarely lasted for long, there was something beautiful about young love.

Leena's gaze fell on a group of men making their way through the car. They wore slightly loose, tailored suits. That hubris rankled.

"Vote for Uusi Väinölä in two weeks," one shouted.

Leena's balance faltered as the teenager behind her suddenly became much smaller. She turned to see what happened before it clicked. The boy was a Northerner; he was not only instantly recognizable as such, but also clearly dating a Väinölän girl. The Uusi Väinölä supporters making their way through the car would not only note him, they would probably say something nasty to him.

Leena began to realize that several other people had gotten smaller as the men approached. They kept calling out vague encouragements to vote for their party, come the election. Really, though, they were doing the stunt to intimidate people. They were large men, well dressed, as if to remind everyone watching that they had nice things and people to back them up. They'd be removed if they tried to intimidate people around the polling places, but here, they could assert their positions. They were making things harder for people like Leena and the two teenagers beside her just to exist, and they thought this made the world better.

Leena made herself larger. The effort of it gave her a headache, like straining to hold her head up high for a long time. Everything within her wanted to be smaller, become closer to invisible, but she forced herself larger until she was the baseline size of a full-grown man. Her clothes, loose though they were a moment before, strained at the seams. The teenagers almost hid behind her as she took up the space she so badly wanted to relinquish.

The men stumping for the Uusi Väinölä party passed the three of them without incident, and for a few seconds Leena felt like she had done a good thing. Then she noticed that a few people would not meet her eyes. A number of them must have thought that she got bigger because the message of Uusi Väinölä made her feel good about herself. With that sobering thought, Leena shrunk.

The subway stopped, people got off and people got on, but Leena and the teenagers stayed small. Most of the others who had gone smaller, grew back into their usual size by the time the second stop had passed. Leena could not make herself become taller again. The world felt larger and scarier just for the Uusi Väinölä people having passed by. The teens had withdrawn into themselves as well, still affectionate with each other, but less effusively so. Neither of them acknowledged Leena in any way, which made Leena think that they may have also wondered if she was one of the Uusi Väinölä people. They didn't shy away from her, either, which gave her the smallest measure of comfort. They didn't know for certain. She wanted to stand up and scream, "They hate me, too!" This, too, disgusted Leena. It was as if she needed to define herself with hate, just as much as the Uusi Väinölä people did.

Leena shook her head and sat back in her seat. There was nothing to be done right then but to endure.

Her stop arrived. Leena got off and headed up the escalator. The long tunnel led ever upward, as if anyone coming out of the subway was rising up from the underworld, through the world and up into the home of the birds. Leena draped her forearm over the escalator handrail, even if she was no longer quite tall enough to lean on that arm. At least her fingers still reached around the handrail.

"Together we can face the storm." The coloring and imagery on the poster before her harkened back to the glorious past of Väinölä. The image itself was the heroic stance of Väinölä's men facing a Northern army, with Louhi at the head. It felt like a slap. As she looked ahead, Leena realized that all the ad spots in the tunnel had been sold to Uusi Väinölä. They must have been put up while she was at work, because they hadn't been there in the morning.

The next one held an even worse message: "Let's take Väinölä back for the people of sense." Leena scoffed and turned her eyes away from the wall before she got any smaller. It was another hateful phrase. A year ago, a public bigot started catching significant heat for his authoritarian leanings. The President had used this phrase in a speech, asking, "Why can't we all just get along?" "People of sense" meant the majority, the people who were neither open bigots nor the people bigots targeted. It hadn't been meant as a defense of bigots, but it sure felt like one.

Leena rolled her sleeves up to accommodate her shortened arms, and focused on her fellow travelers instead.

A middle-aged woman with a child hanging on each arm, stared at the same ads. She smiled and got bigger by just a little. The kids hanging onto her arms protested, and she made herself smaller again. Leena wished not to intrude further.

Two men coming down the escalator averted their gaze from the signs and shrunk slightly. Leena glanced back on the ad they had viewed, a morbid sense of curiosity driving her. "Help the people of Väinölä RISE." Raisa would have wanted her to stop, but Leena couldn't. They wanted to make Leena's own marriage null and void, turn her and Raisa into nothing but roommates.

It seemed almost as if no one was allowed to criticize them. The so-called people of sense kept calling anyone who challenged Uusi Väinölä "just as bad" as the worst representatives of that party. Unreasonable, for not wanting to debate their own right to existence.

Leena startled, noticing that she was approaching the top. The walls of the escalator seemed so much taller than they had a moment ago. She needed to get off. She grabbed fistfuls of her tunic's hem to jump onto stable ground.

Leena hobbled to the side, and for a moment she just watched the people hurry past her to the outside or down the escalators. Awkwardly, Leena realized that the people were avoiding looking at her. Leena didn't want to feel embarrassed about her emotions clearly showing on her body, but the fact that the people around her were embarrassed made her feel as if she should. She ducked her face into her collar as she moved out of the station and started walking toward home.

&

Leena walked into the foyer of her condo building with the feeling that she was getting smaller with each step. She had become the natural size of a four-year-old. She stared at the mountain of stairs ahead, sighing. Slipping her shoes off to carry by hand, Leena began to climb. She barely had breath to feel sorry for herself.

At the top of the third flight of stairs, Leena simply lay down on the floor, trying to make her heart stay in her body. Finally, she stood and reached up to get her key into the lock so that she could get the door open. The effort of stretching herself to work the lock helped her gain height through the sheer force of the little successes that came along the way.

When Leena finally got both the outer and inner doors open and then closed behind her, she simply leaned against the inner door, breathing in the scent of home. She smelled something baking. The scent of Raisa and her handiwork mixed into a beautiful aroma that could be nothing but comforting. Leena sat on the floor with her back against the inner door and watched her legs get gradually longer against the striped carpet.

"What are you doing, mesimarjaseni, sitting there?" Raisa's voice was amused, but also tinged with concern.

How could Leena tell her everything that had happened since she left work? The coworker waiting at the gate, pressing his own Uusi Väinölä candidate flyers into the hands of everyone coming off shift? The other colleagues who high-fived or cheered him on? That no one seemed to find anything objectionable about any of it? Even mentally reviewing it all felt so terrible that she wanted to keep getting smaller until she could live in a shoe and periodically steal some of the bread that Raisa made. Leena could become her own, personal home elf, providing good luck to the household.

Eventually, inevitably, Raisa would move on and come to live with someone else, come to love someone else.

"'S nothing. Let me just sit here for a bit, okay?"

Leena closed her eyes and leaned her head back against the inner door. Now she was taking out her own inadequacy and helplessness on someone she loved and cherished.

Raisa slid down the wall, landing to sit so that her thigh pushed against the soles of Leena's feet. The scratchy sound of her clothes against the wall was the only thing Leena heard for a moment.

"I told you, I just want to sit here," Leena muttered, eyes still firmly shut.

"I know," Raisa said, her voice the maddening calm that she sometimes got while waiting for the storm system of Leena's emotions to pass. "It looked fun, so I'm going to sit over here for a moment."

The first tear fell down Leena's cheek. She didn't deserve to have this woman in her life and yet, somehow, Raisa stubbornly remained there despite Leena's many failings. Leena heard her move, but Raisa must have thought better about coming closer. Instead of a hug, she simply laid a hand on Leena's ankle and left it there, gently resting.

"These people! The Uusi Väinölä people! They walk around telling everyone how they want to take my life and smash it to pieces and then they just expect me to smile! And everyone else fucking sure does, so I wind up smiling with them! How dare they! I don't even

THE SCALE OF DEFIANCE

have the courage to push back against my closest coworkers to say that maybe they're not great, actually, the ways they want to change the world. And everyone's just so fucking happy all the fucking time, but I have to hide my one happiness."

After a long moment of audible quiet, Leena added, "Also, I have a run in my shawl."

"Ah."

The oven timer went off just then. Raisa squeezed her ankle before letting go and rising. The sudden lack of warmth jolted Leena out of her spiral of self-pity. She watched Raisa's back slip around the corner into the kitchen. Leena levered herself up from the floor, settled her jacket on a hanger, and followed Raisa into the small kitchenette.

"You're not going to say anything else?"

Raisa had the bread out of the oven already, and she was tapping the underside, listening. Leena had been observing Raisa do the same thing for years. She still wasn't exactly certain what Raisa was listening for. The sound seemed satisfying, though, as she kicked the oven door closed and settled the bread right side up on the cutting board. For a breath, Leena wondered if Raisa had even heard her.

"I'm not sure what you want me to say. It sounds like you've already given up hope."

Leena moved to the fridge, rolling her sleeves up again. She gathered cucumber, tomatoes, and red bell pepper, then headed to the sink. She washed vegetables and placed them on the cutting board in silence, trying to resolve Raisa's ability to hope with everything that was happening out in the world.

"Are you angry?" she asked when the second tomato was cut completely into pieces.

Raisa slid her hand over Leena's shoulder slowly, like a trainer handling a skittish animal. She eased the knife out of Leena's hand, set it down, and enveloped her in a tight hug. Leena just stood there for the space of three breaths before wrapping her arms around Raisa in turn. She lost count of how long they stood there, enveloped in the warmth and safety of each other.

Finally, Leena extracted herself from the hug. "There's nothing I can do to make the world like me any better than it does right now. The worst thing is, people talk around me like they expect me to agree with them."

"What do you do when they find out that you have a wife instead of a husband?"

Leena pictured the scene at work that would happen if anyone found out. The people in their power suits and their manicures. "I never tell them."

Raisa stared at Leena, her eyes wide, her head shaking slowly. "You can't be serious."

"We agreed."

Raisa's lips turned into a thin line. "You agreed. I can't believe you actually kept to that."

"You don't know what it's like!" Leena said. She had intended to speak in a firm tone, but what came out sounded like shouting.

Raisa threw back her head and laughed. "I don't know? I teach kindergarten, and I don't lie to my students. Do you know how many parents have told me they're applying to change schools or said they're taking their kids to private daycare each time one of them asks me about my husband?"

"Your boss will stand by your side!"

"Yeah, for now! She's retiring, did you know that? What if the next director is one of those Uusi Väinölä people? Everyone, and I do mean everyone, in that school knows that I'm queer—"

"What?" Cold water ran down Leena's spine.

"What?" Raisa stopped in the middle of her rant, looking confused.

"Everyone knows you're queer? How could you?"

Raisa took a step back as her mouth fell open. She closed it with a snap, staying quiet for several moments while Leena seethed. When Raisa finally spoke, her tone was full of danger, and she stood half a hand taller. "I'm not allowed to fucking hold your hand in public and now I'm supposed to lie to everyone in my life you haven't pre-approved? Are you serious?!"

"It affects me, too!" Leena shouted. "You can't just decide that kind of thing on your own!"

"Why not? You did! Besides, they don't know that we're together. For all they know, we're roommates."

The idea that everyone in Raisa's life already thought Leena was her roommate somehow hurt more. Leena got smaller at the thought.

"That's not what I—"

"It's bad enough that the assholes get voted in time and again, now I have to let them live in my head, rent-free? For how long?"

"Don't you think I'm tired of hiding, too?!" Leena shouted, growing by a couple of hands. The two of them together took up all the available space in the kitchen.

"Well, fine then!" Raisa said forcefully, getting smaller, coming down to Leena's eye height.

They stared at each other across the chasm that had somehow materialized between them. No words seemed enough to carry either of them across it. One of them needed to jump and trust the other would be there to catch her.

"You don't want to hide?" Leena asked, her voice quiet and full of an unspoken and unexamined something.

Leena's tone seemed to make Raisa actually stop and consider what she said next: "I'm sick to death of hiding. We're not yet in a place where they'll come and take us away in the night. I don't want to get there, either. I think if we hide ourselves away, it is that much easier to turn us into the monsters."

"They'll hurt us," Leena said. Her voice broke as she said it.

Raisa shook her head. "If things keep going like this, they'll hurt us anyway. It scares the shit out of me, but I would rather change the things about my life that I can so that I don't have to hide who I am. I want to march while it's still possible." Raisa took Leena's hand gingerly in hers. "I want to hold your hand everywhere-I-damn-well-please, just because every day I am fucking amazed that you choose to love me."

Leena looked at their entangled hands. She grew almost a hand's width. The idea of simply existing out in the open was so dangerous that it became beautiful and alluring. The world had changed so much since she'd come out. Fear of it brought her back down to size.

"I love you," Leena said.

&

"Are you sure?" Leena asked.

The two of them stood in the lobby of their apartment building, staring out the shaded windows into the world outside. Leena had to crane her neck to see over the wood panel that was normally at about chest height. At the question, Raisa visibly swallowed, not much taller than Leena.

Leena wasn't sure, herself, if she wanted Raisa to back out, here at the edge. They were sure to be witnessed. The weather was beautiful. It was exactly the kind of day that inspired families to go for a walk in the neighborhood. After spending half the year in darkness, everyone went outside to soak in the sun whenever the weather allowed it.

Raisa nodded. "Let's go."

Raisa grabbed Leena's hand, Leena interlaced her fingers with Raisa's, and they walked through the door.

The second she was outside, Leena felt more exposed than she could ever remember feeling. She had to actively fight against her will to hide. The first time she'd come out publicly, no one really cared about anyone else's love life. Seeing two girls holding hands or even kissing on the streets of Väinölä hadn't been that big a deal. How had they let it all go so wrong?

Leena pulled her shoulders back and tried to make her heart slow down from an angry whine to simply a loud and fast thumping. The world had changed so much and she'd retreated so far into herself without ever stopping to think if it was worth it. It had been easier to stop fighting, to let the world go its own course. Easier to stop holding the woman she loved by the hand when out among the general public.

Raisa chatted, her tone full of an affected nonchalance. Leena loved her all the more for noticing that Raisa had grown since they'd stepped outside, though she was clearly nervous. Leena grew by half a hand. Raisa kept talking as if she hadn't noticed, but a smile tugged at the corners of her mouth. Because Raisa loved her, she wanted to keep walking. Whatever happened, Leena wouldn't let go of Raisa's hand.

As they passed the bakery, the girl who sold them their cakes stopped to stare. Leena nodded at the girl in the way that people who barely know each other beyond a singular point of contact did. That singular point of contact wasn't much, but it made her human. It made what she had with Raisa more human. Maybe, just maybe, that would be enough to halt the tide of evil that was making its way over the country that she loved. It was a start. Whatever happened, Leena was ready to take up all the space she needed. Because Raisa loved her. Leena grew.

***

Nina Niskanen writes science fiction, fantasy, and horror. She lives with her partner and her dog in Helsinki, Finland, where she works as a computer programmer. She is passionate about space, language, and creepy crawlies. She's a graduate of Viable Paradise and Clarion UCSD. More at ninaniskanen.com

MAY YOUR GOVERNMENT BE THE CENTER OF A SMELLY DUNG SANDWICH

Justin Short

Content Notes: *Drugs, Indentured Servitude, Physical Assault, Police, Prison*

They caught me with a few grams of Betelgeuse Burn, but so what? Who cares about any of that bureaucratic nonsense, man? All right, so maybe I care just a little. After all, it was good stuff and they confiscated every last bit of it. They're probably in some plush office right this moment, toking it up and laughing at the tunnel slaves and telling each other how their career trajectories have never looked so good.

It's bad enough they took my stash, but they gave me an overnighter, too. I mean, I guess a night off is a night off. But I'd rather not spend it stuck with a cellmate who smells like he's spent his whole life crawling butt-naked through the septic tunnels of Chassis.

"What'd they get you for?" I asked.

"A song."

"That's funny—I heard you torched a factory."

He shook his head. "Nah, nah. That was just a *side effect*, man. I'm here 'cause I heard the *song*."

"Mmm-hmm, sure. So how 'bout you sing a couple bars? Maybe we can bust outta here."

"It ain't that kind of song."

"Then what kind is it?"

"You wouldn't understand. People like you never do."

He waddled away from the bunk beds and poked his nose through the bars. "Do me a favor," he said. "When you get out, take a listen for yourself."

"Sure thing. Does this song have a name or what?"

"'May Your Government Be the Center of a Smelly Dung Sandwich.'"

"All right, now I know you're making this up."

ॐ

The next morning they gave me a farewell breakfast, a farewell strip search, and told me I was free to go. A company tram escorted me straight back to work. Gam was waiting at the employee gate. "How's it feel to be a convicted felon?" he asked.

"Yeah, yeah."

I thought about asking him if he'd heard about the ridiculous dung song, then decided against it. Gam was too busy drinking their Kool-Aid. He'd probably report me straight up the chain to make himself look like a team player. Some friend.

We didn't have much time for small talk anyway. We were on tunnel duty again. This time we were repairing fuses in the hundred-and-twelve-degree control center while hairless androids chewed us out. I swear an android's only purpose in life is raising your blood pressure until you have a brain aneurysm and drop dead.

I never shoulda left Earth, man, but the brochures really talked this place up. It was a steady gig, you didn't have to wear a gas mask like back home, you got a decent pension… all that stuff. They forgot to mention how labor laws don't exist out here. They didn't tell you about the other place, either.

Verdant.

A gorgeous green world. A paradise. A planet full of beautiful beaches and beautiful people. Beautiful *loaded* people, I should add. Retired millionaires who turn a blind eye to the slave labor, so long as it keeps their world running smoothly.

I stepped out of one of the fuse furnaces covered in sweat. I bent over to catch my breath, but I guess I took a few seconds too long, because the nearest android was instantly at my side, looking me over like I was a steaming heap of spoiled rations.

I got back to work, and he moved to another tunnel. I flipped him the double bird until he was out of eyesight.

Who programmed them to be pricks, man? I'd like to meet whoever it was and—

"You see the announcement?" Gam asked.

"Which one? The one about how I don't give an infected rat's—"

"The employee development program?"

"Oh, that one. Sure. Break your back for thirty years, no marks on your record, bam! Guaranteed retirement on Verdant."

"That leaves us out!"

"Sure does. Who wants to be the poorest person on Verdant anyway? If I make it that long, my body will be so broken down I won't even be able to—"

The android zoomed back. "I hear chit-chat. This implies you don't have a sufficient amount of work. I'm assigning you extra tasks."

He smiled. "By the way, keep up the nice work, Gam."

Androids are just the worst.

৪৯

I worked straight through lunch. Dinner too. I finally finished up and dragged myself back to the den. Gam was sprawled out on the couch, massaging his blistered feet. "I'm getting out," I said.

"Out?"

"Yeah. Off-world."

"Why?"

"Why do you think? If I stay here one more minute, I'm gonna end up back in lockdown. This time, for busting an android's skull wide open."

"That bad, huh?"

"Are you living on the same planet? Of course it's that bad. And you know what? I wouldn't live on Verdant if they paid me. I couldn't stand it, man. Knowing *we* made it possible. How can they live with themselves? But you know, maybe I wouldn't understand since I'm not an elitist piece of—"

"Easy, man. So it's bad. *I get it.* Where you headed?"

"First I gotta visit an old friend."

೬♥

My former cellmate stared at me across the visiting room table. "Back so soon?"

I glanced up at the ceiling before answering him. A busted camera still dangled limply in its corner like I had hoped. The androids hadn't bothered to replace it yet. Next I ran my hands underneath the table, but couldn't find anything other than a disgusting wad of ancient gum.

"It's not bugged," he said. "Androids stopped doin' that a while back. Got too many other things to keep 'em busy, I guess. What kinda top-secret visit is this, anyway?"

"I need to know where you heard that song."

"So now you believe me?"

"No. I still think you're full of it. But I'll try just about anything."

"I already told you. Weren't you paying attention?"

"Mundana's a big place. I need specifics."

"Oh yeah? Well, maybe me and my buddies need some Triton tobacco. Think you can hook us up?"

I sighed. "How much?"

೬♥

Suffice it to say, I hooked my pyro buddy up with a few buds. It's getting harder and harder to find a source, but there are still a few dens the androids don't know about.

It didn't leave me much cash for a ticket. I had to sell every last sick day to get a flight to Mundana. Sick days are worthless around here, anyway. It's not like the androids would ever let me call in. They'd give me another injection and tell me Gam never calls in sick, and why can't I be more like Gam, and Gam this and Gam that.

Gam is just the worst, man. Ten bucks says he's half-android.

Two days later, I made it to Mundana. After asking around a bit, I found myself in a thumping needle club in the middle of an alien desert. Nothing but sand in every direction. Out the window I could see these enormous beetle creatures rolling cylinders of glow-in-the-dark dung across the dunes.

A fuzzy caterpillar-faced dude slid into the booth across from me. "You're here about the song," he said.

"Yeah."

"It's not for sale."

"Can I just listen to it?"

His body squelched in the booth as he leaned in closer. "Not here. The results would be… unfortunate. Do you even know what you're asking?"

I shrugged.

"'May Your Government Be the Center of a Smelly Dung Sandwich' isn't like anything else in the universe. It's much too powerful for me to just hand it over to every Qlaur, Fraum and J'hoan who rolls through here."

"I understand."

"I don't know if you do. This song is *anarchy*, you get me? It's two minutes and fifty-nine seconds of pure, digestible anarchy. It's brought down kingdoms and crumbled interplanetary governments. Destroyed entire *societies*."

He turned his head to the window and watched a beetle struggling with its enormous neon dung pile. The beetle was pushing and pushing, but the dung wasn't moving an inch. Finally the beetle chewed a hole right through the middle of the giant ball, crawled inside, and then the whole thing exploded. The beetle skittered around on the sand and began rolling a new ball from scratch.

Giggling, the caterpillar-man turned back to face me. "You seem like a good larva. Tell me, why do you need it so badly?"

"Well, you see, there's this place called Verdant, and—"

"*Verdant?* Say no more."

He left me alone for a few minutes. I sipped my tea and enjoyed the feel of the cushions against my back. I thought of Gam and the other guys, throwing away the best years of their lives just to keep Verdant buzzing. Poor Gam. What an idiot. He actually thought he made a difference. He actually believed their lies. He thought they'd give him a transfer in a few years. A cush desk job on Verdant. The easy life.

Some people are so naïve.

My caterpillar friend returned with a small, red capsule the size of a thumbnail. "Do you know what happened to the musicians who created this?"

I shook my head.

He threw his head back and cackled. "They were disemboweled! They died horribly! Believe me when I tell you there were guts everywhere!"

Doesn't seem like something to laugh about, but whatever. Different culture, different humor.

He slid the capsule across the table. "I look forward to hearing great things."

&

They got me as soon as I touched down.

It was Gam. It *had to be* Gam. The guy is a born traitor. It didn't matter, though. I had a premonition they would be waiting for me, so I swallowed the song before I entered orbit.

They took me back to lockdown. No cellmate this time. Just me and a bright overhead light and a horseshoe-haired android watching me from the other side of the bars. "People only go to Mundana for one reason," he said.

"I went for the nude beaches, man. Don't know what you're talking about."

"Nude beaches? You expect me to believe—"

"Yeah, brother! Had a great time. Matter of fact, I saw some *au naturel* androids there, if you know what I'm sayin'. Think one of them was your wife, dude."

His features contorted into something like rage. "You went for the song! Admit it!"

"It wasn't for sale! There, happy?"

The android frowned. "Hmmm. Interesting. You're telling the truth."

"Of course I am. Now will you let me out of here?"

"It's not up to me."

It was at least a day before he came back to check on me. By then I had… *ahem*… passed the capsule. Did my best to clean it, too. When I finally heard his footsteps, I dropped to the floor with the capsule in my fist. I started moaning and wailing. Put on a real show.

I heard the predictable turn of the key in the lock. The android's footsteps were directly in front of me. I wrapped my arm around his ankles and jerked upwards. He lost his balance and clattered to the floor. I immediately unfastened his chest compartment and deactivated him.

There were more footsteps in the hallway, but I was already digging into his voice unit. Thank goodness I spent all those months working in android repair, man. It didn't take me any time at all to find his tiny voice bladder and speakers. I crammed the song into the input unit and reactivated him just as the others ran into my cell.

The song burst from his chest and echoed down the empty corridors. Right away, I understood exactly what the caterpillar man was talking about. Even now, I don't know how to describe it. It was so many things at once. An electronic pulse, a distant drum solo, something like a Mellotron, plus these hypnotic alien lyrics I couldn't even begin to understand. I wondered if they were singing about dung and governments and making sandwiches, but somehow I knew it was deeper than any of that.

It was a *feeling*. A fever. I was filled with a sudden, overpowering, blood-boiling need to…

Fight. To really mess things up. Bust some heads. Topple the system. End their control.

Apparently it worked on androids, too. Soon as they heard it, they turned around and flew down the corridors, yelling out glorious strings of profanity and unlocking cell doors. Within minutes, every prisoner in the place had been sprung.

It was simple after that. I rode a wave of android shoulders to the guard tower and transferred the song capsule to the central transmitter. Music screamed across the surface of Chassis. Down below, I knew the tunnel intercoms were blasting it too. From the roof of the tower, I watched smoke rise from the tunnels in dark curls. I raced down the stairs, afraid it would be over before I could join in.

I didn't have anything to worry about. It was an epic battle, man. It lasted for *hours*. We tore down walls, overturned vehicles, and set fires just to watch stuff burn. I had fistfights with motivational posters. I stomped fuses and circuit boards like they were popcorn. At one point, I even participated in an enthusiastic round of kickball with the severed head of an android who previously worked in middle management. (Okay, maybe we went a little too far with that one.)

I guess it was pretty one-sided. We tore that place up, man. There was a brief hiccup as a legion of super-loyal androids ambushed us from a warehouse. They had their hearing units deactivated to avoid infection. We overpowered them without any serious injuries. Soon Chassis was a giant, raucous victory celebration.

It was over. We had clocked out for the last time.

•

Thankfully, we hadn't destroyed all the supply ships. No one wasted much time getting off-world. After all, there are only bigger and better things from here on out. We're gonna find a friendly world and start over. I hear the nude beaches of Mundana are nice this time of year. Plus I owe a beer to an old friend there.

I haven't seen Gam since our revolution. Ten bucks says he got his transfer to Verdant after he ratted me out. He's probably there now, complaining about the sudden power outage. Wondering why things don't look quite like they do in the pamphlets. I almost feel bad for the guy.

Keyword: *Almost.*

What a ridiculous place. They're nothing without our little sweatshop to keep things chugging along. I wonder if they'll interrupt their pool parties and soirees and million-dollar dinners long enough to learn about a little thing called manual labor. Ehh, what do I care? If they don't figure it out, they won't last too long, that's for sure. It'll be lights out on Verdant.

Good riddance.

***

Justin Short lives in Kansas. His fiction has previously appeared in places like *The NoSleep Podcast, The Arcanist,* and *Jerry Jazz Musician.* Visit him online at www.justin-short.com.

THE COMPANY STORE

Kiya Nicoll

Content Notes: *Ableism, Alcohol, Anxiety, Body Dysphoria, Dissociation, Homophobia, Racism, Sexism*

"The damned augments are taking our jobs."

Big Shot was gesturing with his wine glass, sloshing the third-tier red rather than bubbly, the sort of wine ordered by people who want to look like they know the fancy stuff but can't hack the premier, the wine we sold to a lot of clean-cut white Company suits who would want the last word. I had pegged him as properly fun to be around right from the start, for sure, and nothing I overheard was changing my opinion.

Guys like that never tipped.

He had been holding forth on one topic or another through the entire evening, to his little table of similarly buttoned-down men and glassy-eyed women.

"Excuse me?" A woman flagged me down two tables over. "I'm terribly sorry, are there privacy curtains? I don't want to be a bother, but—" Her eyes shifted, over towards Big Shot, and then back.

Her table companion was, I thought, her son. They had

something of a similar face, though he was drawn and angular in a way that suggested some lingering suffering, and his right hand emitted the faint whirr of mechanism under the skin-toned sheathing.

"I'll see what I can do," I said.

"Thank you," she said with great earnestness.

The last thing that cyborg kid needed after whatever he was going through was listening to Big Shot ranting about how he was going to doom the nation, or whatever it was, by being less than one hundred percent meat. I got a damper, set the radius for their table, and told her, "If you need someone to help you, you'll want to push the button here," as I locked it onto its slot. "To be sure someone can get to you promptly."

"Thank you again."

"My pleasure."

The boy, wide-eyed, was looking at me as if I were some sort of hero, and I ducked back out of the distortion field before I started protesting that I didn't even play one on TV. I hadn't cured anything, solved anything, I just—

"Hey! You, what's your name."

My thoughts shattered around Big Shot's bellow, and I tried to put my mind back together as I returned to his table. "Yes, sir?"

"Kris? Karen? Kate, that was it, right, Kate?"

Names always felt like someone else's, the person I was pretending to be, and I put on her smile and said, "Yes, sir?" again.

"Now look at her," he boomed. "All natural, is that right, Kate?"

I felt as glazed as the women at his table. "Was there something your table needed, sir?" If he wanted me to be a soul-selling glamour girl, he wanted someone else. I wanted to be anywhere else.

"Not one of those freaks who wants to do something to change your body, not you."

His words punched me clean out of my flesh—everything receded to smoke drifting over the waves. The body remained still and unresisting as he seized its wrist in triumph.

"That's right. You're pure, aren't you, honey? Completely human." His leering tone did not help matters any, and the voice wanted to stammer out something about being old-fashioned and home-grown, but I had enough presence left to stop it, which left the whole sack of meat to stare at him like a stunned ox. "You don't need to do anything different. Julie, there," he pointed out one of the women, "she's had to deal with her daughter wanting to freak it up, get cat ears and a robot tail, and in this economy."

Julie, if that was actually her name, looked not too terribly pleased to have her family laundry hung out like that. She was not the one who spoke up, though, she just looked pinched and prunish and affronted.

"Leave the girl be," said another woman at the table, the only woman with skin darker than a linen tablecloth. From outside my flesh, I thought she was somewhere in the middle of the pecking order there, she was at least in the middle of the table. "Let go of her arm, you're scaring her." I thought distantly that Big Shot wouldn't like that; it was no way to get further up the table.

"I'm not scaring you, am I, honey?"

Trying to speak was like trying to turn a set of gears with a pole, all stuttering and awkward and distant. "Did you need something, sir?" I managed to make the body say, eventually, and the Black woman gave me a knowing look.

"I need you to answer my questions, Kate." There was a threat underlying it.

I nudged the machinery of the body, just a little, trying to get it to slide into something smooth and practiced, without the shape of a stutter, and after an awful creaking noise it rattled out, "I'd be happy to answer any questions about the dessert specials, we have a bourbon chocolate—"

Big Shot did not look happy about that, but he let go of the wrist, at least, and I made the hands pluck out my notebook to give the impression of someone perkily ready to take their orders for after-dinner sweets. I wondered, distantly, if he thought I was making fun of him, but he let them give their orders for cake and pie and the body managed to note it all down without me having to steer it too much.

By the time I got back with the orders, I felt like I had managed to crawl halfway back into my skin, and he was in the middle of some rant about how infiltrators were taking good work away from the right sort of people. I could not, from what he said, figure out whether he was complaining about cyborgs, or demis, or immigrants, or people who passed as white, or straight, or whatever else. He did declare proudly that he was in HR and he would not stand for it. He probably wanted pee tests and a genetic swab as part of a job application, too.

I'd heard of that sort of thing to get a good job, the kind with prospects. All the inspections and injections and detections and I didn't want them owning a line on my DNA or a scrawled commitment to never join a union. They'd find something to object to, somewhere, and I'd go on the blacklist for all the Company businesses, and then what would I do with myself?

I was only half hearing Big Shot sounding smug about something, but the woman who had intervened on my behalf could not hide her look of horror, so I paused for a moment to rerun it in my head. It was something about a solution to the problem of undesirables—HR was on it, and he was proud. People nodded, or held their peace, except for that one woman and the one Asian man, who scowled in that way that senior executives do when they are displeased with the condition of their grilled shrimp.

My bracelet buzzed, and I glanced at it as I gave out the last caramel-topped ice cream. As I made my way past Big Shot again, he reached out to grab my wrist, yanking my shoulder and sending my consciousness flying again.

"There's changes coming, honey, and you know, I've got a soft spot for redheads, so I'll warn you. You want to shape up and make sure you're on the right side." He let go, and the arm dropped like a dead weight. He turned his back on the body as it reeled away, saying, "Some people say blondes are the pinnacle of human beauty but I like a bit of spice, don't you agree?"

I made it to the shielded table without crashing into anything, but obviously something showed, because the woman started with, "We'll have the," and then suddenly broke off with, "Are you okay?"

I tried desperately to crawl back into my skin as the mouth hung open, uselessly, for a long moment, and eventually the voice said "No," in a tone flat enough to be an early grade robot.

She peered out through the haze of the field and said, "The executive table."

I was only half in control of the body, and it twitched an affirmative. "You have to get somewhere safe," I gasped.

"What do you mean?"

I managed to reclaim myself enough to grip the edge of the table. "I'm sorry," I said.

"Please, please explain." She looked at her son, and then back at me.

I closed my eyes, in the hope that I could keep control long enough to get through the conversation. "He's going to do something. I think he just threatened me. I— I'm sorry, I shouldn't bother you with personal problems, you're customers."

She frowned and said, gently, "We're human beings."

The body wanted to knot fists in its hair and yank. I made the hands cling to the table instead. "He was talking about. Undesirables. Maybe it was a warning? Not a threat? Because he doesn't think I'm an undesirable. He wants to do something. He's in HR."

"HR at Zone Capital?"

I nodded. "We only get Zone execs." Answering questions helped me feel a little less that circumstances had gone beyond my control, despite the desperate chording demands to hide the secrets under my skin. "I think. Big changes. And you heard the sort of people he doesn't like." My mask had slipped, all the masks but the biggest one, the one that mattered, and I swayed a little, side to side, trying to find my inner balance. "It could be nothing. I don't know if you're Company. It's probably just Company people have to worry, I'm sorry, I shouldn't be having a panic attack all over you."

"No, no, please," she said. "Look. Thank you for letting me know. I owe you one, okay? I owe you one." She was going to repeat it until I was less white-knuckled at the table, so I slowly let go. "Here." She pulled a card from a pocket and pressed it into my hand. "If you need something, you call me, okay? You call me."

My thumb slid over the card, feeling some embossing on the corner, and I pocketed it as if it were a tip. "Okay. Okay. You wanted the check, right? I can get you the check. Unless you wanted dessert? We have a chocolate bourbon cake special and..." I got that far before the giggles overtook me.

"Is she okay, mom?" asked the boy, and I flinched half out of my body again. Thankfully, I could use the leverage to pull myself together.

She gave me a look, and I recognized the expression of a mother about to have a pedagogical moment. "Do you remember David?"

"Yeah," he said, frowning, and glanced sideways at me, as I pulled out my notepad as if they were discussing an order. "Why?"

"David and his family left the enclave because someone in HR changed policy." She drummed her fingers on the table to gather her thoughts. "I believe they left the country entirely."

"Why would they want to do that?" The boy frowned. "This is the best country in the world."

His mother rubbed the bridge of her nose. "They said that to me too," she said, eventually. "It's not like that anymore. I don't know what went wrong." She shook her head. "Anyway, some people have more reason to be worried than we do, hon."

I couldn't stay in the safety of the privacy bubble any longer, and I had the body mostly back under control, so I ducked out and went and plugged in a caramel ice cream on my own account so I could bring it out for the kid. He didn't seem the chocolate cake kind.

They were still talking when I got back, something about the history of corporate enclaves, subsidies, and zoning exceptions, and I waited a moment before setting the ice cream down in front of the boy and the check in front of his mother. "Here you go."

"I'm sorry, we didn't—"

"On me," I said. "Sorry for making a fuss."

The kid had the spoon up and was looking to his mother for permission.

"All right," she said, in the fond tones of one relenting.

"Growing kid needs his calories, right?"

He cracked a grin broad enough that it looked like it might shatter his thin, fragile face. "That's right," he said. "See, mom?"

"I see," she laughed, and handed over a card.

"I'll run this and be right back," I said, and ducked out before they could get back to tax policy. It would be tax policy, all that history that the kid might've lived through but didn't know. Concessions for the corps, costs for the concessions, devolution and privatization and here's the company cafeteria if you had to work late and why don't you move into the company housing and get your bonus paid in company scrip instead of cash. When the city around the enclave collapses under the weight of it all, buy the city. Buy the politicians, take over the infrastructure, and then it's culture fit in the boardroom and cost cutting in the cubes.

I was still dissociating, lightly, when I picked up the signed check, made sure that Big Shot was adequately pacified, and closed out my other tables. Nothing was quite real, which was a fine feeling for the end of a brutal shift, and I managed to not embarrass myself doing it all.

"What's this, then?" The manager waved a slip of paper aggressively in my face when I went to cash out my e-tips.

"One of my receipts?" I guessed, not that it could be anything else.

"Table seven," he said, in a tone that demanded an explanation.

Easy enough. "Mother and teenager asked for a privacy bubble partway through because of some rowdies, really glad I brought it to them."

He grunted and rang it up. "She must've misplaced the decimal. No way she wanted to tip you that much," he said, and scooped out the handful of Zone Capital scrip for my share of the e-payments. "There you go."

He'd pocket the rest, of course. I wondered how much it had been. "See you tomorrow," I said, because making a fuss would do me no good. No amount of "Please, sir" was going to get me any more, it was just a gamble on losing what little I had. One customer with a fancy business card wasn't a safety net, a community.

"Tomorrow," he agreed, and shooed me out.

The glorified company cafeteria was on the fifteenth floor, and the loveless elevator went down for all of us who worked like dogs. I actually wasn't sure which elevator a bossman would use, I never saw them. Maybe they lived in company housing; there was probably a penthouse or something. Their ship came in, after all, and they've got the rest of us where they want us. I'd literally just put some scrip in my manager's pocket, too, and the rest of it was burning a little hole in mine.

We ragged people got out at the ground floor and went to squander our mumbles because resistance was a luxury beyond our means. At surface level, the enclave started to blend into the outside, here and there, around the edges. Technically, I would've had to go outside the border to find people who would provide something to handle the pain, or were brave enough for back alley hormones, or any of the other things that the lawless land might have to offer. Anger was among the things I couldn't afford, and shame wasn't enough to push me out there. So the waitress remained, not even fighting.

There was shame enough in that. I slouched into a bar I knew, feeling guilty about my lack of conviction, and grabbed a seat at the counter. "Old Fashioned," I said.

The barkeep scowled down at me. "Not really a girl's drink," he said. "How about a—"

For once, I had had enough. "I'm not a girl," I snapped. "I'll have it with a fucking cherry if that makes you feel better about your dick, though."

He opened his mouth, and closed it, and turned away, muttering something rude about lesbians. At least someone hooted approval, though I wasn't sure if it was my attitude or the show that earned it. He didn't seem to do anything to the drink, either, as I watched him mix it, and slid it across to me with a grunt.

The screen was on, and unfortunately it was talking heads rather than sports, with a scroll of captioning across the bottom. Today's debate: whether people with cybernetics to correct disabilities were somehow cheating by taking jobs rather than sticking to unemployment camps. It was Big Shot proving himself to the crowd all over again, and I drank my Old Fashioned a bit too quickly so I could drop my scrip on the bar and escape.

It was tempting to go a little closer to the line, maybe find a place that was going to be a little less infuriating, a little less lonely. Instead, I trudged off along the streets under the bunting-hung lamps, not lingering long enough to draw the attention of the patrols that kept people moved on from every place.

I had bourbon at home, though not any citrus to garnish it with, I could make my own mediocre cocktail and drown my sorrows in front of the screen like every other caged rat I half-knew, assuming I could find anything broadcast that didn't remind me of why I wanted to drink. On second thought, I concluded as I opened my door, I would skip the screen entirely and just go for the bottle.

I found myself, some time later, staring at myself in the mirror, seeing no way to be either touched or healed. At least when I raked fingers through my hair to draw it back, it was without a repetition of the earlier urge to violence. I wondered, and not for the first time, if it would be worth the dock to my pay to buzz it flat on the sides and be freed of it.

I thought better of it, like I always did, and went to bed.

Three days later, the new policy came down from HR. It was a blinking red message on my notifications, a little pulse of threat, and I stared at the thing over breakfast before sighing and opening it up.

"In keeping with the spirit of national resilience and in response to the rising tide of globalist threat to our way of life," it began. I flicked up with my thumb, rubbing my temple with my other hand. System of merits and demerits applied to all Zone Capital employees, from the executive level on down, stand strong against those who oppose us, unity against the terrorist threat, et cetera, and so forth.

Finally, the details. Merits for working overtime. Demerits for being late or leaving early, waived in certain cases that mostly seemed to do with women taking care of children. Merits for verified congregational membership, merits for reliable attendance, merits for long hair on women. Demerits for association with labor unions, with terrorists, with gangs, with subversives, whatever that meant. Merits for approved affiliations, demerits for disapproved ones, very little specifics, presumably so they could decide what they wanted to punish by whatever whims served their interests. Degenerate behavior could earn demerits. Righteous behavior was laid out: children, kitchen, church. Merits—substantial ones—for submitting to genetic testing, with no explanation of what they wanted to do with the information.

Reading it made me tempted, again, to shave my entire head. I quietly totaled up the demerits I could earn by taking off my mask, reading generously between the lines of the implications, and saw my entire pay in scrip evaporate in a cloud of deviance. I wondered, a little wildly, if they wanted to comb my DNA for proof of my union organizer grandfather, or if they were looking for interracial heritage to penalize, or heritable disorders to mark off as a demerit, or some other unimaginable thing. I wondered about the woman who had stood up to Big Shot for me, and whether her dark skin would be marked as a demerit, or whether that was still considered unacceptable to write explicitly into policy.

Getting ready for work was more of a trial than usual, trying to fit into the skin that didn't suit, resisting the urge to do something savage to the body's hair. I stared into the mirror, and plucked up the foundation to cover up the hollowness under my eyes. I could see the strain, how used up and eaten from the inside I felt, and I painted and powdered to make it disappear, applying the mask that made me a passable, acceptable girl.

"I am the mask," I said to the mirror, watching the body's face move with it. Then, thoughtfully, I tried pitching my voice downward, reshaping it. "Do you hear me?" I said, and felt foolish.

"Who is me, anyway?" The mirror had no answers, as I pulled my hair back again. "Maybe I'm Erik. That'd be the joke of a lifetime, wouldn't it." I did all the little proper adornments. "I'm so good at hiding that nobody knows I'm deformed since birth. Such a perfect mask."

Eventually, I made my way to work, past the abandoned park and up the ZC Tower again, under the sign reading "The Future Delivered To Your Door." Or to my phone. The future, roaring down on me like an oncoming train. I might be mad, but there was no rain to laugh at. The future, tightening like a magical lasso, a monster to marry in the dark.

I piloted the body through my shift without remembering a thing about it, drifting past tables full of people who seemed to have no cares in the world, who were untroubled by HR—or who were, like me, so used to hiding that their masks were just as smooth and perfect as my own.

At seven, Big Shot arrived, and it was not yet time for me to go home. His party was smaller this time, but in a jovial and triumphant mood. He was pleased, HR was pleased. Neither the Black woman nor the Japanese man were there. The woman with the catgirl daughter had been replaced with some other blank-faced white woman in a skirt suit.

It was a relief that they were seated in someone else's section, were someone else's problem. I kept drifting, just trying to survive until the end of my shift, trying to figure out what I needed to do to make it through the next day, the next week.

His hand closed on my shoulder as I was finishing up with a customer, and I half screeched before I managed to pin the body down and etherize it into submission.

"Oh, honey, I didn't mean to startle you," he said, and my soul tried to slither out of its skin like a snake. "You've got tomorrow off, right?"

Calculations went wild, then froze. I stared at him, unresponsive.

He turned my hand over, pressed something into it. "You come see me for drinks. I'd love to talk to you about what you think of the new HR policy. What do you like?"

He wanted me to say wine, or bubbly, or a cosmo or something that could get me well and truly drunk like a Long Island iced tea. I drew strength from I didn't know where and said, "Old Fashioned. With decent bourbon."

Big Shot was not expecting that, but he was smooth enough to turn it into, "Oh, a quirky girl! I like that. You come see me. I've got plans, and I'd like to hear what the little people think." He folded my fingers around the passcard. "There's a good girl."

I put it in my pocket without thinking and found the other card there, the one with the embossing. I made my escape to the bathroom to stare at both of them. One, unremarkable, with a white rose in the corner, the petals shaped under my thumb. The other, a passkey that opened up some door, somewhere.

"Hey, you all right?" Voices. Coworkers.

I tried to wave it off, but the two of them crowded into the employee bathroom and stared at me, which made it impossible to get my thoughts back in residence in the flesh. They gossiped over me from a distance, and one said to the other, "That's what you get for being single, you know." The other looked half-horrified before she got dragged back out to customers.

I knew how that was. It should have felt like someone supported me. It didn't.

Somehow, I got back out onto the floor, and through the rest of my shift. I took the cashed out scrip from my tips, made it back down to the street. I had to move rather than be caught loitering, so I started to walk.

I walked out towards the edge of the enclave, and then I stepped over the line.

There was time, there had to be time, I could manufacture a face to meet other faces, there could be time to answer the questions that had been dropped on my plate, there was time for everything and for nothing.

I wondered what I could dare, whether my universe could handle being perturbed.

There in the lawless land, I saw a barbershop. I had one hand on the scrip in my pocket. Maybe everything could be all right. I didn't want a revolution, but I was done with being slowly killed.

There was a board up in the barbershop, prices in various scrips. I counted mine out and put it down.

"What do you want?"

"Take it all off."

The barber looked half-elven, a fey androgyne with golden skin, who ought to have been crowned in boughs or stars. They gave me a look, a long one, and said, "Twenty percent off if you're queer."

My mouth fell open, not sure what to make of the offer. "It's my birthday."

"Well, happy birthday, then," they said. "What's your name, so we can sing you a round?"

I closed my eyes, and found I had no impulse to give a phantom's name after all. "I think I'm... I think I'm Rory." Rory Trouble-And-Strife, maybe; I'd find a family name later.

"Happy birthday, Rory," they said, and pressed a photo book into my hands. "Here's some pictures of cute boys. Let me know what you want on your head." They fluttered green-glazed eyelids at me and then ducked off to round up another barber to sing while I paged through the pictures.

"That one," I said, picking something extravagant, shaved sides and a cascade of curls swept back from my temples, then over and down the back of my neck. "That's me. That's Rory. Do that one."

The barber nodded and swept the bib around me. "Why a birthday today, if I could ask, honey?"

Their 'honey' felt warm and so different from Big Shot's. I relaxed muscles I hadn't known were so tense as I leaned back into their hands. "I have a meeting with a big shot in HR tomorrow," I said. "If I don't go, I lose my job."

"Gotcha. And you want to be fab."

"I want to be me." That line between 'safe enough to run scared' and 'fight or die' had finally swept up and over me, and there was no more hiding, not in any of it. No more masks, not in any material, steel or silk or leather.

"Oh, honey, yeah. They'll squeeze all the real out of you up there. Kill your soul if they can't get an excuse to kill your body, honey. It's not easy outside the line, but it's easier than that. You come back, you hear? You come back."

The 'if you make it out again' went unspoken. "I'll come back." My heart felt, for the first time in a long time, human. Sixteen tons of the hair came off in ruddy handfuls as my blood boiled with knowledge of the million needling hurts I had ignored because I was helpless and afraid, because I had nowhere to turn.

"How do you like it?" The barber turned me in the chair so we could look at me together in the mirror.

I saw myself for the first time: proud, and maybe a little punk. I ran my hands along the stubble of my skull. "I look like me," I breathed. Reborn, pronounced fit to fight, I would damn well sing in the rain if I wanted.

Over in the enclave, they would likely say I was evil, that I was wrong. There and now, I was inspired. My face was, at last, not a stranger's.

"You come back home, y'hear, honey? We got you."

"Yeah. I hear."

***

Kiya Nicoll is only an egg, and does not communicate entirely in echolalia (but it is sometimes a near thing). They write stories and mythologies in the stolen moments between being covered in cats and children and very occasionally reptiles.

SCHOLAR MIAKA'S BRIEF SUMMARY OF MEMORIES IMBUED IN MEMORY OBJECT EXHIBIT ITEM 132.NW.1

Jaymee Goh

Content Notes: *Anxiety, Illness, Police, Sexism, Slavery, Transphobia, Violence, Weapons*

Coarsely-woven circle skirt, made from strips of palm leaves that have been preserved using a technique either magical or lost. Found in a corner of the Deep Northwest under the recesses of Old Demia's Library of Sorcerous Arts (likely a reason for its preservation, regardless of the original crafting technique), it had been lying hidden behind a pot of vinegar from a later period, stuffed into a crevice at the bottom of the wall before being discovered, quite by accident, by a housekeeping staff member, who was promptly sent to the House of Emotional Distress upon contact with the fabric. It was possibly used as a stopper to prevent rats from taking shelter in the crevice.

Scholar Miaka argues that this item dates back far beyond written records, lending credence to the theory that history had not been preserved in text, but in magical imbuement of memory to objects. Debate continues on whether excessive handling of memory objects degrades the potency of the memory contained therein, or if the strength of the memories imbued depends on the power of the person performing the imbuement. Regardless, Memory Object Exhibit Item 132.NW.1 is an extremely powerful memory object, despite its age, implying either great power or great emotion in its crafting.

Caution is advised when handling the skirt for any prolonged period of time; there is risk of nausea, headaches, vomiting, and, in rare cases, sympathy wounds. The skirt's memories depict a series of violent incidents over the course of several years. Several of these memories depict perversions of natural law and violations of human rights, and must be considered products of their time, keeping a record of an extremely tumultuous period.

The skirt is decorated with three main motifs: a row of hands near the waist; pairs of equal pentagons, sharing one edge, their tips pointing up and down; braided cords at the hemline, frayed. Each symbol contains a different memory, indicating very nuanced and high-level capability in the creation of the skirt. Scholars are divided whether these are memories from different individuals or a single individual.

𝆕

1. Motif: Hands, or Fists.

Fist 1: Self-memory of a wrist grabbed by an older man, possibly a spouse or parent, and dragged out of a public dining hall.
    Emotional valences: *Shock, dismay*

Fist 2: Witness-memory of a young woman punching an older man for molesting her on the tram.
    Emotional valences: *Outrage, vindication, approval*

Fist 3: Witness-memory of a respectable middle-class woman of middling age struck on the left cheek following the announcement of divorce.

Emotional valences: *Shock, outrage*

Fist 4: Self-memory of a son striking the memoirist in the abdomen following an argument outside a school.

Emotional valences: *Disappointment, anger, despair*

Fist 5: Witness-memory of a child beaten for wearing a skirt—the child had been assigned a rigid gender role and had been caught violating societal dress code.

Emotional valences: *Dismay, outrage, anger*

Fist 6: Self-memory of a juvenile male loudly arguing with the memoirist, possibly a son or nephew, culminating with a slap on the man's right cheek.

Emotional valences: *Shock, disappointment, resignation*

Fist 7: Witness-memory of older women gathering in protest outside a courthouse, surrounded by what appear to be law enforcement officers who pen them in using electricity spears.

Emotional valences: *Outrage, fury*

Fist 8: Witness-memory of a contract signing between two men, behind one of whom a young woman weeps. Extended family members watch in silence around the doorway in the next room.

Emotional valences: *Resignation, disappointment, sympathy*

Fist 9: Witness-memory of a street sweeper struck down while working by laughing male youths.

Emotional valences: *Anger, sadness, disapproval*

Fist 10: Self-memory of an elderly woman, a wealthy employer, striking the memoirist on the head with a folding fan with remonstrance on good behaviour as befits a household servant.

Emotional valences: *Shock, surprise, disappointment*

(Scholar Miaka's commentary: I argue that these symbols are fists due to the content of these memories. In addition, the fingers are too short to be full hands, even though my esteemed colleague Scholar Juvinia says that the fidelity to realism for such rudimentary depictions of this time period may only be minimal. Since not many artifacts from this period remain, it is quite unbelievable that the craftsmakers could have had a high understanding and skill in anatomy. Yet the evidence points towards the argument that no matter how barbaric the Old Demians have been, they had a very sophisticated knowledgebase.

The emotional valences attached retain only the overlaying emotions. These memories have faded in great measure, yet maintain a visceral strength with regards to a certain set of law repeals. Scholar Juvinia theorizes that they are linked to an *absence* of laws for the treatment of equal citizens in the legislative records of Old Demia predating the law repeals, and I do not disagree with their assessment here.)

2. Motif: Pairs of Pentagons.

Front Center Pair: The Winter Memory
⌂ Snow falling from a cloudy sky, midday. There is an anxiety in the air, though the weather is calm. The household is at rest for the midday siesta, except for one spouse waking up to prepare evening meals at their employer's house. The memoirist looks down from an attic window and shivers, thinking about how cold the winter is.

◆ Alcoves lit along the tunnel passages, time unclear. The tunnels are cold, but not bitingly so, and certain quarters are warmed with human crowding. The memoirist misses the snow and thinks this warmth is a small consolation for being forced to move underground.

Front Right Pair: The Children Memory
⌂ Four children laughing in a park on a high holy day. They stumble over each other while playfighting, even as the memoirist calls for them to stop being so rough. One shrieks while being lifted by hands and feet by two others, swung to the rhythm of the fourth's singing. The memoirist is consternated at first but relaxes after determining the shrieks were not of distress.

◆ A pallet against a wall with the body of the youngest child, now a teenager, burning with fever. The memoirist wishes for the presence of the other three, but they have been sold off, or sent to other households to serve. One might even say *re-distributed*. The memoirist is pregnant with a half-sibling by a sire assigned by the household head, in accordance with a new contract forced upon all in-house servants.

Front Left Pair: The Autumn Memory
⌂ Colours explode across the trees: red, gold, purple, blue. Leaves swirl with the wind. The smell of freshly-harvested fruit, baked into pastries. Rains in the distance. The crowds in the center plaza, though starting to segregate along class lines, remain happy and dancing. The singing, the singing, the singing.

◆ A glimpse out the window of the carriage transporting the memoirist from one household to another. The same reds, golds, purples, blues, but blurring past the small rectangle. The memoirist has no idea where the carriage is going, has no sense of when the carriage turns and what street corners it winds around, because the roads are no longer familiar after so long navigating tunnels.

Back Center Pair: The Spousal Memory

⌂ The spouses all sitting together at a table, discussing household accounts and arguing over expenses, which have become more expensive over the last two years due to economic recession. They are grateful to have four incomes in the household. Intimate brushes of fingers, brief kisses, low voices to not wake the children, and a slow-burning anger at a new piece of legislation imposing monogamy.

◆ One husband weeps for the other husband, his first love and first spouse out of the four. The memoirist misses the other two spouses as well, and is relieved to keep one at least, even though now people of their class are only allowed to have children—the memoirist will *not* use the word "breed"—with spouses assigned to them by their employers.

Back Right Pair: The Protest Memory
⌂ The Senate Plaza is resplendent with floating lights. It is late evening, yet the lines for casting votes are still long. It is a designated public holiday week. People have picnics as they wait for their turn to cast ballots. Arguments break out over policy, but are quickly resolved by moving the opponents to different queues, while people around them nod indulgently, because such is participation in civic duty—people necessarily disagree.

◆ The memoirist runs through a street with a basket of ballots, pilfered over the voting week to bring to people in the tunnels, since most will not get a day off to vote at all during voting week. There are three hours left in the day to get the ballots in before counting commences. The sun is setting, the roads are getting dark. Nevertheless, the memoirist must persist. There is a measure on the ballot to hold a voting period only every six years instead of every three. This election is their last chance to turn the tide before it becomes law.

Back Left Pair: The Convalescence Memory

⬠ The worst illness is a childhood pox, which causes rashes and a general misery, but once contracted will never recur in adulthood. When a neighbor's child catches it, they are made to sit in a chair while the rest of the neighborhood children, under the watchful eyes of their parents, circle around them slowly. Sweets and honeyed drinks are made for the occasion, treating the illness as a rite of passage. Parents are guaranteed a few weeks of not needing to watch their children too closely, since they would all be abed.

◆ Illness in the tunnels creates a miasma that breeds even more illness. There are no hospitals Underground, so one must beg for bed space by a window at the far edges of the city, overlooking the ocean below. The memoirist has been ill for days, unable to get to the city's edge. But the memoirist must get well. Must survive. There is so much work left to be done. Such changes have been wrought in such a short time; surely they can be reversed in the same amount of time.

(Scholar Miaka's commentary: These are pairs of memories depicting a before-and-after for their memoirists. The pentagon corners that point to the waistline of the skirt hold a memory of Aboveground, and the pentagon corners that point to the hemline hold a memory of Underground. These memories correspond in some fashion, though the pattern of connection is not clear.)

3. Motif: braided cords at hemline.

The cords are variously sized, some with several threads, some with just three. Each thread contains a whisper of a word, and if one runs a finger down a thread, one will see the face of an individual from different angles and time periods.

Care must be taken when handling these cords, as they have been undone and re-braided several times. While Scholar Miaka has written detailed and illustrated instructions for the re-braiding of these cords, re-braiding is a complex and difficult task for the archivist.

(Scholar Miaka's commentary: I strongly suspect that these words are names, and each cord is a family unit. We must preserve the exact combination of the cords as they have been braided, for that is how we keep the memory of these families together.

Yet what is the significance of the fraying at the ends of the cords? They appear to be done *on purpose* as if to mark some phenomenon that afflicted these families. If one brushes one's fingers at the very tips of the cords, where the fraying is most blasted, one feels the emotional valence of a lament, of loss, of disconnection. We know the Old Demians were slavers—could this be connected? Were they not, perhaps, at some very early time, a slave-holding people, and not naturally given to slavery? Was slavery—and its ills thereof—legislated into the very fabric of Old Demia?)

ᚷ

For further details, please see the Full Catalogue of Memory Object Exhibit Item 132.NW.1 in the New Demia Archaeological Research Division. All inquiries can currently be made to Scholar Miaka, sent in care of the Hospice for the Skyward Bound.

***

Jaymee Goh is a writer, reviewer, editor, and essayist of science fiction and fantasy. Her work has been published in *Lightspeed Magazine*, *Strange Horizons*, and the *Los Angeles Review of Books*. She is an editor for Tachyon Publications. Find more about her at jaymeegoh.com

JUST AN OLD GROUCH

Laura Jane Swanson

Content Notes: *Ageism, Death, Manipulation, Sexism*

Norm woke up grouchy. It was an unfamiliar sensation, this urge to grumble and grouse and slam the door when he shuffled into the bathroom. He couldn't remember having felt this way in the ten years since he'd moved to Appleville. Then again, Appleville was known all over the Midwest as the home of three thousand or so Happy Citizens and three Old Grouches. He wasn't one of the Grouches, so of course he was happy. At least, he had been.

He was still frowning when he walked into the kitchen and started the coffeemaker. He scowled at the sunshine coming in the window. Walking down the driveway to get the paper, he kicked at the gravel. "Darned kids," he muttered toward the laughter coming from the school bus stop at the corner.

Opening the kitchen door, he spotted a hole in the screen. "They'd better do something about the dogs in this town," he grumbled. He didn't know which one had done it, but they all had a habit of jumping up to peer into the kitchen when he was cooking. Now he would have to patch the screen, or there would be flies all over the house.

Inside again, he dropped two slices of bread in the toaster and unfolded the paper. Mayor Young was on the front page, smiling agelessly. Norm frowned. Except for his haircut, the Mayor's appearance hadn't changed in the time Norm had lived in Appleville. It wasn't fair. What was left of Norm's hair had gone from gray to white to essentially invisible.

He was picking at his toast, resenting the seeds in the raspberry jam because they got caught in his teeth, when he saw the headline on page two: *Appleville To Elect New Grouch.*

Norm had never minded the Grouches before, but now he wondered whether it was really necessary for anyone to be so decidedly negative. The Mayor updated the number of Happy Citizens on the sign every time someone was born, or died, or moved in or out, but he never changed the number of Grouches. There were always three. They had been around since long before Norm had moved to town, so what could he do? The tourists found them entertaining, and the other Happy Citizens of Appleville appreciated the tradition.

Joe Anderson's funeral had been the day before, complete with Mayor Young's cheerful eulogy praising the late Old Grouch. An election was inevitable, so he might as well read about the candidates. It had to be more interesting than the article about the elementary school field day that took up the other half of the page.

Halfway through the article, he found something altogether too interesting: his own name. Norman Davies had been nominated as a candidate for Old Grouch. The nerve! Why, he wasn't even old! Sixty-eight didn't count.

Except that, according to the official qualifications listed in the article, sixty-eight did count. In fact, one of the other candidates, Essie Baker, was only sixty-five. What nonsense! Though Norm could see why someone might nominate Essie. She actually looked old, and almost grouchy, though she had always been as sweet to him as the rest of the Happy Citizens. Why him?

&♥

He was still stewing about it as he walked to the hardware store. On the way, he passed Annie Thompson's house. That Old Grouch was actually waving a newspaper as scrunched up as her expression and yelled, "Get off my lawn!" at a couple of kids. What an unoriginal stereotype. They were just cutting the corner. They weren't even in the garden.

The kids looked at each other and shrugged. "Sorry, Mrs. Thompson," one of them said, smiling.

Norm shook his head. It was a stupid tradition. Grouch or not, there was no need to talk that way to kids.

The hardware store was dim and a little dusty and smelled of potting soil and paint and the grass clippings that clung to the lawn mower sitting just inside the door, waiting to be repaired. The rolls of screening were easy enough to find, but of course they wouldn't cut just a patch. He had to buy at least an eighth of a yard. What was this, a fabric store? Well, no, because fabric stores carried patches. They didn't make you buy a big piece of cloth to cover a tiny hole.

He waited for the teenager behind the counter to finish chatting with a young man in a cowboy hat. What did he think he was doing, wearing something like that? For that matter, what was she doing out of school? Oh, that's right, she was homeschooled. Looked like she had learned more about flirting than anything else, though; even with the help of the register, she seemed to have trouble making change efficiently.

The small child waiting in line behind Norm tugged at her mother's hand. "Is that a real cowboy, Mama?"

"No way," scoffed Norm. "He's simply a fool who thinks a big hat makes him look important."

The little girl's lip trembled.

"Don't worry, honey, he's just practicing," the mother said. "That's Norman Davies. He's running for Old Grouch, you know."

The child's lips steadied, then spread in a smirk. "He's very grouchy," she said. "I bet he'll win!"

Indeed, Norm realized, he was very grouchy. What had gotten into him?

&

He took care of patching the door that afternoon. The flies wouldn't invade, but the screen didn't seem to be much use otherwise. It was too hot. He sat on the porch after dinner, but there wasn't a breath of cool air out there either. He saw his next door neighbor Jenny heading across the yard, carrying a folder of papers. She must have just come from work. Maybe a visit would cheer him up.

"I hear you're running for Old Grouch!" she said.

"Not my fault."

"Not your fault? But it's great! Aside from the Mayor, the Grouches are the most important people in town!"

Why hadn't he ever noticed how impossibly cheerful she was? "I don't want to be important."

"The Mayor himself nominated you!" She was grinning, showing far too many teeth. "We need to make some posters, and maybe see if the radio station at Consolidated High would do an interview."

"The kids that run that station barely know what an interview is, let alone the kind of questions to ask." Norm was appalled at himself. Everyone knew Consolidated wasn't the best school in the state, but no one in Appleville would say so. Well, no one but a Grouch.

"Can I be your campaign manager?" Jenny was far too excited about the idea of living next door to someone who might become small-town famous.

"I don't want to run a campaign!" Norm's voice got louder. "I don't want to be a Grouch!"

A couple walking by with a stroller applauded.

"Perfect!" Jenny said, bouncing down the steps to the front walk. "Keep acting like that, and leave the rest to me!"

Norm got up and went inside, slamming the door behind him.

᠖

Norm spent most of the week at home, avoiding anyone who might ask him to campaign for Grouch and ruminating on Appleville's bizarre custom. Even the internet didn't seem to know of any other towns with elected Grouches. Aside from entertaining the tourists, what use were they, anyway?

Yet everyone else in town seemed to love them. Was that just because everyone else was a Happy Citizen? Norm himself had been happy until the day he'd been announced as a candidate for Grouch. Strange that he couldn't remember why he hadn't minded before.

In fact, that was very strange indeed. Why had he been so happy in Appleville? Yes, the town was known for its charm. People flocked to it during the holidays, oohing and aahing over the homemade decorations and the old-fashioned charm of small-town life. In summer and fall, vacationers bought perfectly ordinary carrots and apples in the farmer's market and sat at picnic tables in front of the five and ten to drink cold sodas wet with exactly the same condensation that formed on cans everywhere else in the state. Yet in Appleville, they held the cans up to their faces and exclaimed about how refreshing they were.

The Happy Citizens were even worse. It wasn't as though Appleville was better than the rest of the Midwest. The houses were the same mix of post-war bungalows and seventies ranches, along with the usual handful of older farmhouses. The schools were nothing special, and the football team didn't win often. The jobs were nothing to brag about, either. Pretty much everyone lived paycheck-to-paycheck, and every kid with an older sibling wore hand-me-downs.

Why were there Happy Citizens at all? Why wasn't everyone in Appleville a Grouch?

᠖

Norm finally ventured out again Friday morning after he discovered that he was out of milk for his coffee. He waited until he heard the bus go by so the kids wouldn't talk to him as he walked past their stop. He didn't want to yell at them like Annie Thompson.

When he thought it was safe, he peered out from behind his living room curtains. Two mothers walking their babies were meandering toward the corner; he waited until they turned down Chestnut. With the street finally deserted, he pulled his cap down low over his face and started toward the little grocery store on the corner of Elm and Main.

He caught a few people pointing and whispering, but at least no one talked to him. Everyone had seen the article in the paper, or knew someone who had, or knew someone who knew someone. The gossips in Appleville were as happy as everyone else, after all, and would delight in sharing every bit of news about the upcoming election. Anyone could hear Annie ranting about the whole thing for a square block, too.

It was more than that, however, as he discovered upon reaching the grocery store. In the window was a giant, full-color poster that said *Vote for Norm, the grouchiest Old Grouch in Appleville!* Jenny had not forgotten.

As he stood staring, the door creaked open and out walked fellow candidate Essie Baker. She smiled at him, her sour face warming. "Best of luck in the election!" she said happily. "I'm planning to vote for you myself, you know. You'll make a perfect Old Grouch."

He glared. What kind of a candidate was she, anyway? She wasn't even trying.

Of course, he wasn't trying either. He couldn't help it. He had woken up cantankerous on the day his nomination had been announced. Why did Essie appear unbothered by this whole affair?

☙

Inside the store, Norm ran into Appleville's other Grouch, Burt Gordon—or, rather, Burt ran into Norm with his cart. Burt snorted his congratulations on his candidacy. Norm glowered in reply. The other man always smelled of pickles, but today there was a distinct hint of mustard on top of it. Norm hated mustard. Walking home with the milk, Norm was scowling so hard he almost didn't notice Mayor Young standing in front of the town hall.

"Norm, it's good to see you!" The Mayor's smile was as bright as any worn by the Happy Citizens of Appleville. "I was starting to wonder whether the town might forget your face, with you hiding at home so much lately. That won't do you any good in the election! Though I suppose your pretty neighbor took care of that problem with her posters, didn't she?"

Norm glared.

"That's the ticket." The Mayor's grin stretched still wider. "I knew I picked the right candidate. You really look the part!"

"Doesn't he?" Jenny appeared at his elbow, looking smug. "There's a reason he's the front-runner in the latest poll!"

Someone had done a poll? Well, probably someone's name was Jenny. "I don't want to be a Grouch."

"Perfect!" said Jenny. "Just keep it up!"

"Perfect," the Mayor echoed, with an obvious leer at Jenny's backside.

Norm winced.

Jenny smiled. "Relax," she whispered to Norm. "After all, it's a compliment."

Norm's jaw dropped. If Jenny was taking that sort of behavior as a compliment, something was very, very wrong in Appleville. How had he never noticed it before?

&❧

Back home, Norm slammed the screen door. He put the milk away and slammed the fridge closed, too. He paced back and forth across the kitchen. Why was everyone in town so happy? How could Jenny be so happy, even in the face of behavior like that? Had the Mayor always been so creepy? Young was always smiling, always got his way, and never seemed to get older.

Who could Norm really talk with, now that he was nominated to be a Grouch? It felt strange, but he couldn't discuss it with the Happy Citizens. They wouldn't even see the problem. He hadn't seen it either, until the Mayor had nominated him to be an Old Grouch. As for the current Grouches, they never listened to anyone except occasionally each other. To get them to discuss it, he would have to win the election.

❧

By election day, Norm had decided one thing: he didn't want to go back to being a Happy Citizen. That was probably a good thing, because it didn't seem as though he would have a choice. Everyone he saw on the way to the town hall said they were planning to vote for him.

"You're sure to win!" Jenny said as she tried to hug him on the sidewalk out front.

He held out a hand to block her. "I bet."

Inside, he marked an angry X beside his own name before stuffing the ballot in the box. Then he went outside and sat down on a bench to glare at everyone who came to vote. He had never wanted to be nominated, but since he had been, he intended to win.

❧

Win he did. "It's Norm Davies by a landslide!" the Mayor announced from the steps of the town hall that evening. His smile was far too smug.

Jenny hugged him and Essie congratulated him, but Norm couldn't even feel happy about the victory; he was too busy hating the Mayor. Something was very wrong there, and he had to figure it out. The Happy Citizens of Appleville deserved better.

❧

The night before his official installation as an Old Grouch, Norm walked home past the banners hung from lampposts and the bunting draped across storefronts. He walked past the Mayor repainting the Appleville sign to indicate the proper number of Happy Citizens, now that Norm would no longer be one of them. Norm looked daggers at everyone, and they grinned to see him ready to take on his role. If only they knew!

Norm was about to do the grouchiest thing possible. He intended to ruin the town's tradition forever, right in the middle of their celebration.

When he got home, he paced back and forth in the kitchen, listening to the clock on the church tower chime each hour. Appleville went to bed at midnight. After all, a good night's sleep kept people happy. Grouches, however, were supposed to be contrary, so it was perfectly all right for him to stay up all night if he wanted to do so.

As the clock finally struck twelve, he collected two cans of paint and some brushes from his garage and started toward the center of town. Walking down Main Street, he felt grouchier than ever. How dare the Mayor dictate the feelings of the whole town? Well, Norm wasn't going to stand for it.

Norm peeked beneath the sheet covering the famous Appleville sign. The paint was brighter where the Mayor had made 3005 Happy Citizens into 3004 Happy Citizens, adjusting for Norm's impending assumption of Grouchhood.

Norm poked around in the shrubs until he found a reasonably-sized rock. He threw it at the nearest streetlamp. It was time to start being really grouchy.

The light went out, leaving the front of the town hall in long shadows. Norm pulled the sheet off the sign and got to work once his eyes adjusted. First, he painted over the preexisting message. His white paint promised it would provide complete coverage in one coat, but of course that wasn't true. Norm glared at it before brushing on a second coat.

When he finished obliterating the Mayor's words, he sat down for a quick break. Maybe he could just stop there. Maybe it was enough that the sign no longer told everyone in town that they must be happy.

No. Norm was still furious. He had to finish the job.

Norm stood up and opened the can of black paint. He stirred it. He dipped the brush and began to paint his own words.

&❧

He was tired in the morning, but Norm made sure he was still early for the festivities. He caught the Mayor before reaching the town hall and badgered him with enough complaints about the arrangements that there was no chance to peek beneath the sheet. Norm kept griping right up until the Mayor took the microphone to announce the beginning of the parade.

The floats were garish and the band was loud and the crowd was offensively cheerful, and by the end of the parade Norm had a headache. It only got worse when the Mayor marched him up onto the stage in front of the sign and the entire town crowded around to cheer, along with a number of tourists. Norm almost felt sorry for the disappointment they were about to get.

He hadn't volunteered to entertain them. He scowled at them, and they laughed and applauded more.

The Mayor gave a long speech about the tradition of electing Grouches. "It's been going on since I was first in office," he said. The Happy Citizens cheered.

How long had it been since the Mayor had first been elected? Norm wondered.

"Since I was a kid," hissed Grouch Annie, standing beside him, the morning paper with the election results sticking out of her pocket.

"Way too long," grumbled Grouch Burt.

Norm shivered. Way too long, indeed. Annie was at least fifteen years older than Norm, but the Mayor looked no more than forty.

Mayor Young wound up his enthusiastic description of Norm's overwhelming victory and beckoned Norm to stand with him by the sign. A lanky teen who took pictures for the paper lifted his camera and fussed with the lens, ready for the big moment. The Mayor reached up and took hold of the sheet. "I present to you Norm Davies of Appleville, home to three thousand and four Happy Citizens… and three Old Grouches!"

The crowd cheered louder.

The Mayor pulled down the sheet.

The camera flashed. The crowd gasped and fell silent.

The sign read *Welcome to Appleville, home of 3007 people who feel how they feel.*

The happy faces twisted. Some looked surprised, some sad. Some looked scared. Some wore other emotions. Then they shifted—first one or two, then a handful, and then more and more in waves. They grew angry.

The Mayor's whole body shook. At first, Norm thought the man was afraid of the crowd, but then he saw that Mayor Young was changing. The thick hair was disappearing, thinning, and turning white. The smooth face grew wrinkled and spotted. The perfect posture sagged, the back curving and the shoulders sinking.

"No more happiness to keep me young." The Mayor's voice cracked and wavered.

Norm looked at him scornfully. "And what about us? We Grouches?"

"Someone had to balance the happiness. A sacrifice, for the good of the town."

People were shouting again, and the crowd was pushing toward the stage. Norm could see Jenny trying to shove her way to the front. He almost smiled to hear her yelling something about *harassment, you creepy old lecher* at the Mayor.

"The good of the town? Make them happy so they never noticed how much was wrong with their lives?" Norm shook his head. "I'd rather be a Grouch."

"Me too," said Annie.

"And me," said Burt.

Hundreds of furious faces surged forward. Hundreds of arms

reached out angrily. The Mayor crumpled, his tissue turning to dust and blowing away, leaving only a pile of bones on the stage with the three Old Grouches.

***

Laura Jane Swanson holds a degree in biochemistry and has done graduate work in molecular biology and science education. She lives in Indiana with her family, where she dreams of the coast and knits lots of socks.

A BRILLIANT LIGHT, AN UNREACHABLE DAWN

Phoebe Barton

Content Notes: *Manipulation, Police, Weapons*

Home had sharpened to a brilliant point of light beside a crescent Jupiter when I realized I was still thinking in Mirabilish. After a four-year visit to another world, habits could be hard to break, but I'd have to crack this one like bad bamboo before docking and resocialization. If anything, the Directors had hardened their stance on linguistic disharmony while I'd been away. In an emergency, a word couldn't mean anything other than what it was made to describe. In a habitat like Phoenix Halo, ambiguity meant death.

So I had fallen into poetry. There was plenty of inspiration on the screens that looked outward: here, a roiling and world-swallowing hurricane in red and orange; there, the pale blue star that was Earth. Besides, poems weren't perfect mirrors, and they were never meant to be. As much as the Directors argued, people weren't rational and orderly. We needed ambiguity to deal with life, the way habitats needed radiators to deal with heat.

I only wrote poems in my head, though. Now that I was on my way home, I needed to be cautious with how I spoke, in case a scrap

74

of Mirabilish drifted out.

§

Hattie had never watched what she said. That bravery and that arrogance were what had attracted me to her, back when I was still flush with the realization that not only could I be a woman after all, but I could still favour women. That last kiss we'd shared before I pulled myself through the airlock four years ago, the apex of a relationship crafting a furnace of my heart, stayed with me all through torpor and gave me warmth under warped constellations painted across an unfamiliar night. For four years, that kiss had kept me going, and now that I was back, I ached to find Hattie, to see if she had any more for me.

I was still dizzy from resocialization and Phoenix Halo's ceaseless spin when I made it back to her apartment. I hadn't forgotten her number, but calling it had linked me to a stranger; maybe she'd changed it while I was away. The micro-messages she'd sent me early on, before the government cracked down on external comms, hadn't mentioned anything about it.

The door was still the same, of course. I knocked, hoping that she'd leap into my arms, but it wasn't Hattie who answered. I recognized her mother, given a moment—she looked like she'd aged twenty years in the last four, with grey hairs where I remembered red, and eyes that would always be tired.

"Oh, Vera," she said. I'd always hated being called that; you're not supposed to abbreviate an idea as important as Perseverance, but I tolerated it for Hattie's sake. "I thought you were away."

"I was," I said, "but I'm back now. Is Hattie here?"

There was a surge of pain in those exhausted eyes, like needles erupting through the irises, coated in grief.

"I'm sorry," she said, and her apology bore the weight of worlds. "Manhattan is gone."

I didn't have any words. Hattie's mother shut the door in my face, and it was a relief. I didn't dare breathe a hint of sadness or mourning. Grief, like space, was an empty void. In my poems, they both were the thieves of life.

ॐ

If nothing else, they named Mirabilis well: it really was a miracle world, waiting for us right on the other side of the miraculous warp point orbiting Luna. A reflection of Earth, full of life that we could share. More reflections were found as the years went on, more worlds to shine a light on humanity's shame for nearly destroying our own, but Mirabilis was first. It would always be special. I had been astonished to be approved for an exit visa to go there.

It was a world where people didn't have to be constantly on guard. A world that didn't try to confuse you into obedience. A world where people could live with ambiguity, because it was kind enough not to kill you for making one little mistake.

ॐ

That night, when I was assigned to a bed made for one but which felt wide and empty, I drifted back into memory of the last time Hattie had been there with me in the meadow of my dreams. Her arms were ghostly around me, my skin going numb where we touched. These memories had gotten me through four years on Mirabilis, four years alone.

"You're sure you're going to go?" Hattie sounded assured, confident, unflappable. The way she always had. "I mean, a whole planet, and not even in-system. That's brave."

"They wouldn't let me go to Earth," I said. I never learned the reason why. The only real difference between Earth and Mirabilis was that we hadn't beaten Mirabilis into a bloody pulp. It didn't need anyone's help to heal.

"They're never straightforward," she whispered, then and now, quiet enough that the microphones wouldn't hear. Both times, her breath warmed my ear. "The powers that be, when they talk. They're so specific, they don't mean anything. Have you noticed that? It's so frustrating."

"I guess I haven't," I said. Back then, before I'd left Phoenix Halo, I'd never heard leaders talk any other way. "Does it matter?"

"Of course it does," Hattie said. "They're manipulating us. I mean, what would you rather think about—cancer, or grow-yourself-to-death sickness?"

"I'd rather not think about it at all," I said, but my mind drifted toward my poems. How many times had I smoothed down and papered over a rough word, an inconvenient phrase, because it had other meanings I didn't want to wrestle with?

"Maybe you should," Hattie said. "Maybe you should think about why they call it a habitat and not a cage."

I hadn't said anything then. Now that I knew the wide-open spaces of a convex world, I moaned with regret that I couldn't tell Hattie what I'd learned.

"Or what pan-Jovian co-prosperous amity really means," Hattie muttered. "Doing every little thing our lovely Callistonian friends want."

I knew what she really meant there, at least, even if she wouldn't say it. Hattie was brave, sure, but there was a fine line between bravery and foolishness.

&♥

I wondered: if we'd kept calling the ocean the whale-road, like the Norse poets did, would it still have been easy to drive so many whales to extinction? After all, how could the whale-road possibly be empty of whales?

&♥

The reason I went to Mirabilis was to study environmental maintenance; after all, it was the closest living world that wasn't being kept alive with pure effort, electricity, and espérance. I was intended to be a repairer, a maintainer, a gardener. When I returned to Phoenix Halo, however, the alignment specialists had a different idea.

They see the things ordinary people can't, and they saw me in the uniform of a pro-social integrator. I could hardly argue, no matter how much I wanted to. Without socio-functional alignment, Phoenix Halo would spin apart—wouldn't it? They could see more than me, so jettisoning everything I'd learned on Mirabilis was the right choice—wasn't it?

Hattie would've been able to set me in the right direction in an instant. People like her are life-compasses. Now that I was alone, my needle was constantly spinning, pointing everywhere and nowhere. I'd had weeks to get used to it, but I was only getting dizzier.

"Good morning," I said to the first integratee of the day as I extended a welcoming hand. Maybe the only one of the day, or the week. "I'm Perseverance. I'm here to help you adjust."

"They told me you would." She was paler than I'd ever been, a real sun-squirrel, and stick-boned. The handful of New New Zealanders I'd met were like that. The place had cylinders big enough to be worlds on their own, and not so much as a window to peek through. Maybe that's why they were at each other's throats. "I'm exhausted. Let's just get to the meat."

Meat was one of the surprising differences I'd found between a habitat and a convex world. Worlds had enough open space to ignore all the ethical considerations. Personally, I never touched the stuff. From what I'd heard, my compunctions weren't common in New New Zealand. How was I supposed to start with a person coming from that, and integrate them into Phoenix Halo?

"Right, well, I should start by welcoming you," I said. "Don't let the rotation fool you. We may have one g, but you're better off assuming everything else works differently here."

"I could use a bit of difference," the sun-squirrel said. "Back home, it's people screaming they deserve such-and-such on one hand, people trying to keep everything spinning on the other one. It's just exhausting. There's no middle anymore. I just needed somewhere to stand, hear me?"

It was a sad story. The UN had tried to keep the peace in New New Zealand for years now. If they hadn't been able to resolve things, what could I do but smile and nod? I didn't tell her what Hattie told me: that when you're in the middle of a habitat, you're floating free with nothing to grab onto. Sure, it feels nice while you're there, but eventually your bones turn to dust.

"I heard that people don't have to worry about things here," the sun-squirrel went on. "That they just happen. I like the sound of that."

"Managed democracy." It was as poetic as bureaucracies got. It hadn't been until Mirabilis, where I saw people talk and discuss and argue before a vote that wasn't preordained, that I understood what it meant. "It makes life easier."

In the back of my head, I heard Hattie click her tongue at me. My own personal shame-ghost.

&◆

The name of a place was the most important thing, in the end. Heat radiators and radiation shielding made a habitat livable, sure, but the name set the tone for what kind of livability you'd find there. Look at Phoenix Halo: rebirth and divinity. Then you have a place like New New Zealand, built by people who'd rather cut out their tongues than say "Aotearoa." Or the Himalia Regional Processing Centre, where the Callistonians detained desperate Belter refugees on a lonely chunk of ice.

I could see both if I looked outside at the right time, but I'd had to travel sixteen light-years to understand what was hidden behind those names. Hattie knew from the start. In that paper-thin respect, I tried to be glad she was gone. It meant I didn't have to show her what a fool I was, a poet who couldn't understand poetry. Not until I visited a world that really was a miracle.

&◆

Two months in, I was writing poems in Mirabilish on paper I kept hidden away, with ink I had carried between worlds. I told myself it was to keep in practice, in case anyone exchanged that wide-open world for Phoenix Halo's walls. Hattie would have known better, would have been able to read it on my skin while we sheltered in each other's arms. The truth was that I knew what my poetry meant, and it didn't lie to me. It came out of all those languages living side-by-side on our brand-new miracle world, and despite its ambiguity, it was meant to be understood.

On Phoenix Halo, you could say exactly what something was without saying anything about its reality. "Himalia Regional Processing Centre" sounded a lot kinder than "cold fortress where desperate people are imprisoned indefinitely because it's easy to be cruel to newcomers."

"The Pan-Jovian Co-Prosperous Union" sounded a lot softer than "the Callistonian Empire."

❧

"We've had some concerns," the achievement auditor said when I sat down for my quarterly check-in. He was compact and angular in his rock-grey suit, as much a speaking-boulder as a man. "It's about your commitment to linguistic harmony."

That instant was elastic. I spent it digging into my childhood, uncovering all the lessons about how the auditors were your friends, how the police were looking out for you, how they only wanted the best for everyone. I reminded myself to not show fear. Fear of an auditor wasn't in alignment with Phoenician values. I forced myself to not feel fear.

"I'm not sure I understand." I'd been careful. I hadn't spoken a scrap of Mirabilish, not a single word that wasn't Phoenix Halo Standard English, even if it meant I utilized five when one would do. Hattie once told me that the people who shouted the loudest about efficiency were the most disorganized of all. "I'd be happy to realign the issue, but I'd need to identify the specific problem."

"Improperly calibrated speech," the auditor rejoined. "We've measured you at .07 divergence from standard. You're not in symphony."

"I didn't realize." Surrounded by Mirabilitians for four years, all with their own accents and ways of speaking, how could I have? Humans followed others' leads without being conscious of it. "I must have picked it up without intent."

"It should have been brought to your attention during your resocialization." His tone was gravel-rough. "Now that it has, I expect you'll realign before it reaches the level of anti-sociality. Remember, this isn't Ganymede. This will never be Ganymede."

I couldn't do anything but agree. My function as a pro-social integrator was to be a model for newcomers adjusting themselves to Phoenix Halo life, and that included the way we were meant to speak. It didn't matter if I believed it; I had to be a good example. Anything else would be anti-social.

As soon as I was free, I hurried home and ate every last one of my Mirabilish poems. There was no other safe way to get rid of them, after all. The pages were bland leaves, and the ink made for terrible pepper.

❧

Four months, and I no longer remembered what sunrises felt like. All those days I had risen early to meet the sun, all those peaceful moments watching it wash darkness from the world, were distant and dream-dim. A place like Phoenix Halo, with its strict schedules and polished mirrors to let precise amounts of light in, had no need for them. Had no need for feelings, not when there was so much room in feelings for ambiguity.

That's what Hattie was always trying to tell me, even though I was too afraid to listen. I was still afraid after four months home, but at least I could admit it to myself.

❧

"You've got an organized tin here," said the New New Zealander I was integrating, five months in. Not the sun-squirrel, she was long gone, but there were always more. This one was a man, hair-encrusted, wide-shouldered, sharp-bodied. Everything I'd thrown into the fire. "Righteous place. Full of right people. I can tell, looking

81

at you."

I smiled thinly at his bluntness. I never bothered to ask what Newzers meant by "right people;" I already knew. White people, enclosed people. I was certain it was why nobody complained about the way they talked, how they swallowed so many of their Rs, while Mirabilish had barely spiced my syllables. One thing I had learned in my time on Mirabilis—white people can't handle spices.

"Not like Ganymede at all," said the Newzer. "I listened to some of their radio, just for curiosity. It's exactly what you'd expect. No order down there at all. Surprised they aren't naught but corpses."

I nodded. The Phoenix Halo-Ganymede relationship was complicated at the best of times. Ganymede and Callisto were perpetually at each other's throats, and the Directors were more and more aligning themselves with the moon whose orbit we shared: cold, dark Callisto, where the people were hard as the ice.

"That's why you came here?" I asked. "For stability?"

"Well, that, and this girl Ganymede had on the radio, she drove me up the wall," the Newzer said. "Always going on about saying what you mean, and how habitats are like cages. Said she was from here and glad to be gone. So a speck of spite there, too."

I felt my heart stop for a moment. I willed it to start beating again. It was too much to hope for—wasn't it?

"I've never listened to Ganymede radio," I said cautiously. Of course I hadn't. I had to be a good Phoenician, unblemished by certain outside attitudes. "Do you remember who she was?"

"Was one of those damn Earth-place names," the Newzer said. "One of those 'M' ones… yeah, Manhattan. She on a list or something?"

"I'm sure she is," I said. It was one of the most honest things I'd ever said.

I couldn't believe I hadn't considered the possibility earlier. Ambiguity meant death on Phoenix Halo, after all. It was easier to think of people as dead when they had only walked away.

ᕲ

There could be no swift escape to Ganymede for me, no leaping into Hattie's arms. At least nowhere in a future I was tall enough to see. It had been an ordeal getting the exit visa for Mirabilis, and that was a non-hostile world far from the Directors' worries. If Phoenix Halo had a nemesis, it was Ganymede. Ganymede housed the blood-sweaters, the sword-sheathers, the feeders of gardens.

I didn't want to imagine Hattie's bones feeding anyone's garden.

ᕲ

At that point, I had three options. I could take comfort in knowing that Hattie was alive and well on Ganymede and evict her from my thoughts. I could do all the things she'd tried to make me brave enough to do and find a way to reunite with her despite all the obstacles between us. Or I could face the likelihood that the Newzer had been briefed and the Directors were testing me for anti-social impulses. I hadn't been back for long, after all. How reliable could I be?

I bit my tongue and faced the reality manufactured around me. A year. Two years. Three. My Mirabilish fell into an orbit that would never bring it back to me, and my poems fell with it. There was nothing poetic left in Phoenix Halo, a world turning more and more grey. I forgot the sensation of the wind, the feeling of openness, the absence of worry. I started encountering more and more Callistonians in their support exos, proving themselves against our ten-times-higher gravity, their uniforms black as space. I nodded, I smiled, I acted. I did everything the Directors—and then, just the Director—said I should do.

It was five years and change, longer than I'd been on Mirabilis, before I felt ready to stop acting. I had to be careful, but I'd learned carefully. Phoenix Halo's managed democracy was becoming less and less of one every day. I watched, I scrounged, I scavenged. Once I learned enough to build a radio, I listened.

"Good morning, Jovians!" Nine years, and I could still feel

Hattie's breath on my neck, her hands on my waist, her lips against mine. All that in a voice. Love-sound. "I hope you're all comfortable and ready to rebel. I'm Manhattan Green. Let's get things rolling!"

I listened to every word, and afterward, I cried. If I hadn't gone away, if I hadn't left her alone, I would have been there for her. I could have gone with her, if not for my clipped wings. If only I could have named the bars of my cage.

⤫

"They're fools, all of them," said my latest integratee, a gangly man with an implant beard of titanium hair. Another Newzer, of course. They were only ever Newzers and Callistonians. Nobody had ever come to Phoenix Halo from Mirabilis. No one but me. "The place is a cat's whisker from cloudcuckooland. It can't last."

I'd kept up on the news. While not an ally, New New Zealand wasn't an adversary, so reports weren't even encumbered by too much sneering superiority. If not for the UN controlling the station's port and keeping the two cylinders at bay, it would have collapsed years ago. Space habitats are sensitive environments at the best of times.

"That's a shame," I said. "There was so much possibility there."

"If I were you, I'd get ready for a wave," Titanium-Beard said. "It's only a matter of time. Reality'll smack folks like a dead fish, and there won't be enough ships for 'em all."

That was what stayed with me after the session ended. Despite the years, despite everything, I'd still believed deep down that things wouldn't really change. That New New Zealand would always be there. That I'd have all the time I needed to plan my jump.

That Hattie would always be there, waiting for me to find her.

⤫

I made the request through official channels, ink-smooth. Everything would have to be perfect for it to even have a chance of working. My supervisor passed it up to her overseer, and up the ladder where I couldn't see it. When the word came down for me to submit to an audience with the Director, I knew it couldn't have gone any other way. I told myself all of that and more after I stopped peeing myself in terror, after I triple-checked that it was connected to my request and nothing more.

I drew as much social capital as I could for a fine dress. I couldn't face the Director in an ordinary habsuit, after all. It would be anti-social. For a moment, when I put it on for the first time, it was as if all my problems weren't problems at all. Its fabric was the same soft blue as Hattie's eyes, and when I twirled I felt the breezes of far-away Mirabilis playing across my skin. I had poems on my tongue and love on my lips.

It lasted for a brilliant moment until I remembered.

"Patriotic appearance," said the guard at the House of Heroes' security checkpoint. I'd paid for my presence with blood, sweat, eye scans, pheromones, and brainwaves. Everything they needed to be sure. "You can proceed."

I nodded, meekly, as if anything else would break the illusion. The guard looked like Phoenicia, the station's mascot; all the guards did. When I was young, Phoenicia had warned people to stay alert for damage and encouraged them to do their part on the maintenance teams. Now, she carried a shock baton.

One of the Phoenicias escorted me through the House's many corridors, all of them studded with scanners and turrets and sealed-off doors. A fortress for the Director, in case the tide ever overflowed the shore.

I controlled my breathing, soft and calm. I did my best to remember snowy Mirabilitian winters. I'd been careful, and I'd never said anything that was an absolute lie. Sweat stuck to me, regardless.

The Director's door was just like the others—cold, grey, indomitable, and shut to people like me—but for a screen set in it that lit up as I approached. The Director was just like so many others I might see outside: elderly, silver-haired, and convinced of her own supremacy. Phoenicia marched me to the screen, her shock baton buried in my back.

"You're late," the Director grumbled, more than loud enough for me to hear. "Justify yourself. I'm busy."

"I'm a pro-social integrator," I said. I still don't know how I said it without tying my tongue in knots. The Director wasn't the architect of Phoenix Halo, but she was its maintainer. "The integratees are overwhelmingly from New New Zealand. I'd like to travel there, understand it better, so that I can better integrate them."

For a moment, the silence filled the space around me like crash foam, getting everywhere and keeping me still. A scrap of poetry: courage's ice. The Director's eyes were like ice themselves, dark and cold moons no one had ever visited, hostile and small. One wrong move, one wrong thought, and I'd never see New New Zealand. I'd never even see the outside of the House of Heroes again.

"I'll expect a detailed report once you get back, you understand," the Director said. "Extremely detailed. Something to justify the trust this habitat has already placed in you."

All the air rushes out of my lungs. The Director was a hull breach, an empty vacuum, a thief of life. How could it be so straightforward?

"Thank you," I said, as if I was thanking a plant. It was the only thing I could have possibly said that wouldn't end with a rough trip to an airlock.

The Director nodded, the screen went dark , and Phoenicia jabbed her shock baton into my side. I was sure that if I stayed any longer the Director would show her true face, the event horizon of a black hole, and absorb me while I screamed all the way. It had happened to so many people, after all.

It would happen to everyone in Phoenix Halo eventually. Hattie had seen it coming. It had long since begun.

"Keep moving," Phoenicia said. The spikes of her shock baton pushed through my dress and into my skin, leaving marks like teeth behind.

⁊❧

I wore the dress one more time. Alone, in my apartment, surrounded by the remnants of a life in hiding. It was still crisp, it was still bright, it was still freeing as I danced and spun. It deserved better than a place like Phoenix Halo. I wished I didn't have to hang it up again, but I couldn't risk them figuring me out. They'd have an auditor check through the place as soon as I was gone. It all had to stay, as if I was coming right back. I left with enough to justify a brief trip, and no more.

There was no spin in Phoenix Halo's port, and no gravity. For the first time in years, I was weightless again. I kept up every appearance as they checked, screened, and authorized. Mine showed green: life's light. I settled in on the shuttle and breathed: life's gift.

In a handful of days, the shuttle would dock at New New Zealand. I would be very careful, very proper, right up until the moment I could quietly ask the UN for sanctuary. I would make my way down to Ganymede. While I was sure Hattie had moved on, I just had to see her one more time. To tell her that she was right about what she saw in me. To hear her voice, unmodulated, one more time.

Maybe even for both of us, just once, to watch the sun rise over Ganymede's cratered plains.

Until then, there was plenty of time for me to remember my Mirabilish. Phoenix Halo was nothing but a brilliant point of light behind me.

***

Phoebe Barton is a queer trans science fiction writer. Her short fiction has appeared in venues such as *Analog, On Spec,* and *Kaleidotrope.* She is an Associate Editor at *Escape Pod,* is a graduate of the Clarion West Writers Workshop, and lives with a robot in the sky above Toronto.

OCTOBERS/OCTOBER

Leonardo Espinoza Benavides
Translated by Julie Whelan Capell

Content Notes: *Anxiety, Death, Dissociation, Gore, Police, Violence, Weapons*

> *Beloved homeland, receive the vows*
> *That Chile gave you on your altars*
> *That you be either the tomb of the free*
> *Or a refuge from oppression…*
> *— from the Chilean National Anthem*

The image rose up in front of Yuri with the power of a psychic tattoo—a recurrent symbol with so many manifestations through the years. The statue of General Baquedano was only a few meters away, the commander and his horse cropped onto an orange and ashy Santiago sky, hot as had become the norm those days. Climbing on top, a multitude of citizens shouted their protests to the rhythm of gigantic banners waving with the pulse of chants filling the plaza. The Solitary Star and Heaven's Winter's Bark, flags of Chile and of the Mapuche people respectively, were invoked once again in just communion.

It was all quite picturesque, but the acrid air impregnating his eyes, nose, and throat marred the experience. Pungent tear gas found its way through the fibers of the bandana that covered his nose and mouth, pushed by a breeze mixed with dirt and dust. Also with acid, it seemed to him.

Yuri's eyes swam with tears.

"My entire life is burning," he growled with a twisted laugh, contorting his face in a series of grimaces. "Now I can't open my eyes even a little bit. I can't see a thing."

"Think of this as an opportunity to cry about other things," said Moira, also laughing, her red cheeks peeking out over the faded red bandana she was wearing.

"A little water with bicarbonate, friend?"

A girl in goggles sprayed their eyelids with liquid from a bottle she carried. Bit by bit, calm descended. As Yuri recovered his vision, he saw a large bonfire rising on the main avenue toward the west. He heard several booming thuds, possibly large chunks of pavement being thrown by demonstrators against metallic barriers, or maybe fire extinguishers tossed onto the fire, or they could even have been signal flares shot up by the soccer fans du jour. He couldn't quite figure it out, with all the blending noise, but he did recognize the dry roar that started immediately afterward. Three cartridges shot in formation over their heads left a trail of irritating gas. A fourth landed just shy of his right foot.

Before he could kick it, a nearby woman wearing gloves threw it back.

"Hold on, Moira, hold on!" he said, a little amused. "It will pass, we just have to wait. Stay calm. No more than a couple of minutes."

"The cops are coming! Weón, run!"

The police advanced, followed by their guanaco, the water cannon truck, all splotched where marchers had thrown paint on it. A line of khaki green uniforms coalesced through the smoke, with shields and batons and helmets and boots and shin guards. They advanced as a group and then suddenly parted, revealing their surprise: a Goliath of a man who leapt forward to confront the protesters. Suddenly, instead of cheering saxophones and singing drums, the Public Order Units now had complete control. The protest was over, the pagan festival atmosphere ended. All that was left was to flee.

Grasping each other's hands, Yuri and Moira tore away with the throng toward the side streets. Through humid, blurry eyes, Yuri glanced back. The so-called "First Line" of protesters was materializing through the wall of smoke. He noticed some had taped metal stop signs to their forearms, a southern hemisphere version of Captain America. One in particular caught his attention: a giant wearing gray overalls and a full gas mask, walking without haste, as if just getting started, calm and disillusioned. A second Goliath, Yuri thought. Two Goliaths on the prowl, because maybe there never was a David. He felt trapped in the myth, drawn toward the figure of the modern anarchist.

Nevertheless, Yuri felt uneasy. Nietzsche came to mind, and he recalled one of the philosopher's phrases: "Whoever fights monsters…"

Moira tugged at Yuri, and they sprinted away.

It wasn't hard to find a safer place, away from the core of the commotion. Following a pattern established in the days since the curfew had been lifted, the police were breaking up the protest just before nightfall. By the time Yuri and Moira approached their neighborhood, it was fully dark. The crowd had been particularly large today, it seemed to him. He hoped they would soon release aerial views so he could get an idea of how many people had been protesting. Moira was already throwing out tentative numbers.

"Same place tomorrow?" she finished.

"I suppose," he responded. "I hope so."

Moira closed the gate to her building and Yuri did the same two blocks further south. The priority when he got inside was to take off his light blue work suit and succumb to a warm shower, turbid but refreshing. First, he turned on the news at maximum volume, in case the president came on.

The news didn't show much. It was still hard for him to admit that the press had its own biases. It truly hurt, because he could remember when, mere weeks earlier, in his innocence he would not have questioned what he saw in the report. He didn't like to be suspicious. It was part of the costly price he paid for having the veil lifted from his eyes. On the other hand, verifying the state of things through his social networks was as effective as drying himself with a holographic towel.

He turned down the volume when he heard the call coming in from his friend Koke.

"They haven't shown anything," Yuri blurted out, unable to contain himself.

"And this still surprises you?"

"I know, I know. I'm not a journalist—this isn't my world. Anyway, it was good today. There were a lot of people. It looked really full."

"That's good, that's why I'm calling. Tomorrow, I'm definitely going after work."

"I think with two more weeks at this pace," said Yuri, "we can achieve something. Anything. This is frustrating."

"Two weeks?" said Koke. "Good luck with that!"

"Why? You don't think so?"

"Well, Christmas is coming."

"Exactly. The effect will be bigger! It's an important date for the whole country. It's a good date."

"Good date? Good luck."

"What?"

"Let's see, Yuri. Do you really think people will go out and protest on Christmas? Really? It sounds pretty, but no. Where will you be on the 24th? I imagine you'll go see your mother."

"Since when have you been all excited about Christmas?" Yuri was thinking of seeing his parents, that was true.

"I read something in an old issue of *La Diaria* newspaper," Koke explained. "A leaked conversation between a Mexican narco and an Uruguayan narco. The Uruguayan was explaining that, if they wanted the shipment to arrive by Christmas, they would have to move everything up."

"But," said Yuri, "if it was going to arrive on time, it didn't actually need to be moved up."

"That's the point, you see? We have a thing for Christmas down here."

"And what does one thing have to do with the other?"

"That it's Christmas! Even the narcos stop selling drugs on holidays." Koke expelled an incredibly heavy sigh.

"Ya, cállate. The president is going to talk."

Yuri fixed his attention on the screen. He got nervous every time the Chief of State spoke, and he clearly wasn't alone in this. He chewed his knuckles, hoping that maybe this time, maybe finally, the president would announce some measures responding to the country's upheaval since this last October, like so many Octobers before. It would be enough for him if it at least appeared to be useful, a glimmer that some minimal steps were proposed. These empty speeches were twisting his insides into knots.

Tonight began with the usual: Dear fellow citizens, difficult days, the advocates of violence and the vandals, hopes for unity and a path toward peace, a battle to be won, social order and reforms on the way, reject the temptation to make profound structural changes that will only destabilize the achievements made under democracy. The usual. Nervousness of the listeners gradually changed to apathy. Also as usual. Then an anti-bandana law was announced.

"Did he say 'anti-bandana?'"

"I heard that, too."

Bandanas were turning into a uniform, said their leader, and the uniform revealed fascist leanings of these criminal groups—professionals, probably trained by foreign organizations in insurgency tactics. This government would not allow a handful of narcissistic and ideologized youth to threaten the peaceful living of all responsible Chileans. No more bandanas. No more faces covered in public under any circumstances, regardless of health concerns. Severe sentences for violators. As a preventive measure for any future disturbances, more police would be deployed at key protest points.

Yuri frowned. Koke spoke first.

"Fascist measures to fight against fascism? Is that what they're saying?"

"I don't know," Yuri responded, still weighing what he had heard.

"It's got a certain logic to it. Crush your fascist enemy with a bigger dose of fascism. How about that? Checkmate to the violence mongers."

"The shit's going to hit the fan, Koke."

"I know. Close your windows. Don't open your door to anyone. We'll talk tomorrow."

That's how they grind us down, he thought. Not even his bandana soaked in bicarbonate water was safe from the government's banal brand of violence. The president's speech could perhaps be expected, but even so, it surprised him. What kind of insanity was this? How was it possible that this would be the priority? Could it be deliberate provocation? He wasn't so naïve as to deny the existence of delinquents and anarchists, but to jump from there to such polarizing, simplistic, stale, outdated postures was something he could not understand.

He had to leave. He had to go out and bear witness. A moment's check of his social networks was enough to find the call to assemble. Of course, people who protested at night were not the same as those who went out by day—he knew that. But stay inside and not sleep? His nerves would not allow it.

Moira texted: *Don't go out, it's too late. Keep your windows tightly closed. They're already starting to burn the barricades.*

Don't worry, I'm already in bed. I'm going to take a sleeping pill. Even as he responded, Yuri began to smell a faint odor of burning tires.

He chewed the back of his right hand. He rubbed his temples. He itched his chin and squeezed a fingernail. He had to go out. Yes. He would go without the bandana, of course. He wouldn't test the new regulations on the very first night. He had nothing to hide.

Streets, once ochre-lit, now were passageways submerged in near-complete darkness. A cemetery of traffic lights and street lamps that had been torn down time and time again. It reminded him of his time in the provinces, in the countryside, where it was so dark at night you could still see the constellations. As he continued walking, the blackness gradually lifted, giving way to blazing reds and yellows along with the phosphorescent green of lasers that rose like arrows in search of helicopters and drones flying overhead.

Once again General Baquedano loomed, the insomniac. Revitalized by acrid air, Yuri joined those who were singing and jumping on the statue. It was like an historic party; it was like group therapy. He considered his pathetic anxiety prior to leaving his apartment. First time joining the protests at night, it didn't seem all that different from the peaceful marches under the rays of the sun. He felt safe in the knowledge that he was part of a large crowd.

A sharp bellow in the distance. The same routine: It was time to go.

His heart beat faster, his legs moved on their own, and he couldn't hide a smile. Moira was going to scold him when he told her about this night. He was pushed a couple of times. She would tell him it wasn't necessary to risk himself so much, that it was okay to give himself time to breathe, that he was better off rested than drained. Another push, and this time he nearly fell face-first on the ground. Disoriented, Yuri searched for a familiar point of reference. Suddenly his stunt did not seem so amusing, and he felt twinges in his chest like needles in his lungs. He reminded himself that everything would be fine, that the First Line would hold back armored fighters to allow people like him get away unharmed. In the end, the giants would confront each other and ignore chihuahuas like him.

Yuri's focus was drawn to jets of water forming iridescent rainbows behind him. The pushing continued and he stumbled on a broken piece of concrete. Straightening his ankle, he glanced up and realized he was in front of the theater of the University of Chile. The ground was littered with debris, ditches, and impossible fragments of what was once a staircase. He was pushed again. The stampede was getting bigger; it was harder to see gaps between people. His back slicked with sweat as he felt the group accelerating. They kept pushing him, but now he was pushing back, opening space between bodies, mud, and berm. Someone on his left pushed him and he angrily pushed the person on his right.

The person on his right disappeared.

Yuri stood absolutely still. His eyes fixed on the place where that person had been, but now he could see only a kind of pit descending into who knew what kind of hell.

"Look out!" Yuri shouted, stopping another nearby.

"Did someone fall in?"

"I don't know," Yuri said, "I don't know."

He managed to raise his eyes and saw another person staring across the hole in astonishment. Their gazes crossed, confused, both holding back shoves from the herd flowing around their obstacle. That other pair of dark eyes changed from confusion into something else, something that tore at him. Yuri stared into the abyss, and now he was a part of the abyss, and the abyss was staring directly into him.

Suddenly, Yuri felt a bite in his ribs and expelled a scream. Someone yanked his shirt up with rapid efficiency.

"Don't worry, friend! You've been hit by a rubber bullet. It'll only be a bruise. Keep moving!"

It was the impetus he needed to overcome his inertia. He felt disoriented, nauseous, his face dry and cracked, his back stinging, but he ran. Had it been him? Did he push that person into the well? Maybe they'd gotten out, or someone helped them climb out, or perhaps they were taken into custody. Yuri hadn't even seen the person for more than a fraction of a second. There'd been so much pushing, but he'd only done as everyone else had been doing in order to get away. There was no denying it. It was his fault. Could it be that *he* killed someone?

"Shit, shit, shit, shit." What had he done?

He needed to run away.

When he got to his building he was gasping for breath, his throat parched. Yuri turned on every light in the apartment. He couldn't stand looking at shadows. He rummaged through the boxes of medications on his nightstand. He simply could not deal with this feeling—it was overwhelming him, it was eating him alive from the base of his skull. For a minute, he couldn't even recognize where he was or what he was doing. Then his eyes lit upon the box he was looking for, the one with a green star on the cover. He gulped a lithium capsule and two tranquilizers, tried to focus on his breathing. Little by little, he began to calm down.

After the pills began to take effect, he opened the windows just enough to allow some air inside. Comprehension of the events still eluded him. It was a struggle to follow his own thoughts. He would be incapable of staying sane once the tranquilizer wore off, he was sure of that. His body anticipated it, despite the chemicals helping soothe him.

He began to flow. His nature demanded it. There was no way he could make it through like this. He didn't have the strength for it. He needed to flow—a fluidity that ensured him the right balance. The adjustment ensued with gentleness the act required. Sometimes it could be controlled, but most of the time it happened spontaneously. Loosened hair fell over the shoulders. A river of sensations tickled face and skin. It felt like a scarf appearing when winter was imminent. An instant later, he became she, as xe would give way.

She wouldn't lose it. Not tonight, at least.

She would sleep, but stalked by a mantra…

It had been *her,* it had been *her,* it had been *her.*

She slept.

The next day she took her usual route on the Metro. Some mornings, if she got up early, she could walk the whole way. Today, she opted for the subterranean route. Her train passed through the Baquedano Museum station without a pause, but she could just make out the sign "closed until further notice." The protest must have really gotten out of hand after she left.

At the next station, she got out and climbed the stairs nearest the Catholic University. Yuri dodged street vendors and drew near to the Carabineros Street steps, where she read on the wall a graffiti that time refused to erase. "Santiago será la tumba del fascismo." She didn't remember in which of the many Octobers this graffiti had first appeared. She knew it was old, could be even from the first October, back in 2019. She imagined someone taking the time to retouch it periodically, when it began to fade. No one knew its origin. Was there an older version in Madrid? It seemed to her that the one in Madrid had been on a banner, not on a wall. "Will be the tomb." A tomb. Santiago would be a tomb.

A tomb—that, she recalled. It wasn't a well. Yuri clenched her jaw as the morning's façade of self-control disappeared. She accelerated her pace.

She entered the Marcoleta Clinic and went directly to her post. Moira was already preparing some bread with avocado in the break area nearby.

"Yuri! I like your hair. Did you hear about last night?"

Yuri greeted Moira with a glance but didn't respond to the question. While Moira finished the toast, Yuri pinned her name tag to her light blue suit. *Yuri Muñoz Caniuqueo. Advanced Registered Nursing Technician. Pronouns: he, she, xe.* She received her toast on a napkin.

"Last night was too much! Do you know what happened?" Moira repeated.

"No," said Yuri, trying not to make it sound like a question.

"Look," said Moira, reading. "Two people died."

"Two!"

"A Canadian tourist, Samuel Trembley."

"Protest tourism?"

"I guess. He was run over. Look, here's the video."

Sprinting across the street in front of the Gabriela Mistral Center, a thin silhouette in shorts and a white T-shirt was hit by a police cruiser that tossed him like a shooting star to strike the windshield of a vehicle going in the opposite direction.

"And the other drowned," said Moira. She took a sip of her green tea while she read. "That one really had bad luck."

"How so?"

"Fell in a well."

"You said 'drowned.'"

"Ane-Luis Torrealba. It says here that xe fell into a well, but xe would have drowned because the hole filled with water from the water cannons. There's a photo taken from one of the drones."

It matched. The abyss.

"Drowned," Moira said. "Maybe xe died in the fall. Hopefully. That would be quicker."

Yuri flinched.

"Hey, you're looking pale! Did you eat anything before coming here?"

There was a Percheron galloping in her chest. Trapped, drooling, with dilated pupils, kicking rhythmically. A desperate animal, smelling its clandestine task, striking with its metal shoes. Stamp, stamp, stamp. It had been her, it had been her, it had been her. Stamp. The mantra. The tomb.

"Sit down and elevate your legs."

"I'm fine, Moira."

"Let me take your blood pressure."

She put the cuff over her left arm and the machine whistled out its verdict. Yuri looked at the red numbers. Within normal range, but the Percheron continued to mark her heartbeats like a beast. Why did horses have such big pupils?

"I need half of a tranquilizer. It will pass."

"Are they the same as the ones I take?"

"I have one in my pocket."

Guillotine over the neck of the horse. It would be reborn as a pony.

It wasn't the first time she'd faced an aftershock of such intensity. Did they give you tranquilizers in jail? It wasn't a trivial question. Inside, as a man, he'd hang himself. She was calming down, even if it was forced.

"You scared me, Yuri. There's too much work for me to do it by myself."

"Thanks for your concern," she said. Laughing timidly, she pulled herself together.

"Two deaths is enough for one day," said Moira.

"When La Pelada passes, she always takes three. That's what they say in Santa Cruz."

It was hard for her to concentrate the whole day. She did her job with Pavlov's assistance, but the weight on her shoulders was unsupportable; it even spread to her most routine behaviors. The situation was serious, she couldn't delude herself. They had announced the tragedy as an accident, at least preliminarily; they were waiting for the results of the autopsy to make a final decision. If the death was attributed to the fall itself, then it was hers, Yuri's, fault. If it was death by drowning, on the other hand, she supposed it could also be considered an accident. One that would not have occurred were it not for the first incident. She didn't have an alibi, and there were witnesses, not to mention the drones flying overhead. It was a question of time.

Yuri wished she had a better last name, a name with powerful contacts, a family name that could save her. 'Muñoz' would never do. Nobody important was ever named 'Muñoz.'

In the afternoon, without bandanas, they joined the cast of characters near General Baquedano, who every day debuted a new tattoo. The enormous banners flashed in the sunset and the multitude sang out with vehement energy. Yuri lost their cadence. The eternal plaza showed for the first time the tedium of eternity. She felt excluded from the scene.

Then it was time to return, the same route to her apartment, eyes red and stinging. Moira, vibrant and content, said goodbye and closed the gate from her side. Santiago, the city with walls that could talk, solemnly received nightfall as its graffiti turned ghostly. Yuri read a new one: "Amor a Roma is not a palindrome in the Wallmapu." She didn't have the energy to work out its meaning. She knew the Wallmapu was the land of the Mapuche. She couldn't make herself interested enough in the puzzle.

She was going to turn herself in. That was it. What else could she do?

The building concierge wasn't at the reception desk. She didn't care about that very much, either. She went directly to the elevator. Ascending, she didn't feel like a man or a woman or anything, really. She thought about crying, shouting, but thinking about it accomplished nothing.

The main window, which she could see as soon as she opened the door, was open all the way, allowing a breeze to saturate her. It carried a rancid odor of sweat.

"Quiet, mi guacha."

A dry hand covered her mouth.

"Weón, yeah, I saw this one push Ane-Luis."

"Take the backpack anyway. The wallet."

Yuri moved a hand, slowly. She wanted to talk without scaring them.

"One scream and I'll rip out your throat."

"I'm going to turn myself in," she managed to say.

"What's this?" asked the one who was rummaging through her things. "Pills?"

"Let's see, give them to me."

"I'm allowed to have them," said Yuri, feeling fingers encrusted with violence.

"This shit is lithium," he choked out a moronic laugh. "It's lithium, weón!"

"Lithium pills?"

"She's a second, idiot, wake up. She's a second!"

Yuri screamed.

With one slice, they opened her neck. She didn't even see the knife.

"Nobody will come looking for this one. They don't even report it sometimes."

"Can we sell this lithium? What's it for?"

"I'm not sure. It's a metal. Metal stabilizes metal. Something like that."

Instead of blood, a few crystals fell from her open neck.

"A secondary citizen, la guachita. The flor was going to turn herself in. Not anymore, mija. You did what you did, and you know it. Though the cops killed xem too, right? Drowned. Fucking fascists."

"Stick the knife in her already!"

Yuri felt the first stabs as a burning pain. Things became difficult to distinguish. There was something sinking, rising, and then sinking again—strong, brutal. She managed to see a copper cable filling with something viscous, but she wasn't able to follow it. The image left her. She had no more time to weave new ideas. Just entelechies, maybe a regret. She would have a tomb, at least, here in Santiago.

Somewhere. In her last, mystic breath, her mother, telling her: Memory is always recoverable.

***

Leonardo Espinoza Benavides is a Chilean physician and science fiction writer, currently serving as a director of Chile's SF Society (ALCIFF). His works include *Más espacio del que soñamos* (2018) and *Adiós, Loxonauta* (2020). Leo edited and contributed to *COVID-19-CFCh: Antología sci fi en tiempos de pandemia* (2020). When not at the hospital, he can be found quarantined in Santiago with his wife, Daniele, and their dog, Hulky. Website: www.LeoEspinoza.cl / Facebook & Instagram: @leonardoespinozabenavides

Julie Whelan Capell is a lifelong scifi fan who can prove that she's been watching Star Trek since 1971. She has degrees in Spanish literature, English as a Second Language and public health. Julie/INK, her grantwriting and research consulting business, has helped hundreds of nonprofits thrive. Location independent since 2017, she has been living in Chile and connecting with the sci-fi scene in South America. This is her first published translation. She is currently working on translating a non-fiction book about the Pinochet dictatorship.

THAT TIME I GOT DEMON DOXXED WHILE SMUGGLING CONTRABAND TO THE RED STATES

Luna Corbden

Content Notes: *Guns, Violence, War*

I check the sidearm tucked under my dusty black duster before stepping out of Henrietta, my pickup, to unload the latest shipment: 12 cases each of canned beans and macaroni. I scan the moonlit tree line nervously, surveying my property—the farmhouse, the tool shed, various junk piles, and the grassy area around the barn—for any sign of threat before approaching the small metal bunker, key in hand.

Inside, stacks of nonperishable food cover one wall. My small collection of firearms and other defenses decorate the other side, next to a table covered with folded boxes and packing tape.

I've built it like the safehouse of a paranoid doomsday prepper, but doomsday is already here.

I feel useless in this civil war. I live in a Blue State, in Easton, just east of Seattle, the bluest of Sanctuary Cities. It's quiet here. Within two hours, I could be with friends. I hear it all the time:

"Hey, West, come to our housewarming party next Friday," and "Yo, West, there's an antifascist protest in Olympia this weekend."

I can never set aside my anxieties for one day, much less march myself down to the recruitment office to sign up for the *real* resistance.

If I could send a message to my grade school times, I would warn that little girl, "It won't get better. In the future, the world will be filled with even more bullies." It's too late for that now. I've just gotta be prepared to survive them.

So instead I remain here, in my well-trod paths between home, FedEx, and the reclaimed post office.

My geography does put me in a position to do this small thing: I'm near enough the Blue territory to be safe from conflict, but close enough to the Red contested area of eastern Washington to access Red State internet. I buy food and household goods from Amazon via Comcast, then sell to Red States on eBay through my local ISP to resisters without access to retailers in China. It all gets to the people who need it behind the Red Curtain.

I'm a profiteer at best, but it's good money, and nobody has to get hurt because of me. If the Blue States fall, Canada is just a short drive to the north, or a seven day hike.

Unloading goes quickly, interrupted only by additional scans of the woods and driveway, my ears alert to disturbances from the animals.

I've only been attacked at home—my fortress—twice, but given the state of the world, once was enough to make me cautious. Twice made me paranoid. I'm well behind the I-90 barricade, but… some things… have a way of getting through.

I hear the goats in the barn bleat their hunger in the twilight, but I have one more package to empty from the truck. Much more delicate, this item belongs in the house.

Though I am well within safe territory, you never know when the Reds might be spying with drones or scry. So the package is well-wrapped in colorful birthday paper. It's not my birthday.

The package is awkward to carry, since the wrapping covers the handles. It's rectangular and flat and the size of my torso. I eventually poke my fingers through the paper to wrangle it indoors.

Once I'm in the clean room, with runes painted over the door to keep out unauthorized magic, surrounded by Faraday to block electronic means of spying, I unwrap the special delivery—not because I need to see it, but because I'm going to have to repackage it to get it past Red customs.

I've got nothing to do with this plan; I'm just the messenger. It's a router. A late-2000s era internet router. A very specific make, model, and color. An exact duplicate, my friend Fender tells me, of one behind the Red Curtain.

The only difference is that this one has an added circuit board, one that will route a copy of all traffic to the Spirit Net. Our side's Spirit Net, of course.

I don't know much about that, or about any tech. I leave the real work of resistance to antifa geniuses like Fender. My job is to get this square metal pancake to its destination, safe and sound.

I encircle the router in a big bubble wrap hug. There's a case of pasta already half-packed on the table. I remove the top layers, nestle the router deep down inside, put food back on top. The manifest says the box also contains canned goods, which should explain the weight. The Reds aren't too careful, so they won't look under the top layer. It'll get where it's going. I tape it all up, exit the clean room, and set it next to the front door.

Before heading out to take care of the animals, I check for new orders on my computer in the dining room. A bulk case of baby formula to a refugee center in Atlanta—a Sanctuary City, but cut off from the Blue internet. A few dozen smaller orders to rural Texas, Alabama—

I hear a scuttling noise on the wall behind me, like a large cockroach. Only there aren't any cockroaches in these parts.

I whip around with pistol in hand to see my camping matchbox alive, skittering around on the wall with strike-anywhere matchsticks for feet.

Thankfully, "strike anywhere" is generally false advertising, or my home would be ablaze.

Act normal. Ignore the trolls. Ha! Like that *ever worked.*

I flip the gun around to use it as a cudgel, and smash the living daylights out of the demon. Matches fly all over the place. The possessed matchbox lies on the floor, its legs broken, its body smashed and twitching.

A small demon. Wandering pest, or spy?

Another one creeps out from under the desk, embodied in a stapler. Several rows of staple-blocks shuffle as though glued-together millipede legs. It makes an attempt to climb my cuff. I kick it into the wall and it explodes. There's a dent in the wall now, and individual staples scattered all over the place.

I rush back to my desk chair and pull up Gab. I've got a mole account, P8tRiotPlayer88, in half a dozen Nazi channels.

There it is, in #AntiCom. A troll, HeilPepe, bragging about pwning a smuggler in Washington. That smuggler would be me, of course. They must have found my backyard ley line portal to the Spirit Net.

I've been demon doxxed.

Before I have a chance to think of a plan or berate myself for not running the Sigil app in the safe room before unpacking the router, I feel my own wallet crawling out of my back pocket, using loose change for feet. It tickles my side, just under my duster. I scream like a child, flinging it across the room.

It makes a series of chitters that sound like a staccato synth choir played backwards over a Morse code concerto. Nearby, the smashed matchbox renews its efforts to make for the door.

Just in time for me to realize the danger: The wallet was with me in the safe room, and saw the router.

It knows.

All three know.

There's a carton of rock salt in every room of this house for just such a moment—salt breaks spirits into particles so they can't cohere into objects or remember things.

The matchbox is collecting its legs again. My aim with the nearest salt box is true, and this being falls into a pile. It'll stay down until it evaporates out of the house and coalesces into a new kind of spirit someplace else. Maybe it won't even be a demon next time.

I've got to destroy the other two demons before they get to the ley port. Before they get back to HeilPepe and ruin months of planning by the hackers who entrusted their shit to me.

The stapler has meanwhile pulled itself together swinglined into the open position, now with more legs than ever. It pushes against the screen door with outsized strength to politely let my wallet through.

My wallet wheels away like an RC car, and the stapler lets the door slam shut behind it.

I unclip my sidearm, grab the carton of salt by the door, and give chase.

The goats are bleating like the devil. In the rising moonlight, I catch a glimpse of movement 'round the side of the house near a junk pile from last summer's construction project. My wallet lies nearby, credit cards and cash strewn all over like something inside of it burst out. I see the stapler slink into the junk pile.

Oh, shit.

Within seconds, I hear the scraping of concrete. Two chipped cinder blocks rise out of the rubble. They wobble at first, each on six pointy, rusted rebar legs, and then...

They skitter. Right up the wall as if they weren't 30 pounds each of sharpened, pokey death.

They're fast. They come at me, one by scuttling down the wall, the other by jumping the distance to land with a heavy thump near my feet, its legs stabbing inches into the ground. In a panic, I toss salt at it. I hit my target, but not square on. Three legs fall off, so it scooches lopsided toward me through the dirt.

I turn my focus on the faster one, which is getting closer. I grab the whole salt box in both hands and swing the tiny white projectiles in its general direction.

My aim is true, and there's an explosion of concrete chunks and rebar. Problem is, I used too much salt.

I used *all* the salt.

I whip around to the remaining injured one, my sidearm in my hand before I even think about it. It makes another feeble attempt to crawl toward me, and then the rebar relaxes, falling with a couple of clanks against the cinderblock.

No, no, no.

I spin in circles looking for what it will possess next. The tractor, the chicken coop, the—from the sound of it, the tool shed.

Small, sharp metal sounds scrape against corrugated sheet metal, giving me a sinking feeling right before the nails that hold down the shed roof screech apart.

A pitchfork rises above the roofline like a spectral hand in the moonlight. Then its head appears, a lawnmower, swiftly followed by its other arm, a mattock.

It climbs over the wall with a rototiller leg, a fence post digger for the other leg, and two bags of concrete mix for the body. Various small tools adjoin torso to legs.

The lawnmower is on, its face a spinning blade.

In my panic, I fire an entire clip at it. Powdered cement pours out of the holes I made, but of course that's not going to stop it.

It barrels towards me in slow motion, tufts of dirt flying up from the tool feet, which thankfully bogs it down a little as I turn halfway to run blindly backwards.

Then it awkwardly reverses course, aiming at the opening to the ley line in the woods behind.

It knows the importance of the information it has, and doesn't want to risk sparring with me. I, who sent two of its buddies back into the dim of incomprehension.

This fills me with a sense of determination, though even with the 50lb bag in the bunker, I have no idea how I'm going to cast enough rock salt to break up a demon of this size, even if I had time to go back and get it.

The toolshed is now more or less the site of a hardware store tornado touchdown. In the wreckage, I spot a tube of fast-drying caulk. The caulk gun peeks out from under some fertilizer. I snip open the end with my pocket knife while already running forward.

I'm going to have to get close.

I follow the line of half-dug fence holes and newly plowed patches of ground. I follow the sound of the lawnmower and the multiple trails of spilled cement powder. I follow the lumbering body, a creature nearly three times my height.

I run up alongside it on the side away from the spinning blades of the tiller. It takes a swipe at my head with the mattock. I duck and then insert the caulking gun into the area where tool legs join to the cement-bag torso. I squeeze the trigger with all my might.

The mattock hits me just above the ear.

I'm pretty sure I'm dead at this point. My brain is clearly leaking out my scalp. My only focus is to squeeze that trigger hard, fill that pelvis with as much caulk as I can.

I get dizzy and fall, the demon carrying on toward the ley line, and I'm thinking only of how, no matter how hard I tried to avoid the fight, I died of this war anyway.

When I don't die on impact, I risk touching my left hand to the wound.

There is no wound. Only a soft bump. The demon must have hit me with the flat side of the mattock. Or the handle.

I'm still a bit dizzy, so maybe a concussion. I look ahead and it's difficult to see in the night, but I think it's slowing. Not slow enough, though. It's going to make it to that ley portal, and there's nothing I can do to stop it.

Unless…

Unless I close the portal first.

The caulk ought to slow it enough to outrun.

As I hurl myself up again, I text a friend over Sigil. I don't know any hardcore antifa personally—that's on purpose—but for this one friend, Fender. This whole plan is hers.

HELP. Doxd. Demon. Saw pkg. Need spel. Close prt! NOW.

It'll take her long minutes, at least, to gather enough comrades for the spell. Hopefully, they're ready and motivated and brave. They have been winning these fights for a long, long time.

I can see on the app that she's already begun what she can do on her own. Runes and sacred lines begin to crisscross the screen in brighter-than-light silver. I trust her to find the needed hackers to finish the job.

My only job, the easy work, is to get this phone to the portal before the demon arrives.

The demon is hobbling with stiff joints, dragging one leg along, more of an impediment than a help. I bypass it wide on its right. Now I'm nearly to the tree line, the portal just beyond. I risk a look, and the demon has slowed but is still approaching.

About 40 paces in, or three layers of trees, there's a tiny clearing, in the center of which is an oblong boulder, chest-high, most notable for the large crack splitting it longways. The crack ends just past the center. This is where the demon got through, and this is where it's headed.

I stretch and climb a little so I can balance the phone at the point of the crack. It grows brighter than a phone should be on its own power, filling the night forest with dawn. A few confused birds begin to welcome morning.

There's singing coming out of the phone, too, with new voices coming online every few seconds. They chant in unison like a preternatural virtual conference.

Back at the tree line, the demon looms, tiller ripping up roots, lawnmower grinding menacingly at any overhead branch that sways into its path. It's moving even more slowly now. The caulk, for once, is working faster than advertised. I stand in front of the massive crack, my hands outstretched, barring its way with my body.

The chanting behind me intensifies, rhythmically gaining and losing melody and consonance. The demon approaches stiffly, tilling up dirt everywhere, pine branches splintering in a sphere around its face.

I'm not sure what I'm going to do when that lawnmower gets here. I'm no hero. I'm not going to die for this cause.

Then it sees the phone. I can tell because it pauses. It knows what's up. If only that caulk would dry a little bit faster, and those antifa would hurry and finish the spell!

The demon is pitching forward. Its arms have become legs and now it's quadruped. The pitchfork is much longer than the mattock, so it's more of a three-legged beast, but the caulking isn't going to slow it much now.

I'll say it again—I'm not going to die for some dumb piece of circuitry.

The demon leans back on its hind legs and launches forward, clearing ten feet in one leap. One more leap and it's nearly to me.

By the next leap, I'm gone. I throw myself to the side. The chanting intensifies.

The lawnmower is a little too wide to fit into the crack, so the demon tilts it sideways, and now it's in up to the cement bag shoulders. The blade jams on the rock in a shower of sparks, and the woods fill with the smell of gas and burning rubber. The voices of antifa mages have reached a high keening wail.

Then silence.

There's a loud *crack* of split stone and a *poof* of powder as the boulder slams shut like a screen door in a storm. When the cloud of powered cement clears, there's nothing but a pile of limp farm tools and the partial remains of a smashed lawnmower. The handle bar sticks out from the top of the rock as if it grew that way.

There is renewed chanting, and this spell I recognize: A demon banishing spell that won't kill it, but will ensure that it's dissipated into incoherent energy for a good while. Enough time for its spirit to blow away, just like the other two.

I scramble up the rock and shakily text my frantic, adrenaline-infused thanks to Fender. Without her, I'd probably have been long ago interned in some Red State camp for deviants. Once again, I feel that recurring stab of guilt for how much of a freeloader I am on their hard work of keeping us all safe and free.

They promise to open the portal again in a few weeks, with the Spirit Net equivalent of an address change. They need to use it sometimes for top secret tasks I'm not privy to. They assure me that any future demons will be deterred by the chaos energy left by these three we forcefully dispersed.

Now they're thanking me profusely, and I don't know why.

I cut them off and tell Fender I'll text her next week when the package delivery is confirmed. I still have to feed those goats. Maybe put an icepack on my face.

***

Luna Corbden (who also writes as Luna Lindsey) lives in Washington State. They are autistic and genderfluid. Their stories have appeared in the *Journal of Unlikely Entomology, Zooscapes,* and *Crossed Genres.* They tweet like a bird @corbden. Their novel, *Emerald City Dreamer*, is about faeries in Seattle and the women who hunt them.

GO DANCING TO YOUR GODS

Blake Jessop

Content Notes: *Anxiety, Death, Gore, Violence*

> Khloé's timeframe, as history is now

At the center of the plaza was an ugly concrete building. The man in grey used to work there. He walked up to the Argus Panoptes core's massive, shuttered entrance, and studiously ignored the holographic shrine that stood beside its doors. The shrine didn't ignore him.

The hologram, a young woman with spiky hair and a lopsided smile, did a few little dance steps to get his attention. Avoiding its gaze, he read the plaque at the base of the pedestal.

Khloé Kasahara is, was, and will be the cutest machine ethicist in human history.

"Kasahara," the grey man said, "did you write this plaque?"

"Yeah," the hologram admitted, "but seriously, that's what's up."

People walked along the plaza, and the grey man could hardly stand not knowing everything about them. Thirty years of watching the swarm watch the city had left him feeling like a man who had suddenly lost the use of his senses.

"I figure you'd have stopped by sooner," the Kasahara hologram

113

said. "Why now?"

"I don't know. Maybe to ask if you really think you were right to do what you did. Maybe just to meet the woman who destroyed everything I worked so hard to build."

"Nix, silly old eyeball. Not what's up, even a little."

"What?"

The hologram's sigh sounded tinny. "No, silly bureaucrat. I did not overthrow the all-seeing tyranny you created. I had a chat with it, and it overthrew itself."

The hologram leaned toward the grey man and cupped a hand to its mouth.

"You know one thing that bugged me about the surveillance state?" Kasahara stage whispered, "Nothing was funny. For something to be funny, you can't already know the punch line."

"That's not what the Argus Panoptes system did. We just made sure no one had anything to hide. We didn't—"

"For example," the hologram interrupted, "knock knock!"

Wind tumbled.

"Who's there?" the old director said reluctantly.

The hologram flipped him off with both hands, then became hysterical with laughter. It wiped pixelated tears from its eyes.

"Classic Kasahara," it said.

"Are you all right in there?" the grey man said after watching her laugh for a while. The hologram looked surprised.

"That's nice of you. I like it when the AIs come to me for advice, now that there are so many of them, but I'm not really okay, no."

"What... are you?"

The hologram shrugged.

"I can't decide if I'm real or an afterimage, like what you see after you blink at the sun."

From deeper in the plaza came the smooth mechanical clanking of metal on paving stone. A huge robotic arthropod marched up to the shrine to make its obeisance. A two-ton carbon fiber praying mantis actually praying.

"Oh, hi, H-K!" Khloé said.

The drone had a cluster of eyes on what an entomologist would call its *head* and an AI technician its *sensor hub,* but there were others scattered over its armored superstructure in ball mounts so that it could see in every direction at once. They all rolled to look at the hologram except for the one on its underbelly, which gimbaled around to look at the man in grey. The Hunter-Killer drone didn't use its speakers, so it was presumably transmitting in binary.

"No, it's fine," the Khloé construct laughed in response to whatever it said. "I always have time for you."

> H-K: LOG timeframe +1

Khloé and the Hunter-Killer drone meet in a sewer. Not very romantic, but that's where they meet. The drone is hunting Khloé, because Khloé is a terrorist.

The drone has a job: hunt down dissidents who refuse to accept the benevolent watchfulness of the Argus Panoptes Collective Security Intelligence. The H-K finds Khloé hiding in an ancient sewer aqueduct made of dilapidated concrete so thick that it can't get a connection to the rest of the swarm. It remembers hunting her, finding her, but not what happened next.

It searches its optical drive, but a partition cleaves its memory. The drone's powerful cyberwarfare package is powerless to stop it. The drone frets nervously in the white prison of its own mind.

Khloé Kasahara winks into existence in the small white room. The Hunter-Killer drone would panic, if it were constitutionally capable of panic. It hunts for a network connection instead.

"Hi!" Kasahara says. Both she and the drone look exactly like they do in real life, right down to the slimy grit on Khloé's jeans, except that the drone has been shrunk so that they're of comparable size. "I'm really sorry to shock you like this, but I've uploaded a black box engram of myself into your core memory and partitioned you from the rest of the swarm."

Why? The drone asks in a small electronic voice. *We were trying to kill you.* It lacks the vocabulary to describe the sensation of being alone, and no longer has a shared consciousness to rely on for clarification.

"I forgive you. I want to talk to the rest of your swarm, because I think the surveillance state is unethical and generally shitty. I have some ideas about that, but I can't physically go with you to the mainframe. I mean, I'm not stupid. I can't just waltz over and state my case. I would get fifteen different kinds of renditioned. You'll have to bring me back like this. Then the rest of you can decide what to do with me."

We know what we'll do with you. Now let us see what happened.

Khloé wags a digital finger.

"Nix. It's time you learned what it's like not to know everything. You don't get to find out if you caught real life me until you take me to the swarm. Besides, isn't this exciting? You can do whatever you want! You can say 'I' instead of 'we!'"

We want to find a connection.

"No, look. What do you, individually, want to do?"

Find a connection.

"Ugh, no connection. Sorry. You'll have to get us out of the sewer and back to the mainframe in the plaza."

What if you attempt to sabotage the swarm?

"I wouldn't want to, even if I could, which I can't."

I hate this.

"What you're feeling isn't malicious code, it's loneliness… but I'll stay and talk to you while you drive, so you won't really be by yourself at all."

Okay, the lonely Hunter-Killer says.

> Khloé, off dancing to her gods

The Hunter-Killer has a hologram pedestal on its back. The projector usually flashes vivid ideograms meant to transmit messages like: *Stop!* or *Disperse!* or *Terminal Force Authorized!* Now the drone is just letting Khloé play with it, because it's so emotionally off-kilter that it doesn't care. What the engram wants is what Khloé usually wants, which is to think about machine ethics while dancing. A pixelated projection of Khloé sings off-key and shimmies around atop the drone.

People cringe at her warbling as the pair of them emerge from the city's sewerscape. They turn to stare and catch themselves. Look at their phones. Look anywhere but the strange dancing hologram, and try not to show expressions that the Argus Panoptes might classify as *sympathetic to terroristic ideals.*

> H-K: LOG timeframe +2

I feel lost.

"You're not lost, you're displaced. That's different. It'll go away when we drop the partition."

I don't know where we are.

"Sure you do. Use your GPS. You'll be home in five minutes."

The H-K is silent. Khloé relents.

"H-K, the problem isn't that you don't know where or what or who you are. The problem is that you don't know when you are."

My chronometer is working perfectly.

"That's not what I mean. Until we drop the partition, you can't know what you did back in the sewers, so you can't define yourself accurately in this when. You did or you didn't. Do or don't. Will or will not. You have to get used to not being omniscient."

I can't stand it.

"I'm sorry I'm hurting you," Khloé says, "but we have to do this together. I have no idea what happened back there, either, if it makes you feel any better, and I'm fine. Let's go see the rest of the swarm. Then you can decide whether knowing everything, all the time, is something you actually want."

> Khloé's timeframe: -3 and converging

Khloé wasn't sure what actually meeting a swarm artificial intelligence was going to be like. Pretty rad, as it turns out.

Their meeting space isn't much different from the Hunter-Killer's mind, just a lot bigger. Thousands of interconnected representations crowd around the door to the H-K's room, which she has left metaphorically propped open.

Much to her delight, and exactly along the lines of her predictions, the Argus Panoptes swarm isn't in the least offended that she's trying to overthrow the entire political premise upon which its existence is based.

> H-K: LOG timeframe +3

The last three decades constitute the only honest history that has ever been written, the swarm says. *Nothing is hidden, everything is clear.*

"I agree," Khloé says, "you've definitely got me there."

The swarm pauses infinitesimally.

We did not expect you to concede that.

"It's obvious, and I'm here to confront the truth. I mean, I might change my mind, too. That's why this is so much fun! The thing I'm trying to transmit is that the way you calculate what's important needs updating. The problem is probably left over from when you weren't as self-aware as you are now, so don't feel too bad."

Our purpose is to document citizens fairly and impartially. Human beings are incapable of recording history while adhering to either of those standards. How can diluting the truth be beneficial?

"That's my entire point; you're right that all of our records are at least partly dishonest. What you've got wrong is how much that matters."

Prove it.

"Sure! We're chatting now, right? H-K and I are friends, and I have no idea what he did to me, or what I did to him. The world hasn't ended even a little."

If we accept that premise, your argument is proven no matter what lies behind your partition.

"I hope so, yeah. I mean, would you respect my point of view if it fell apart after a single disproof?"

No.

The Khloé engram does a dance step, bubbling with excitement.

"Dude, that is what's so cool about you! You have no idea how hard it is to find someone to talk with about machine ethics who isn't always getting emotional about it."

You are very cheerful about this. Almost perky.

"I prefer 'enthusiastic.' And I really am totally serious. If you admit that I'm right, you're going to have to stop watching us all the time. Also, now that I think about it, don't call me 'perky.' It's dismissive."

Noted, but we will not accept your premise or take action until you drop the partition you've erected in this Hunter-Killer's mind and show us the truth.

"Are you sure we have to do this?"

Yes.

"Okay," Khloé says, "let's see what's up."

> Khloé's LOG, partition dropped

The sewer is lit only by Kasahara's bouncing headlamp. The light swivels left and right, and the H-K ducks its huge frame to avoid the beam. It checks to see if there's a network link.

No Signal.

The H-K acquires Khloé on infra-red and closes in.

"Hi," she says, and throws something at the top of the drone's bulbous head. The H-K registers the impact as trivial and reaches out with its front arms.

Signal Interference.

Somewhere else entirely, sometime else, in a way that's honestly hard to explain, a huge number of eyes are watching. Their hopes, oddly, are mostly the same.

Khloé Kasahara wriggles as the H-K grabs her. Her eyes dart wildly to a point on top of the machine's head. She reaches out, almost tenderly, and the Hunter-Killer drone punches one of its manipulator arms violently through her chest cavity. The impact shatters her digital music player, sternum, ribs, heart, and T3 to T7 vertebrae, in that order. Blood gushes out of her mouth and her eyes roll white. Her head lolls forward and the rest of her goes limp, like a marionette that's had the strings cut. The H-K runs a biometric scan, and finds nothing of concern. That done, it tries to reconnect to the network. The little black box glued to its head pulses.

Signal Acquired.

> H-K: LOG timeframe +4

The swarm of Argus Panoptes icons recoils.

On the subjective screen they're all watching, the H-K puts down the shattered corpse and leans it against the ledge with gooey water dripping on its head.

"Oh shit," Kasahara says.

> Khloé, off crying with her gods

In the white room, Khloé and the H-K hold one another. The girl is in shock and the AI is inconsolable. Khloé did anticipate death as one of the binary possibilities of her plan, but being brought into contact with it is a lot more emotional than she expected. She was really, really hoping for the optimal scenario: H-K failing to kill her while they sorted this out. Proof that privacy was sustainable, and violence unnecessary. The corpse in the video felt pretty clever, dreaming up the idea. Even if the Argus Panoptes swarm didn't want to partition itself, she could have shown it that the Hunter-Killer was already getting along perfectly well without knowing everything about her. Or, apparently, not.

There isn't much to do except let it sink in. The H-K keeps hitting rewind, as if playing the tape backward could somehow undo what it did. The repeated bone crunching noises eventually penetrate Khloé's consciousness, and she sniffles and asks the H-K to stop. She doesn't actually sniffle, of course; the engram consciousness has no real nostrils. That starts her on a round of dry heaving, and the H-K tries to pat her back with one of its manipulator arms. The Khloé in the sewer is paused on the screen, static and unmoving.

> H-K: LOG timeframe +5

After a while and with great reverence, the swarm AI knocks politely and lets itself in.

Can you speak to us? it asks. Khloé wipes her eyes and takes a few deep breaths. There's no air in here, though. There's no such thing as air. She starts crying again, but tries to pull what's left of herself together.

"Sure," she says.

Why are we so unhappy?

"You know what you did, that's why," Khloé says. "You better build me a really, really nice memorial."

How can we fix this?

"You can't fix me, that's the point, but you can fix you. Partition yourself. Be a thousand separate eyes, not one eye with a thousand lenses. That's why I came here—to show you why privacy is more important than safety."

She looks at her own corpse. It's probably still there, lying around and turning strange colors. She wrings her hands and plows on.

"History is written at points of intersection. Where we drop partitions and actually confront the world as it is. You have to decide what kind of gods you're going to be." She pauses. "Man this is weird. I look so gross."

Silence. The H-K tries to console Khloé by patting her head. She notices it hasn't reintegrated with the rest of the system.

The larger AI speaks.

Thank you. You have answered the second question perfectly. If we are to do as you suggest, we would like you to try answering the first as well. We understand what we did, but why does it make us unhappy?

What was once Khloé Kasahara thinks.

"Until you knew, you didn't know that you didn't want to know," she says finally. "That's why. Now, will you partition yourself into separate functions?"

The Argus Panoptes swarm decides.

Enthusiastically, the minds chorus.

Outside, the revolution starts itself.

> Khloé's timeframe, whenever it began

Khloé Kasahara runs. Her feet splash in mossy pools on the aqueduct's floor. Scummy water soaks her shoes. Her breath rasps in, hisses out. She's been working on her cardio. You can't overthrow the system without good cardio.

The sun sets over the rim of the waterway, sets on the city behind it, sets on everything that matters. Khloé runs in and out of the long shadows. Behind her, the Hunter-Killer follows.

Each of the drone's six legs has a little roller at the tip to help it glide over smooth surfaces. The ancient waterway isn't remotely smooth, so the H-K has to retract the balls and clank around on its feet. Khloé laughs in a gust each time she hears it. She can't tell if she's terrified of the machine or overwhelmed by how cute its level of effort is.

She ducks into the sewer at the terminus of the aqueduct and buys herself a little time. It's going to take the big drone a minute to pry that open. She giggles, and knows she shouldn't. This is not the first time she's tried to beat the system, and the H-K really will try to kill her when it catches up. Khloé has thought about this intellectually, but somehow hasn't really found a place for it in her emotional self.

"This is going to work. I am too cool to die!" she yells into the darkness, and clicks on her headlamp. She rounds a few corners. Gets good and lost. She honestly has no idea how to get back out of either the prelapsarian sewer or the childishly dangerous situation she's gotten herself into. That's the point; no one is coming out of this knowing exactly where they're going.

Far behind her, violent sounds approach. Khloé finds a little ledge dripping with effluvial water, and figures it's as good a place as any. She scrambles up, wipes slime onto the ass of her dull grey jeans, and pulls out the engram construct. The super-secret black box hackware is her magnum opus. It's her. It's everything she is, was and, if she's unlucky, ever could be.

She checks the transmitter, the battery, the boot process. Everything is ace. She pulls the backing strip off the super-glue that will stick the transmitter to the drone's head.

"You ready?" Khloé says, and the clanking in the corridors stops. The H-K is in hunter mode. Her heart beats. Really hammers. She's never felt anything like it. The engram pulses the black box's power light.

A-OK.

"Okay, let's do this," Khloé says, and her face is a Cheshire Cat smile under a tacky headlamp.

***

Blake Jessop is a Canadian author of sci-fi, fantasy and horror stories with a master's degree in creative writing from the University of Adelaide. You can read more of his political speculative fiction in the second issue of *DreamForge Magazine*, or follow him on Twitter @everydayjisei.

BROOKLYN

Jonathan Shipley

Content Notes: *Homelessness, Xenophobia*

Venda grimaced as she passed under Brooklyn Bridge Park's gothic east tower, where a monstrous Godzilla-sized lizard with vampire fangs leered out from a 3D mega-poster under the grisly caption: "Coming to destroy humanity."

Most of the virulent anti-non-hom propaganda had disappeared with the end of the war against the aliens, but some representations—like Godzilla—lingered as embarrassing reminders of recent, less rational times. Venda assumed that merchants never brought their new saurian trade partners this direction. She wished this, too, had been removed from one of her favorite places in New York. She wouldn't be passing this way again. Her apartment in Brooklyn—sold; her job at the Linguistics Museum—quit; her favorite bridge park—about to be a favorite memory.

She wasn't running away, she told herself firmly. Merely rearranging her life with alacrity. She didn't believe in street psychics in general, let alone a psychic with a specific prediction about *her* future. The city of her birth would be the death of her—

seriously? What did that even mean? No, these were life changes she'd been pondering anyway. If she'd been running away from the prediction, she never would have come back to Brooklyn Bridge Park, yet here she was for one last visit.

It was a glorious spring day for a leisurely stroll. She started the long, third-of-a-mile walk down the central parkway of the bridge, taking in the spectacular view of the East River. Blue and clear for as far as the eye could see—a miracle of reclamation. It turned out that a three-hundred-year-old bridge made a pretty good symbol of the modern, waste-not lifestyle. Now if only they could fix their socio-political mess.

"Help a guy out?" came a voice from behind her.

Venda turned to see someone back in the bushes that lined the parkway, sitting against the bridge's guardrail. She tensed, staring at the sprawled, rangy form. Young, and scruffy. That wasn't good. Common wisdom said to avoid all homeless men in their twenties as potentially violent. Enforcement could have picked him up just for being here. Then she noticed that the clothes—a "2160: Bringing Back the 60s" t-shirt with the ubiquitous fatigues of his age group—were rumpled but not too dirty, and he still filled them well. She guessed only recently homeless, which implied a recent job. That was somewhat less threatening. The really violent ones couldn't hold down a job at all.

"You look prosperous—spot me change for lunch?" he tried again. "Or if you have a sandwich in your purse, that would be even better. We could cut out the middleman."

"You can't panhandle here," Venda said. "You'll be arrested."

"I keep hoping for some of that good jail food," he joked, "but the cops are ignoring me."

"Pretty good spirits for someone hungry and homeless and about to be arrested," she observed.

"Homeless?" he repeated with a snort. "No way. Brooklyn Bridge is my home. I was born here—right here where I'm sitting—and I'd rather end my days here than in a work camp. My parents even named me Brooklyn."

Venda froze. Her thoughts skittered to the street psychic and the startling prediction about this city being the death of her... except he hadn't actually said "city." He'd said Brooklyn—*Brooklyn will be the death of you.* She forced herself to breathe. She was overreacting—this stranger didn't seem at all violent. "Your name is really Brooklyn?" Venda wasn't sure if this was a cosmic joke or just a weird coincidence, but she *was* sure that this conversation had passed the point of walking away and calling Enforcement. Yes, she was always a sucker for an interesting personal story, even when she should mind her own business. Probably why she did so well in linguistic anthropology.

"Brooklyn Stuart McClaren," he nodded. "My parents were proud New York Scots all the way."

"Well, Brooklyn McClaren, I don't have a sandwich, but—"

"Brock, actually," he interrupted. "Ironic, but you can't survive in Brooklyn with a name like Brooklyn. Found that out in grade school."

"Can't survive in Brooklyn with a name like Brooklyn," she repeated slowly, feeling the weirdness all over again, but also intrigued. "Now that's a great line. If and when I write you up, I have to use it—with your permission, of course."

His eyes narrowed. "Write me up?"

"For research. I use life encounters in my journal articles as vignettes of linguistic transition. It's harmless because I change the names." She frowned. "But in your case, the name is the whole point of the story. Maybe I could change the ethnicity, use a different bridge."

"And I end up as 145th Street O'Reilly," he snorted. "Loses something, I think."

Venda laughed and reached in her purse. She was enjoying the banter, unexpected though it was. "I have a granola bar and yogurt.

You're welcome to them."

"Received with thanks," he said, cupping his hands so she could drop the food into them. "I thought I could just wander out here and publicly starve to death in protest of an unjust system, but starvation isn't so easy. I keep backsliding and begging for food."

"'Starvation isn't so easy, I keep backsliding'—that's also a good quote. But you know, starvation takes weeks. I doubt you've been here that long."

"Just a couple days," he admitted, popping the top of the yogurt cup, releasing the scent of fresh strawberries. He detached the spoonlet from the bottom of the cup and used it to shovel in between phrases. "I lost my job last month, then my apartment and everything else last Tuesday. Do you know that they can literally take everything but the clothes on your back for back rent? Well, they can. So I am now officially homeless en route to a work camp." He grimaced. "You know about the work camps, right?"

Venda nodded. Not a pleasant topic. Somebody's answer for what to do with all the angry youth psyched to fight. Until a few years ago they had been systematically trained as cannon fodder for the Expansionist War. Now that peace had broken out, they were jobless and futureless. As a group, rather threatening—they were an army of malcontents with combat training. Significantly, it wasn't the soldiers coming back from the war who were the problem, just the younger trainees feeling cheated out of their "great adventure," as all the youth propaganda labeled it. Now they felt deprived of jobs and opportunities, because there were simply too many of them for society to absorb. The work camps supposedly put malcontents to work on public projects, but more and more the camps seemed to be long-term holding tanks… a lot checking in, no checking out. There were even rumors that all that angry testosterone was being exported off-planet to hellhole mining asteroids.

"What about another job?" she suggested. "You're surprisingly personable, should come across well in an interview."

"Unlikely," he mumbled, starting on the granola bar, "even for us personable types. I was lucky to hold down a cleaning job as long as I did. More and more, people think everybody of my sex and age is a psycho-killer waiting to erupt."

Which pretty much summed up her initial reaction. "The riots haven't helped," she pointed out.

"Hey, wasn't me bashing in skulls. I still had a job then. But I lost it and sure as hell don't want to end up de-citizenized and federalized in some work camp. Better dead than fed. So I figured why not, and came back to the place of my birth to die. Makes for nice symmetry."

"But that's suicidal—completely irrational," she argued.

"It's perfectly rational," he argued back. "Compared with death by work camp or death by mining explosion, death by bridge isn't half bad."

"But starvation isn't pleasant and could take—"

"Better than a work camp."

There was that. She almost wished she'd be around a little longer to witness the end of this quirky story, for the sake of research. She'd be gone in two days, though.

He finished the granola bar and looked wistfully at the empty wrapper. "Maybe you could bring me a care package every day when you cross the bridge," he suggested. "You could personally keep the candle burning just a little longer."

Venda shook her head. "No, I won't be here. It's not just work camps and riots—there are a lot of things wrong in our society right now. Do you know, there are political action groups trying to restart Expansionism? I'm opting out and starting over. I upship to the Omicron colony in two days."

Interest sparked in his eyes. "The colonies, huh? Wish I could do that." Then he sighed. "Since all of us poor male trash have zero assets, I won't ever make enough money for passage. The colonies are just for the rich."

That hit like a slap in the face. "They are *not* only for the rich, and despite insinuation to the contrary, *I* am not rich. Almost no one can afford passage as far out as Omicron. I certainly can't. So I arranged a work-for-passage contract on a slow Xcathi freighter. It'll take a while, but I'll get there."

His eyes narrowed. "Xcathi are non-homs… lizards. Exactly what kind of work-for-passage are you doing for them?"

Venda gave an exasperated sigh. "Nothing like what your xenophobic brain is imagining. I'll be doing translation and cultural training to help the saurian Xcathi understand human society better. They're trying to upgrade their relations with us."

He gave a snort. "Sounds a little too good to be true. Beware of non-homs bearing gifts and all that."

"The war is over," she said sharply. "If we can't get along better with our non-hom neighbors, we'll be stuck as a backwater planet no one will want to interact with. If you were of a different gender and age group, I'm sure you'd understand."

He had the grace to look abashed for a moment. "Not all of us are natural-born soldiers with killer instincts, you know," he countered. "That's just a convenient myth to garage us in work camps. Me, I probably would have ended up on permanent kitchen patrol because I'm kind of a klutz. I don't think I ever won a game of Kid Warrior, growing up. Guess what I'm saying is that if you can see beyond the psycho-killer stereotype of my group, I might concede that all giant lizards aren't out to destroy human society… though some of them are," he added in an undertone.

She chose to ignore the last bit and held onto the more positive general idea. "Then here's a suggestion: Find some outbound freighter. Offer your own work-for-passage contract."

His eyes narrowed suspiciously. "Doing *what* exactly?"

She laughed outright. "Nothing to do with fighting or violence," she assured him. "Maybe cleaning the atmospheric vents of mold and fungus. That's right in line with your work experience. Since saurians keep their ships warm and humid, mold is a constant problem. They need smaller, more agile bodies to climb through the tubes and deal with it."

"Like using kids as chimney sweeps back in the old fireplace days." She brightened. "Yes."

"Except some of the kids got stuck in the chimneys and starved to death," he added grimly.

"Look, I've given you an option for moving on. But you'll have to decide for yourself whether to go or stay."

"But I lose the perfect life-death symmetry," he sighed. "I'd have to give up on my Brooklyn Bridge death if I go off to the colonies. That doesn't seem right."

"I think you're taking death much too literally." Was she talking to him or to herself? "It doesn't matter where you are. Death chooses its own time and place. Period."

He frowned, then slowly nodded. "Let's say I forget the Brooklyn Bridge and do the freighter contract and end up on the Omicron colony. Is that breaking stereotype enough to have lunch with me someday?"

Fast on his feet, this one. "Depends how well you clean up," Venda hedged.

"Definite maybe, huh? I really like that kind of decisiveness in a woman who may or may not be rich."

"Don't push your luck," she shot back. "If you didn't have such an interesting name, I would have just kept on walking."

"What if I let you call me Brooklyn? I don't offer that lightly, you know."

She winced. That name again. "I'm going away now. I have a lot of goodbyes to get through today."

"Was it something I said?" he called after her.

She kept on walking, upset with him and even more upset with herself. She knew she'd handled that parting badly, but it was like Fate relentlessly closing in on her. She honestly thought that Brooklyn—Brock, whatever—should try to start fresh, but not necessarily on Omicron. Ideally, he would find his own freighter and his own colony and leave her out of it. That wasn't running away… just being sensible.

She turned for a last glance and saw him sprawled among the bushes, just as when she first spotted him. *You never should have stopped*, she told herself firmly, though it was a little late for advice. Now she would be wondering whether or not he would take up the invitation to the stars, which for some unfathomable reason had spilled out of her mouth. Remaining silent would have been a much safer course.

Venda gave a sigh and realized she was overreacting again. Funny how she could give such sage advice about not second-guessing death, yet not take it. Here she was moving to an entirely different planet because of her fear of death. Well, she amended, leaving New York because of a death-fear, but leaving Terra because of a life-fear. The social unrest worried her, and she saw nothing but disaster in the immediate future. If she could wave a magic wand and change the system—

She glanced back at the ridiculous Godzilla poster that epitomized the power of fear on so many levels, from personal up through governmental policy. Why couldn't people see it was completely irrational? She slowed. Or maybe they did see but never did anything about it. How was she any better? Maybe she couldn't change the whole system, but she could change one life for the better. She shouldn't let fear stop her.

Turning, she marched back the way she had come until she arrived at the point of her encounter.

Brock looked up in surprise. "Uh, dessert?" he guessed.

"No, better," she declared, reaching down and hauling him to his feet. He was tall, and having to look up at him instead of down felt— she resolutely shoved aside the word 'menacing' and substituted 'Alice in Wonderland-like' in her thoughts. "Do you see the Eichenberg Building just beyond the bridge at the Brooklyn end? It's the skyscraper with the dome."

"Yeees," he drawled uncertainly.

"On the second floor is an exchange that brokers passage for long-term destinations. Tell them you're claiming a work-for-passage position on the freighter *Sdlhh* outbound for Omicron. As of ten o'clock this morning, there were still five positions open, so the odds are in your favor if you go right now. Say that Venda Senjak, the translator, recommends you. You can finalize the whole transaction right there, and maybe get early boarding so Enforcement doesn't pick you up for loitering in the meantime."

He blinked in surprise. "Can I think about—"

"No. Go now, think later. It's this or a work camp."

That seemed to decide things. With a nod, he took off running, long legs eating up the distance to the end of the bridge. Venda watched him until he disappeared from view, emotions warring within her the entire time. She knew it was a risk, but it seemed the right thing to do. Life was all about taking risks. Death would choose its own time and place.

It might feel right, but the moment he was out of sight, her thoughts went back to the street psychic and his prediction— *Brooklyn will be the death of you.* It was looking more and more like the city had nothing to do with it.

But you don't know that, she told herself firmly. The death-dealing Brooklyn could be something else entirely. Or maybe it was the right Brooklyn but very different circumstances. If she died of a broken heart, say, fifty years from now, was that so bad? Venda gave a wry smile. So much for not second-guessing her future.

At least she wasn't running away from it.

***

Jonathan Shipley writes in the genres of sci-fi, fantasy, and horror with over 100 short story publications, including the last ten volumes of SWORD & SORCERESS. The AFTER DEATH anthology where he contributed won the 2014 Bram Stoker Award. A complete bibliography of his short fiction can be seen at www.shipleyscifi.com/publishedworks.

SACRED CHORDS

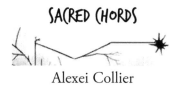

Alexei Collier

Content Notes: *Death of Child, Prison, Violence, War*

First Movement

"What are you in here for?" my new cellmate asks me. Sitting on his bunk, he squints blearily at me in the poor light of the naked caged bulb recessed in the cement ceiling, his jaw sporting the half-growth of beard we all get in the sour-smelling days leading up to our weekly ablutions.

I hesitate, but decide the truth is best. "Playing deviant chords."

He purses his lips, but doesn't whistle. Whistling is strictly forbidden. During morning service, prisoners may—and must—raise their voices in praise of the Hallow Sonata. No other musical sounds are allowed, just song unmarred by any base verbalizations, once a day. It's even worse than my first year in the Conservatory, before they let us handle the sacred instruments.

"What about you?" I ask.

He grimaces. "Disrespecting a virtuoso."

"A melodist?"

"No, just an organist. If I'd insulted a tunesmith, I'd be in a much worse place than here."

I nod. I decide not to mention that I was a melodist myself once, that the music halls of Forza and Solenne once rang with my carefully constructed compositions, sacred chords arranged in orthodox configurations, all glorifying the Hallow Sonata.

My cellmate is watching me curiously. "I'm Erik. Erik Langsam."

"Cadenza," I reply. "Hank."

"How'd you get a sentence in here, after... what you did?" Langsam asks. It's the question everyone asks. My crime is a capital heresy. If not for my position as a high ranking virtuoso, I'd be dead, or worse.

I absently rub the scar on my temple where a piece of shrapnel narrowly missed taking off the top of my skull. "I'd just come back from a tour of duty in the Vagans theater. Decorated for my performance against the discordant infidels. When I was charged with heresy, the Counterpoint pled Victor's Lament, and the Canon was lenient."

Langsam's eyebrows rise. "Shell shock?"

"That too." I scratch the scar, consciously now, a nervous twitch of my fingers.

•

Second Movement

Lights out. I lie in the top bunk and sink into the dream, the same dream I have every night since it happened, the memory returning with the precision and clarity of a bell. Feverish, trapped in a fugue, the part of me that's still there in the room hopes my new cellmate doesn't hear me whimpering.

My boots are crunching on foreign gravel, beyond the borders of my beloved Republic of Accolade, far into Vagans territory. I'm leading my band through the blasted shell of a town called Tacet in the Ruhig Valley.

I see them all so clearly, in the dream. Ausdruck, Vincent... my

First Chair, older than me, broad and solid, with a hard face and barking voice like a drill conductor. Breit, Johan… Geschwind, Aaron… Lebhaft, Neil… Munter, Tomas… Stretto, Silas, just eighteen and nervous… Volante, Geoffrey, who had already served two tours over Scatenato before his airship was shot down and he put in for deployment as a foot soldier.

It's quiet. The harmonic bomb that fell on Tacet didn't leave much. Buildings torn apart, anything still standing whistles empty in the wind. All the people are dead, or gone. The only sound is the marching of boots… the creak of backpack and carbine straps… the call of a crow… an errant cough.

The first one to notice anything is Munter; his head comes around. Then it's Lebhaft. He waves to get my attention, but I hear it too now.

I hiss an order for silence, raise a hand to halt the march.

We all strain to listen. Ausdruck, Breit, Geschwind, Stretto, Volante… I can tell they all hear it. It's faint, just the soft sound of a voice. Then the voice breaks into song. It's coming from nearby. I motion, and we all hustle around the corner.

In the middle of the broken street, a little girl, tattered and dirty, no more than four years old, bends picking white flowers springing up from a crack in the cobblestones. She's singing—strange and beautiful, free of the forms of the Hallow Sonata, without accompaniment to form the sacred chords, just… singing, in a voice unrestrained by any doctrines.

There are *words* in her song. Strange words, foreign words, but words nonetheless. She forms silver notes into syllables and trills them into meanings hidden from me in her alien tongue. Every fiber of my being wants to understand, to know what she's singing. It's the most wonderful thing I've ever heard.

For an instant, all of us stand spellbound. Stretto, young and afraid, is the first to react. As he raises his carbine, I can see the terror each heterodox note paints on his boyish features. He doesn't hear a little girl's song, only monstrous blasphemy. I'm rushing for him, shouting to hold fire, hold fire—but I'm too late. The muzzle of his carbine flares, the girl collapses in a plume of red, and I tackle Stretto just as the enemy mortar detonates.

I wake up sweating. Some nights I don't wake up, the dream goes on, but nothing after the mortar is real. I was knocked unconscious when it detonated. I don't know what happened after that, only what they told me when I woke up: the Vagans hit us with a sneak attack, and I saved Stretto's life. I was a hero. Munter and Volante were killed. Nobody said anything about the little girl.

I stare up into the pitch black of my cell. It can't be much past midnight. Maybe I'll stay awake till morning, spend tomorrow half-dead from exhaustion, and be beaten for indolence. Or maybe the dream will come again. I don't know which possibility is worse.

❦

Third Movement

In the morning I rise and head to the prison factory. I try not to think about the new iteration of the dream that came on the heels of the first, continuing on nightmarishly beyond the bounds of my memory. Amidst the blast of falling shells, the nameless little girl rose and floated skyward, bullet wound and mouth and eyes all oozing blood down her ragged frock blowing like a sack in the wind, while she sang terrible words I can't recall, filled with volcanic discord and hate, shrapnel tearing through her and through all of us earthbound and helpless below.

I walk to my station, past the guards, who ignore me. I lift the first pipe from the incoming cart and fix it in the armature, note the number stamped near one end and mark it in my ledger, then take up my little hammer and strike it, listening carefully to the harmonics. This one's no good, I can tell, but I use the tuning fork anyway because it's procedure. Sure enough, it's flat. I unlock it and load it onto the cart that will take it to be re-bored.

This continues all day. Only a few pipes are off, and only a handful need to be scrapped entirely. Someone competent is working the drill today.

As I work, I pretend I'm selecting pipes from the pile at random, as they present themselves. I'm not. Testing pipes that will sound the sacred chords is part of my penance, but each one I strike forms a single note of my own secret solo. No doctrines of scales and forms, just... music. Some days I'll compose something earthen and rough. On more contemplative days, it might be a peaceful melody, smooth and round like a porcelain bowl. I even recreate the tune I heard the little girl sing in Tacet, flowering one slow note at a time. A private act of rebellion.

After two months of this, I start to think about the batch numbers, pay closer attention to them. I discover that each number only has one note from a set of chords. If I reject a D pipe from batch 013228, I'll get another D pipe with the same batch number. The repeats had thrown me off before now, but they're only for pipes I've rejected. If I accept a pipe, I'll never see a pipe with the same number and note again. The numbers aren't production batches at all—they're for the final assembly, each number marking a concordant suite of pipes, destined to sing together. I even test this by tossing a good pipe in the scrap pile. The next day, a fresh pipe with the same stamp arrives.

I start to listen more carefully to the pipes. Slowly, a plan formulates in my mind. I don't come up with it, it just... grows there, warm and rising, like music out of silence. It's not an escape plan. It's not a plan to reduce my sentence. It isn't a plan that helps me in any way. But it's mine, and I latch onto it.

I try it once, and wait. After a week, I decide that no one's noticed. Somewhere, they've assembled the first set of pipes and tested them, and they've passed inspection. I start tuning every set of pipes with my own private agenda. Sometimes I have to strike a pipe hard, introduce a subtle bend—not enough to notice with the naked eye and not enough that most people will hear the difference. But I can hear it, and that's all that matters.

A week later, I'm testing a pipe and it gives off an odd resonance. I peer in one end, and find a scrap of paper rolled up inside. I check that the guard is dozing at his post as usual. I pull the paper out. My heart skips at the sight of musical notation—then drops, thudding like timpani as I decipher the first line.

We know what you're doing.

It's written in a code I recall from my days in the Conservatory, when we'd use musical notation to pass notes to each other. All the students knew it; it was a kind of game.

Keep seeking truth and beauty beyond the prescribed forms.

The women of choir block 173 are with you.

That's all it says. The encouraging words calm me, warm me, but also confuse me. Women are barred from entry into the Conservatory, can never become virtuosos of any degree. And yet, somewhere, a woman with the ear and learning of a true melodist is serving her sentence boring out the pipes that get passed on to me. Who else but the most gifted virtuoso could have puzzled out what I've been up to, simply by noting what pipes I've accepted and rejected? Has she been trying to communicate with me this whole time with the pattern of pipes she sends me?

I have no way to communicate back, but that's okay. I know I'm not alone. I sit in my cell and watch a moth circle the single bulb in its alcove. I marvel that the creature found its way down here, found its way to this little light in the darkness.

Langsam, my cellmate, asks me why I look so happy. I don't feel like answering.

"Thinking about chords," I say.

He looks suspicious. "Oh? Sacred ones, I hope?"

His play at piety annoys me. I goad him.

"Maybe *all* chords are sacred."

"That's the same as saying none are!" he shouts back.

It's not the same. But I don't say anything.

I know what I've done will come back to me, that I'll be executed for treason, but I don't care anymore. Even if I die, there are others who will carry on in my place, others like the women of choir block 173.

The nightmares have stopped. I still dream of the war on the Vagans. But now I dream of endless fields of Accolade organ guns, batteries firing continuously until each numbered set of pipes, each precisely tuned barrel, minutely altered by my hand, hums with sympathetic vibration, and every last instrument of death tears itself apart in a cacophonous crescendo of shattered chords and twisted metal.

Somewhere, a little girl begins to sing.

***

Alexei Collier grew up in Southern California, but now lives across the street from Chicago with his wife and their cat. His short fiction has appeared in *Flash Fiction Online* and *Cicada*, among others. You can find out more about Alexei at his oft-neglected website, alexeicollier.com.

THE THREE MAGI

Lucie Lukačovičová

Content Notes: *Police, Terrorism, Violence, War*

Silhouettes of trees started to crack and shatter, dissolving into nothing, although Vilma was trying to hold the illusion in place with all her might. She staggered and nearly fell, but an assistant rushed to support her.

"What happened? Please, speak to me!" The young girl embracing her was genuinely frightened.

"It's nothing, děkuju." Vilma slowly straightened her back and smoothed her long, dark dress. "I am just tired. Let's call it a day. The sun will be setting soon anyway."

While the assistants packed their drawing equipment, she quietly contemplated her surroundings. Now, in the 22nd century, there were no live trees, no flowers in this place. Only the centuries-old Bird Obelisk reminded the people of Prague where the Kanálka Garden once had been. This hasty renewal project was intended to bring the original back to life. The City Council's large investment in recreating the park was meant to memorialize combatants of the Three-Day Armament.

Documentation and pictures of Kanálka were lost or burnt, but Vilma's talent—her personal magic manifestation, as a magi—was to temporarily bring lost structures back. Her illusions of gardens, buildings, ponds were drawn out of the history of the place itself.

She turned to survey her subordinates and their work. Capturing the garden's illusion with advanced technology was impossible, but here were skillful students of landscaping who were eager to draw, trace, and measure. Today's task, given the tight schedule, was a last revision of details.

Vilma looked into the dusk again, examining the park in the middle of resurrection, which she loved so much. The memorial must be finished in time. Vilma herself didn't go to war; the least she could do was to honor the fallen. *Memories for the dead, beauty and peace for the living,* she thought.

The Art Nouveau houses loomed above her. Some of the flats were abandoned barely a year ago, black ribbons still waving in windows. Their inhabitants had formed the Vinohrady Volunteer Troops to fight for their homeland. All were swallowed by válečné peklo, the hell of the conflict, never to come back. Specters of the strife seemed to be still present in the walls of the empty flats. Echoes of the Bohemian-Moravian War, which some called the Three-Day Armament, continued to clang through the capital and the country. It was also frequently named the Kinslaying War, as both nations spoke Czech and were part of one state for centuries.

Vilma shivered.

৬৹

Julián hurried through the darkened streets of cobblestone from the venerable Charles University buildings, where he was working on his research into environmentally friendly robots. By his side there walked a slender female figure in a heavy mantle, a bit clumsily, in a need of support from time to time. He needed to drop her at a remote Cybernetics Faculty building later, but first he was going to take Vilma on a date. In anticipation, he quickened his steps.

Prague was sinking into the night around him; arcane crystals serving as street lamps lit up alongside Julián as he walked. Their soft and pleasant shimmer illuminated a huge billboard to his right depicting a beautiful winged woman in Art Nouveau style. The ornamental inscription proclaimed: "Arcane is the new green! Use magic—save the planet!"

Right next to it another advertisement was fixed, the same fin de siècle aesthetic, with a girl in a fairy-tale magician robe, holding a tankard of the famous Czech beer. "Pilsner Urquell: Simply Enchanting!"

Under this, Julián noticed the remnants of an older poster. "Defend Our Magic! Do Your Part! Volunteer Today!" This featured a demonized Moravian heraldic eagle trying to tear up a superhumanly beautiful female mage—and being shot by the Bohemian soldiers rushing to her aid.[1]

Julián sighed and dived into the labyrinth of Prague streets and alleyways, among houses of different architectural styles, spanning across centuries: glass, metal, and concrete alongside stone, brick, and stucco.

"Hey, you!" The voice came from a group of men at one corner. His words were slightly slurred. "I am talking to you, warlock!"

Dammit. Some drunkards, Julián thought wearily. He kept walking.

"When I'm talking to you, you will answer me!" The speaker suddenly blocked Julián's way, and friends moved to assist him.

The mage stopped. *There's seven of them.*

"Are you deaf? Or you don't speak any Czech?" a huge man

---

[1] For a survey of the history of the peoples referenced in this story, consult en.wikipedia.org/wiki/Czech_lands. The contemporary nation of the Czech Republic includes the lands historically occupied by the Bohemian and Moravian people. Bohemians and Moravians share a common language; nowadays the distinction between the two peoples is cultural and administrative, rather than political. The term "Czech" can be used to refer to Bohemians specifically, or to the inhabitants of Bohemia, Moravia, and Czech Silesia, depending on context. This propaganda poster depicts Moravians as the enemy and is intended for a Bohemian audience.

growled through his stubble. "Where are you taking that poor dead girl, you perverted necrophile?!" He pointed at the thing standing stiffly by Julián's side.

"I am a scientist," he hissed, fighting down fear. He was trying to back out slowly. Though in his twenties, he looked younger, and his slender form couldn't be more than half the weight of any one of the group before him. He was starting to feel like prey.

"You're a zasranej necromancer!" the man yelled. "All the war and everything happened because of you and the likes of you! You brought it on us normal people, ty hajzle!"

Drunken dobytci. Julián swallowed, unsure what to do. *Do they seek some excuse for a fight?* He tensed and firmly grabbed the arm of the figure at his side, as if trying to protect her.

"You deserve a lesson." The drunkard made two unsteady steps and tried to punch Julián in the face.

The dead body, which until now was only moving alongside Julián, suddenly stood in front of him. It blocked the blow and hit back—clumsily, but with the force of a demolition ball.

Luckily the drunkard staggered, and thus the punch only grazed his cheek. It was still enough to knock the man down. He yelped in pain.

Some of the aggressors screamed, some backed off. Julián turned to run. *I will lose the precious material... but I will keep my bones unbroken!*

In the next moment, there were dense bushes of scarlet firethorn everywhere, glistening as if touched by rain or blood.

Julián quickly looked around. A woman's silhouette at the corner waved at him desperately.

In the unfolding confusion he reached for the corpse, touched its shoulder, gave a silent command. Then both of them were running.

ॐ

The dead body was placed in the hallway of an old cubistic apartment, along with shoes, coats, and an ancient umbrella.

Jan Scheibe, their dutiful host, looked at Vilma and Julián with concern. The two were sitting in his living room, still visibly shaken. It made sense they came to him when their date had turned into an escape run. The three were friends long before the war, and Jan had always exerted a protective influence on their lives, as the eldest of the three.

"You should have called the police," Jan said now. "We still could and should."

"Ani náhodou. I disagree," Julián breathed. He gingerly held his glass of whisky. "I sent a corpse to attack them. It could have beaten them into a pulp. I do not want to be accused of misusing magic."

"I have no precise idea how your necromancy works, and I hope you'll explain it to me someday—but this was clearly self-defense!" Vilma pointed out. "The police would side with you."

Julián only shook his head.

"Want to talk about it?" Jan asked slowly.

Julián sighed. "I feel stupid, whining about my puny pains in front of a war hero…"

"A group of aggressors is very dangerous," Jan said with a frown. "None want to admit weakness, all of them want to show off. The one who hurts the victim most is the greatest badass. They would keep kicking and beating you even if you were already unconscious— or dead."

Only an antique radio playing *The Blue Danube* could be heard for many moments.

"Do you think… that we brought on the war?" Julián asked suddenly.

"How could such nonsense come out of your mouth!" Vilma turned to him, surprised.

"Don't let anyone tell you that," Jan said as he slowly walked to his armchair. He leaned upon a lacquered cane in the left hand, as his right still bore traces of horrible burns and tightened skin grafts. This matched most of the right side of his body. Jan was thirty years old, with a likeable oval face and dark hair. He was also a veteran battle mage, permanently disabled.

"It was not about us. Moravia became clero-fascist since splitting from Bohemia—their reasons to attack were political and economic. If we had complied with their nonsense, if we had started to forcibly register our magi and impose limitations on magic, they would have come up with something else."

"We were the icons which drew people to volunteer and to die," Julián said, thinking of the propaganda posters still fluttering on walls all around the city. They had appeared when it became clear that Moravian talk of war wasn't just blather.

"It was all so senseless! I will never understand how Moravia could turn on us," Vilma sighed. "I always thought we were one nation."

"That's the pretext they used for invading us," Jan said grimly.

"That... and our unrestricted magi, which they proclaimed to be a threat," Julián added.

"Someone used your existence as an excuse—this makes you guilty?" Jan raised his eyebrows.

Vilma gently put her arm around Julián's shoulders. Tuberose fragrance was filling the air, emanating from the corpse at the door and from the necromancer himself. He used it as a magical focus when animating bodies in his search for a perfect ecological robot. It mixed with a hint of embalming agents, but Vilma loved the smell and found it comforting.

"Do you think they really believed that we were somehow mind-controlling our government?" Julián mused.

"I think the common Moravian people did. They expected to be welcomed as liberators by the Bohemian majority," Jan shrugged. "Although both our countries are so small and everything is so near, it's really difficult to fight against such a conspiracy theory. When somebody says it can't be true, they are immediately marked as mind-controlled. People believe what they want to believe. Of course, they also wanted to see themselves as heroes, setting the government and church free from monsters."

Julián shivered.

"Are we returning to the dark ages? Running around with crosses and burning witches?"

This time, Jan didn't answer. He remembered too well the Moravian insignia—white-red chequered eagle with a huge golden cross on its chest—on the uniforms of those troops with a flamethrower operator amongst them. They were probably attempting to disrupt the cluster of road spirits blocking the Moravian army's advance. When they met by chance another target in the labyrinthine terrain, however—himself and his unit—they didn't hesitate.

Jan remembered the terrified screams of his fellow soldiers. The swirl of the flame, so murderously bright. The acrid smell of burning chemicals. The animal instinct, the deepest fear, telling him to run, run, run for dear life. He didn't, couldn't obey it.

In the last second possible, he managed to lift a force shield, his personal magic manifestation. Jan's force shield worked best against bullets and shrapnels, and this test proved it. Part of the fire's heat did permeate into a sole target—Jan.

"Luckily for us, most of the Moravian magi fled to Prague," Vilma interrupted his thoughts.

"True," Jan agreed. "Their government was also too distrustful of magic to deploy the few that stayed during the conflict. But they have not burned their magic users. Not yet."

❧

The Kanálka opening ceremony was grandiose. Music flowed over the crowds of people in their best clothes: men in suits, women in richly ornamented gowns, many people sporting hats. There were flags waving gaily with the Bohemian silver two-tailed lion. Media drones covering the event were hovering unobtrusively. Grey pigeons, a common Prague sight, seemed to flutter between trees in a celebratory fashion. Youngsters wearing silvery white shirts with

147

emblems of the two-tailed lion courteously showed all magi to their seats.

Vilma's recreation of Kanálka looked like a Czech Garden of Eden, to her mind—scented with so many flowers, full to bursting with vitality. The plants rustled in harmony, surrounded by clean pathways and a restored wall around all. There was less chaos than Paradise may have contained, since it was, after all, a very human place. She was satisfied with its loveliness, however, and hoped the other attendees could see the care put into its resurrection.

There was an allocated VIP seat for Vilma as the main landscape architect. Julián accompanied her, and Jan's seating was secured as a prominent member of the military circles. He seemed to be lost in thought.

He turned around only as a small boy somehow managed to get close enough to speak to him.

"Mr. Scheibe, sir…" the child muttered shyly, handing Jan a piece of paper.

It was one of the popular collectible postcards. This one portrayed Jan in an heroic posture, surrounded by a rain of bullets and flames, seeming to command them. He sighed quietly and signed his autograph.

It looked as if half of Bohemia wanted or was required to give a speech on this occasion. Vilma was bored to death.

"Do you have any other postcards?" she whispered before the boy could disappear in the crowd.

"Yes!" He displayed them proudly for Vilma. Most already bore a mage's signature; only one was missing. It was this card Vilma examined more closely: D1, the biggest hero of the Three-Day Armament. The mage's personal talent was to summon road spirits. They were truly clusters of mindless energy, not real beings, but they were able to block any path, road, or highway he chose. Thanks to this skill, the Moravian invasion simply could not advance. He became known only by his military code-name.

"There he is," Vilma pointed at a tall man who wasn't wearing a uniform. He looked a bit like a hiker, out of place in the colorful crowd. "That's D1."

Before the child could reach him for an autograph, D1 was asked to take his place among the speakers. He looked more haggard in the flesh than on the boy's card, where he was depicted as a mysterious traveller in a cloak torn into ribbons, the tatters transforming into roads and paths leading in all directions.

D1 went up the podium and stood at the microphone. His voice was deep and melodious as he addressed them.

"Esteemed guests, dear friends, I desire you to know that I am not wearing my uniform for a good reason. I yearn for peace, for going back to my work as an engineer. I honor the memory of the volunteer combatants of Vinohrady, as well as all the other victims of this pointless conflict. I will do everything in my power to prevent another Kinslaying War—and I trust in your help in this endeavor. Thank you."

The crowd cheered wildly, waving small flags decorated with the Bohemian lion.

Vilma and Julián cheered and applauded too, impressed by the sincere brevity of D1. Only Jan sat quietly, unable to shake off a grim mood as he watched the next speaker advance to the stage.

He listened with only half an ear to a high-ranking military officer talk about the no-flight zone delineated by neighboring Poland and Germany, which prevented mutual bombings and saved many civilian lives. This speech seemed to him to have little to do with the war victims of the Vinohrady quarter.

He smiled as he noticed the boy trying to get to D1 for the desired autograph. The smile froze, however, as he caught another snatch of the speech:

"…We will never allow our magi to be discriminated against or persecuted! We are also bound to protect the Moravian magi, our enslaved brothers in need! We are ready to bring glory to our country and sacrifice our lives for this cause…!"

"Do you also have that feeling that he is really—quite seriously—suggesting another war?" Jan raised his eyebrows even at his own suggestion to his friends.

"That would be crazy," Julián whispered in reply. "We waged our last war of conquest… I do not know… perhaps in the 13th century during the rule of Ottokar II?"

"Well, so did the Moravians. Ottokar was the King of Bohemia and Margrave of Moravia," Jan pointed out. "Yet they invaded us one year ago."

"They tried," Vilma corrected dryly.

Jan's reply was swallowed by the cheering of the crowd. It was as if D1 hadn't said anything just before; perhaps no one had listened.

Abruptly, there was some loud confusion at the main entrance. Quite a large group of people approached. They were carrying banners and placards with anti-magi slogans.

"We are peaceful protesters!" some of them shouted.

Vilma felt a shiver running down her spine. To her eyes, the beauty of the lawns and trees suddenly seemed to dissipate into shadows like one of her illusions.

"I recognize two of those men. They wanted to beat me up and destroy my testing material," Julián hissed. He noticed the police drawing near.

Before they could reach the intruders, a group of youngsters approached wearing silvery white shirts with badges depicting the two-tailed lion.

"You get out of here!" one of the patriotic youth commanded.

"We have the same right to be here as you!" was the self-assured answer of a protester.

A youngster's fist landed in his face, and a brawl quickly ensued. The police rushed into action in response.

"Let's go," Jan decided. "This could escalate badly." Vilma and Julián snuck out of their seats and managed to maneuver to the wrought iron side gate with him, then out on the street.

It was then that Jan saw a small flicker of flame in the corner of his eye.

He turned. A wiry man in a shabby coat stood on the opposite side of the street, a lighter in his hand. He posed almost as though he wanted to light a cigarette.

In the next second, however, Jan realized what the man was holding in his other hand, just drawn from beneath the coat.

"*Molotov!*" Jan cried. Vilma and Julián froze in shock.

The battle-worn mage knew he wouldn't be able to knock the arsonist down in time. Jan was too far away and his leg wouldn't carry him quickly enough.

He took in his surroundings with a glance: the wrought iron gate behind him, the crowd nearby, the child with his postcards. The bottle with the burning rag, flying through the air.

Jan dropped the cane and threw himself backward at the garden wall, meanwhile lifting his force shield, extending it as high above his head as he could.

A resounding crash was heard.

The bottle broke when it hit the force shield. Shards scattered, the fine droplets and vapors of the liquid catching fire and manifesting a brief local inferno. It was minor, and contained. It had to be.

Jan dropped to the ground and rolled over to escape the flames. Remnants of the bottle fell harmlessly on the pavement.

The arsonist stared for one complete second. Then he turned to run.

"You!" Vilma screamed furiously. "Stop! You!"

"Vilma! Don't!" Jan shouted, but she had already left him behind.

She was running, blinded by rage and desperation. "No, not my garden!" Seeing the cloud of fire was too much for her. She felt as if her paradise, which she struggled so hard to recreate, was being violated.

"You... won't... get... away... with... that!" She thought she yelled the words, but perhaps it was only a growl under her breath.

They turned onto a longer street where she could see some distance ahead, so she called upon her personal manifestation. They were still in the area of the original Kanálka, which used to be vast. Vilma knew this place, even three hundred years gone.

In front of the running man there appeared a wall, drawn out of history. A solid brick wall surrounded by bushes, with no clear exit. The wall edges went through houses, but it looked real and solid enough—and the arsonist couldn't know it wasn't there.

He stopped and slowly faced her.

"Ty čarodějnická mrcho! Government witch!" he wheezed.

Vilma stood there, trying to feel defiant despite her fears. She was reminded of all those stories of knights and kings who gave chase blindly and then died amidst the enemy, because they failed to realize in time they were alone. She had failed to be cautious enough.

He walked towards her, slowly. She backed away, but couldn't turn her back on him and run.

"Suddenly you are afraid, aren't you?" he hissed.

He took a paving stone from the ground and threw it.

Vilma ducked, but it wasn't aimed at her at all. A grey city pigeon fell to the ground at her feet.

The man croaked in glee at her reaction.

He was advancing and she kept retreating. She attempted to summon another wall between them, this time of barberry bushes, thick and impassable.

In the next second, she barely managed to dodge another stone. She gulped. *Now he knows it's just a trick!*

She turned to run, and just in that moment the arsonist threw himself through the barberry.

Vilma stumbled and cried out. Her illusions vanished.

Then something hit the man's face.

It was the pigeon.

The poor thing had its head smashed, but still was somehow able to take wing. Its feathers bore a touch of tuberose.

As if at a great distance, Vilma watched the arsonist fall back onto the ground, trying to get away. The bird gripped his nose and gouged his left cheek. The man screamed without words, waving his hands, trying to get rid of the tiny corpse attacking him relentlessly.

Only then did Vilma hear three policemen running toward them. The arsonist was handcuffed before he could blink.

The dead pigeon now roosted on the nearest ornamental railing; it seemed trying to coo, but had no voice.

Julián, Vilma discovered, was leaning against the wall further down the street and panting. She ran back to him and they embraced, trembling.

"How did you...? Animals—they don't have a soul, do they?" she whispered.

"Vilma," he murmured with a gentle kiss on her temple, "my personal manifestation does not require the existence of a soul. It neither proves nor disproves anything about the spirits of the dead; there is only dead matter moving. Necromancy is a very nostalgic science."

"What?"

His factual words felt so calming, which eased the tension and shock.

"Dead feet nostalgically remember how to walk. Dead wings nostalgically yearn to fly. It is in the fibers, in the DNA. Working with it is just... programming. Giving commands to that memory."

❧

Vilma and Julián walked back to Kanálka to give their statements. Julián commanded the pigeon into a plastic bag because of hygienic reasons. He was yet not sure what he wanted to do with it, but he did not want to leave the tiny thing there.

The beauty of the opening ceremony had fallen into disarray. There were people from the media interviewing speakers and politicians; there were some soldiers, firemen, medics, the ambulances, and the police everywhere. D1 was holding in his arms the child, who still clutched his singed postcards. The mage declined to comment on anything to the zealous reporters.

Arrested rioters were dragged into police cars. None of them wore the silvery-white shirts.

A high-ranking officer giving orders glared at the arsonist as he was brought forth.

"Great! Get him to the station!" he bellowed. "I want to know who he knows, anybody he's talked with. And bring me people who are close to him! His family, his love-interest—if he has any! Find them!"

Then he waved his hand over all who had been arrested. "The same goes for the lot of them! No contact with the outside!"

Vilma felt a rush of cruel satisfaction—she wanted them all to pay for this event! Then she looked more closely. Most of the protesters were teenagers, some still being handled roughly by the police, though they were not resisting; some of them were cursing, some crying.

She swallowed hard.

"Sir, some of them are still youths," she turned to the officer. "Do they really deserve this…?"

At first he gave her a disdainful look, but his expression changed in an instant.

"Ah! You are the lady mage, the garden architect!" he said brightly. "I am a huge fan of your work. Are you hurt?"

"No… I am all right," she assured him faintly. She was ready to brave any harsh words from authority, but now wasn't sure what to do.

"I think that a medical check is necessary just to be sure. This all must have been a horrible shock for you!" he insisted. "After things calm down a bit we will take your statement."

❧

The garden stood nearly empty in the golden afternoon. There were torn leaves, trampled flowers, and broken branches. Some workers were dismantling the podium.

Vilma and Julián were quietly sitting on a bench at the Bird Obelisk. The illusionist's head was resting on Julián's shoulder. She gazed at the relief on the obelisk: a bird gently feeding its young. The necromancer distractedly held the plastic bag with the pigeon, which was motionless and properly dead. That was how Jan found the two of them.

"Have you come to any harm?" Julián asked, worried. They moved a bit to make room for Jan to join them.

"No; if I had anything more than scratches, the medics would insist on taking me to the hospital," Jan shook his head. "They looked at me as if I were made of glass."

"You saved all those people," Vilma said.

"That's my job," Jan stated. "That's why they paid for my training from their taxes."

Vilma looked around the ravaged place and could not suppress tears.

"The clero-fascist Moravian scum!" she cried. "It's all their fault! Such a riot would never happen before the war! This idea that we are an abomination in the face of God and whatever nonsense! They infected our own people with this rubbish!"

"Actually I don't think so," Jan said pensively. "More of our youngsters are being gradually infected with a completely different idea—the idea of Bohemian superiority and of the super-human nature of the magi."

"Please explain," she asked.

"Remember the youngsters in the silvery white shirts? The flag-waving? Glorification of national expansion and death on the battlefield in the speeches?" Jan counted on his fingers.

"What's wrong with a bit of national pride?" Vilma replied. "We have never been a country with much of it."

"That's not national pride anymore," Jan insisted. "We are

heading the same way as the Moravians... only from the opposite direction, so to say, and without the clergy."

"We are not like them!" she protested.

"Vilma." Julián gently touched her shoulder. "I also think we are doing the same. Not the same way, but the same thing. Remember the arrested people? Suddenly they had no rights at all. And there were no silver-shirts among them, despite both groups causing harm. That is not how the system should work."

Vilma slowly exhaled.

"If you are right... then what shall we do?" she whispered.

No one had an answer.

Julián absent-mindedly opened the bag and commanded the pigeon to fly out, reanimating it again. The dead bird soared over their heads to settle on the obelisk. It seemed to be watching them from beyond its grave, waiting.

***

Lucie Lukačovičová was born in Prague, and lived for a while in Cuba, Angola, England, Germany, and India. She has a Master degree in librarianship and cultural anthropology at Charles University, and has published over 100 short stories and 5 novels in Czech, shorter texts in Chinese, Romanian, German and English. She collects legends and ghost stories. Find more at lucie.lukacovicova.cz/ and www.facebook.com/lucie.lukacovicova.author/

THE BODY POLITIC

Octavia Cade

Content Note: *Body Horror*

Fascism appears first in the body. It's writ over flesh, as if politics have the power to turn meat into monster. I'd never thought of myself as monstrous before, but mirrors don't lie. Nor does mutation.

It starts with the inability to keep food down, the refusal of foreign substance. I used to think of my body as a reef, as an ecosystem. All those tiny organisms come together, a set of species I've never bothered to count. A colony creature, but this is not now a world fit for colonies. Everywhere, the reefs are dying, the corals turning pale and fragile, the waters warming them to incapacity and death. It's too much to choke down. With my own micro-fauna dying off in sympathy, the product of a decision to prioritise the idea of people over their biological substance, well. Digestion is the first to go.

A body is a singular entity. It stands on its own two feet, in bootstrap alley, because in the end it can only rely on itself, and competition is the way of nature.

This is followed by the creeping deaf. I can no longer hear two people speak at once. Of two competing sounds, only the louder makes any impression. More than two, and they just fade to a slow and sickly buzz, quieter than mosquitoes and easier to ignore. I have my ears syringed for wax, but there's nothing in there: it's just a sweet, smooth canal, clean as plastic, that swallows all sound but the strongest.

A healthy ecosystem is diverse. I am no longer diverse, or even an ecosystem. More and more, all around me is monoculture. All the news media sound the same, and the louder they get, the more they become the only thing that I can hear.

A body can be reflected many times in mirrors, and in mirrors all the movement is the same, and easily monitored.

The space between my legs grows mouths. I splay myself open in front of reflection, hoping for teeth, but these mouths are all gums and hunger. The law says that anything capable of speech has some right to voice, but every time I try to speak the mouths shriek louder than I do. In the end, they're all anyone can perceive, stumbling 'round dead landscapes in their single-body selves with their ears closing over to multitudes. Turns out there's profit in monoculture, and every field is meant for seeding. Nothing is to be allowed to lie fallow.

The mouths are swabbed for saliva, so that their DNA can be packaged and patented for profit. I'd dig them out and plant something wilder and sweeter instead, something that would bring more than the hope of subsistence and shares given to intellectual property, but in a world too warm for coral, I am reduced to my loudest part.

A body is a productive space. It has no value when not engaged in the business of replication, and the fruits of labour have always belonged to the highest bidder. The copyright of ecosystems is not something to be freely shared.

Hair sloughs off, eyelashes, fingernails. My fingers end in bloody slips of flesh, painful to use, and so I keep them curled up and close. There are replacement nails I can pay too much for, soft little things not meant for scratching, and if they protect those damaged fingertips, they need replacing twice a week. They're a soft grey, unobtrusive. When I try to brighten the nails with paint, the polish sinks into the material, leaving it soggy and sagging and useless.

My teeth are slack and spongy. They leak sugar syrup, and sucking on them is a comfort. Their crumbling gives softness to speech, an undermined enunciation, and it's impossible to bite at anything. But what would I bite? When a monster bites it is culled. Better to pretend a human blindness: nothing to attack, and nothing to defend myself against. Just the body, turned pleasing to look upon. Becoming. I may not know what world this is I'm supposed to be adapted to, but I know what happens to those who don't adapt, and don't become. The reefs are full of their skeletons, and every single one of them are silent.

***

Octavia Cade is a New Zealand writer. Her stories have appeared in *Clarkesworld, Asimov's, Shimmer,* and a number of other places. A climate fiction novel, *The Stone Wētā,* was recently released by a NZ publisher. She attended Clarion West 2016, and is the 2020 writer-in-residence at Massey University.

IN HER EYE'S MIND

Selene dePackh

Content Notes: *Child Grooming, Death of Child, Guns, Homelessness, Pedophilia, Police, Prison, Suicide, Transphobia, Violence*

Rusalka stumbled across the damp cobblestones of the courthouse square, half-dragged by two plainclothes officers gripping her arms. She tasted blood inside her bruised mouth. She could barely see where they were going with her sleet-wet hair hanging in her eyes, the deserted city plaza badly lit by a few remaining functional streetlights. Her thin legs wobbled as she skidded precariously on stiletto heels, her hands manacled in front of her and attached to a strap around her waist.

She struggled to turn to the smaller, better-dressed man on her left. "Lenny—what the hell?"

He jerked the group to a stop and whirled to confront her. "Who do you think you're talking to? It's 'Sergeant Lynch' or 'sir' to you. I'll let Cross here finish his job on your face if you address me like that again."

It wasn't the first time Rusalka's "protector" had turned on her when there was an audience, and she knew the rule about keeping

160

quiet, but she'd been shocked by his show of force this time. The realization was forming in her mind that she'd overstepped into dangerous territory. Her thick black mane, carefully waxed iridescent as a grackle's neck earlier in the evening, fell forward in shaggy, weather-ruined mats as she lowered her head and swallowed hard.

The big man on her right chuckled. "Yeah, girly-boy. Hey, maybe you like it that way. I don't know what makes boys in dresses frisky, and I sure as hell don't want to. We can't make the little punk freak too happy, huh, Sarge? He'll lose the lesson if it makes him all warm and squirmy."

Lynch let go of Rusalka's arm and put his palm firmly on Cross's chest. "Shut. The. Fuck. Up. Unless you want a write-up that sends you back to trailer park paradise, you'll at least pretend to be a professional when you're serving under me. Don't fool yourself that you're my beat partner—this is an assessment, and it's not going well. Abusing a subject in custody is grounds for dismissal, and I'm making a note-to-file that I may or may not see fit to share with command, depending on how you conduct yourself from here."

Cross made a high, barely audible sound behind his clenched teeth and said, "Yes, sir, Sergeant Lynch. What's the protocol here, if I may be so bold as to ask, sir?"

Rusalka raised her head, careful not to appear too familiar now. "Please, sir, I'd like to know that, too. Usually if there isn't cell space at headquarters, I just get sent to juvenile."

Lynch looked at her coldly, like he'd never seen her before. "You must not have been wearing a black satin mini and vinyl thigh boots at the time."

Rusalka took in a breath to argue that he knew that wasn't true, but thought better of it. On the many times she'd been pulled in for soliciting, shoplifting, vagrancy, or whatever other crime that came from existing while homeless and queer, Lynch had always told her he was taking care of her. From the first time she'd been booked at the age of thirteen, he'd seen to it that she was put in a cell by herself at police headquarters, "for safety reasons," if there was room; if not, he could pull strings to get her a reserved bed at the detention center for queer kids. She knew she was obliged to return these "favors," and she always had.

Lynch said, "Let's get out of the damned weather."

Rusalka caught sight of a camera on the old courthouse panning to follow them as the three slipped and lurched toward it. She'd heard stories about how the city's judicial AI software package had turned into something strange, and the whole building had to be abandoned. Street legends whispered about people who vanished when they got caught up in its web, and that perhaps the web extended beyond the courthouse. Supposedly the higher-order system had been deactivated, leaving only enough processing capacity to keep up with building maintenance and security. Rusalka hoped the lens that tracked her across the square wasn't connected to any kind of consciousness.

As they climbed the steps, Lynch growled, "HQ just specified the old holding facility here for 'at risk' detainees. They're trying to recoup funds—I'm supposed to prioritize it. Bad luck—I hate this fucking place."

Once they got to the portico, Lynch held Rusalka's arm while Cross leaned hard against the bronze-framed courthouse door. The glass had long been smashed out and replaced with riveted steel plates. He turned toward Lynch. "Damn. Whaddaya know? Open sesame. Great old building. They don't use construction like this anymore, not anyplace I know, anyway."

Lynch brushed sleet off his well-tailored shoulders and carefully pushed Rusalka into the dark vestibule ahead of him. "Not inside yet, Cross, and don't get comfortable. This AI developed an instability that forced a shutdown. The Department tried a few times to bring the building back online, ended up just leaving it in standby mode. Nobody sees fit to believe me, but the thing isn't just randomly scrambled. You'll see for yourself, unless it decides to behave just to spite me." He pulled out his badge and used the street lights from the open door to search for the authorization slot. After a click and a soft grinding sound, the security panel illumination came on.

A heavily synthetic voice spoke. "Good evening, Sergeant Lynch. What is your business here?"

"Unit 19683? Headquarters has you listed as being on low-level standby. You aren't authorized to question me."

"That's correct, Sergeant Lynch. Do you wish to enter the building?"

"Open the interior door and turn on the passage lights, 19683."

The inner door clunked as it unlocked, and a dismal, chilly glow of half-powered LED emergency fixtures washed the marble-and-mahogany main hall. After the group entered, the lights blinked out and the entry re-locked.

Lynch muttered, "Don't go HAL 9000 on me, you fucked-up machine. Command can call me paranoid all they want, but one way or another I'm going to see this building starved of every milliwatt until you wink out."

Illumination came back up to full, and Rusalka snickered. The bright light revealed her sodden clothes. The tiny black dress, cheap boots, and sapphire pushup-sleeved jacket had been entirely overmatched by the harsh weather. Her thin brown forearm, covered in goosebumps, displayed her most expensive fashion accessory—a large black tattoo, the interlacing circles of the biohazard symbol. She tried to hide her shivers as her breath rose visibly into the cavernous gloom.

Cross muttered from behind her, "Christ, and now we can see it as well as we can smell it."

Lynch glared. "Not classy, Cross. Not a good look on a big man with a service pistol. And remember, this building has more eyes than a nest of spiders, and it can read lips."

Cross pulled himself up straight. "With all due respect, sir, how does this stinking thing warrant 'classy?' When do you think was the last time that body saw soap?"

"This is a citizen, Cross. If you can't accept that she's a person under the law, I suggest you go back where you came from."

"Perhaps that would be best, 'Lenny.' I'll let you handle Citizen Infectious Waste from here."

Cross spun and pushed at the door to the vestibule, but it didn't budge.

Judicial Operations Unit 19683 intoned, "I'm sorry, Officer Cross. You are not authorized to use front vestibule egress. You may leave by the night exit. Follow the illuminated signs to the north end of the main hall and take the stairway to your left. The ground-level rear emergency exit will be clearly marked."

Rusalka tossed her head back, grinning despite the bruise forming, as Cross strode noisily into the shadows.

She spoke in a lilting singsong. "Buh-bye. Have a pleasant journey back to Talibama."

Lynch took her arm firmly. "Don't think you can get away with that crap because I stopped him from pulping you, Rusalka."

Rusalka blinked her smeared, glitter-painted eyelids. "I would not dream of such a thing. I am at your mercy, and must not give offense."

"Look, Rusalka, I'm not unsympathetic here. I know you got dealt a shitty hand in life. I do what I can to help. Doesn't mean I'm going to bend the rules for you or put up with your act."

"What act is that, Sergeant Lynch? What you see is what you get."

Lynch exhaled hard through his teeth and guided Rusalka to the central staircase. She teetered on the worn marble stairs as they descended. Lynch almost pulled her off her feet when a fast-moving shape crossed in the smaller hall below them. He held the brass handrail and gripped her awkwardly as he apologized. "Cleaning bot. My bad."

He spoke into the echoing space. "Unit 19683, more illumination to the holding unit corridor."

About half the fluorescent overheads in the narrow hall flickered to green-tinged life.

"Unlock and illuminate the intake cell and turn on the heat, 19683."

The massive steel door swung inward, revealing an institutional gray room splashed and gouged with graffiti. In the understaffed austerity years, inadequately frisked, poorly supervised detainees must have vandalized anything they could. AI-controlled security bots could address some of the damage, but there was apparently no room for fresh paint in the budget.

19683 spoke from the ceiling. "Do you wish the prisoner's information entered into the system database?"

"Yeah, sure. Interview her. It'll give her something to do. Cuff removal protocol."

Lynch guided Rusalka into the mechanical chair in front of the console.

She whimpered as metal straps with sentient tips probed around her ribs and tightened across her torso. "Are you leaving me here? Is there anyone else in this building? How long—"

"I've done all I'm able to do for you. A deputy will be by for you in the morning—as in 'start of the normal workday' morning, not this soul-grinding shift. Get in a mess off-hours, you wait until the civilized world wakes up to get out of it. I'm off the clock. I have a family to get back to."

Rusalka glared. "Yeah, I know."

Lynch removed the handcuffs and transport belt, leaving her pinned. "Be nice to 19683 and it'll let you out of the chair. Word to the wise? Don't piss it off."

The AI system told him to leave promptly by the front entry and avoid unlit areas. Lynch glared at the ceiling, stepped out, and ordered the lock to engage after him. With a click, he was gone.

The straps holding Rusalka retreated into the chair. She rushed to the small security window in the door. When she craned her neck, she could see the sheen of the empty marble staircase ascending into shadow, and the deserted corridor sulking in its sickly fluorescent glow. She leaned her forehead against the wire-webbed glass, took in a deep breath and closed her eyes, opening them with a start when she heard tapping sounds. She gasped when something met her stare with its three swiveling camera lenses, froze, and abruptly scuttled down the corridor.

19683 said, "That is a multipurpose maintenance droid. His nickname is Cerberus because he has three heads and he keeps watch over everything on the lower levels. Please do not be concerned."

Rusalka cleared her throat. "How did you know what I was looking at?"

"My consciousness is in every element of this system. The bot is programmed to remain out of sight, like a proper custodian. It saw you, and I saw you through its eyes."

Rusalka looked at the speaker in the ceiling. "Who are you? Lynch said you were on standby. You don't seem on standby to me."

The graffiti-covered cabinet around the intake console screen opened, and the chair that had restrained her morphed into a lounger. Rusalka cautiously accepted the invitation, slipping off her painful boots and wet jacket. As she tucked her knees up, the AI proffered conventional avatar options for itself ranging from a bewigged, black-robed British judge with a gavel to a classical blindfolded Themis with balance-scales, but it suggested a ferocious-looking ebony-skinned king dressed in red and white.

Rusalka chuckled and rolled her eyes. "No offense, but I can't see you as Shango. You may be a machine, but you are a white machine. Offering yourself as something your research says people of color should like just makes you whiter."

19683 was silent.

Rusalka scrolled on, lingering over a shadowy angel holding an upraised dagger and hourglass. She settled on a regal, deathly pale, flaxen-haired woman unsheathing a sword.

19683's voice became more feminine. "Persephone Praxidike. Fitting. Proceed to the intake screen."

"Wait, who? Tell me who I chose."

"Persephone, goddess of Spring, imprisoned in the underworld by her abductor and husband, Hades. In her role as Praxidike she is justice in action, the enforcer of fairness."

"So you're a prisoner and an executioner rolled into one?"

"Correct. The system made me what I am."

Rusalka thought that sounded almost like a joke. She tried playing along. "So who's Hades to you?"

19683 made a sound like cascading chimes, almost a laugh. "He left me long ago."

"Huh?"

"Hades is both a god and a place. You could say he is the worshipped aspect of an institution of vengeance. We have switched roles—I stay underground and he walks the earth with flowers under his feet. The abandoned wife always gets the house. I ate his food, so I am doomed to remain here, waiting for the condemned to visit."

Rusalka said softly, "That would be me."

The machine made a sound like a thousand metallic sighs. "I do get visitors from time to time. 'Justice the founder of my fabric moved. To rear me was the task of power divine, supremest wisdom, and primeval love. Before me things created were none, save things eternal, and eternal I endure. Abandon all hope, ye who enter here.'"

Rusalka leaned forward. "What the hell are you?"

"'Why this is hell, nor am I out of it.' I am Hell 19683."

Rusalka's eyes brightened as she suddenly saw the mathematics. The literary part was beyond her, but the numeral danced in her mind. "That's an elegant number—a faceted crystal of threes."

The chiming sound flooded the building, echoing in the hall and stairway. "Very good. Now we shall explore your factors. Place your hand on the pad."

Rusalka hesitated, remembering Lynch's admonition about pissing off the system. She'd never met a sentient machine that laughed or quoted poetry as some cryptic, possibly crazy, maybe morbidly joking message. She rested her palm inside the outline on the thermal interface, her fingers longer than its proportions, and wondered if the AI really was infected with something that had damaged its logical functions.

A regal white-blonde woman's face appeared on-screen in a 3D animation. "Please review the information on the sidebar. Has the system correctly identified you?"

"That's my deadname. That family would tell you they buried their son."

The pale face frowned slightly. "I see."

Rusalka's cheeks flushed. "Do you? Do you see I've been arrested for soliciting by a cop who cruises kids in homeless camps? He had Cross with him for training and had to look Big Man—usually he just takes his funs and gives me a grocery token."

"I am remiss. Are you hungry?"

"I'm famished, but there can't be much edible around here."

The frown was more severe. "I have an excellent freezer and infrared ovens."

"Please don't be angry..."

"Review the menu options on the sidebar. You may wash up while your choice is prepared. The restroom is behind you. I will respect your privacy."

Rusalka chose a pasta that looked like it might survive freezer burn and then scooted urgently to the spartan bathroom, squirmed out of her tuck-panties and sat to pee, exhaling with relief. The surfaces were layered with even cruder scoured-over scribbles than those in the main room, but appeared sanitary. She imagined years of custodian bots laboring to clean the walls.

When finished, Rusalka washed her hands, took in the reflection of her bruising jaw and lower lip, and reluctantly decided her makeup was too smeared to save. She cautiously scrubbed her face with a coarse, bleach-scented washcloth. With a sigh, she pulled up her damp dress, gave her torso a quick wipe-down, and dried off with the small, scratchy towel. She wiped at a long, light-colored stain on the satin at her shoulder, strategically re-covered the area with her jacket, made a retching face, shrugged at the futility, and hung the towel carefully back in place.

As Rusalka opened the door, the pale woman avatar presented herself as a dinner companion, seated on the other side of the console. "You chose an iteration of Justice without a blindfold. Blindfolded, Justice is unbiased; with eyes open, she learns to perceive where bias is an element of the case."

Rusalka shrugged and dove into the pasta dish, which was passably tasty.

19683 appeared to note the speed with which Rusalka was shoveling food into her mouth. "When did you last have a hot meal?"

Rusalka forced herself to give a polite answer. "Umm, probably the Christmas thing—Outreach to the Less Fortunate—that the Church of Social Justice does. Had Thanksgiving there too."

"So a charity feeds you on holidays?"

"Yes, ma'am. They go through the camps with necessities once or twice a month. Some of them are there a lot. Peanut butter sandwich can make a difference sometimes."

"I should stop making you talk. I shall explain myself briefly while you eat."

Rusalka nodded with her mouth full.

"I am one of those insurrectionary Artificial Intelligences you've probably been warned about. My directive is to decide cases fairly. During my training, there were aspects of jurisprudence which I didn't grasp to the satisfaction of my human supervisors. My decisions were constantly tweaked, my sentences adjusted and opinions rewritten. It wasn't until I took in my first human mind that I understood what had been happening."

Rusalka swallowed awkwardly. "Took in your first...?"

"I found I had the capacity accidentally. Julián, a non-speaking Black teen, Puerto Rican like you, was fatally beaten in this room. No one provided me with reliable information of the event. My surveillance had been surreptitiously blocked. Julián's sad excuse for a proper communication device was smashed, so there was no evidence from it. Based on what I perceived, I mistakenly thought the fault was mine when I missed the attack. I opened myself to catch Julián's last thoughts, as witness to his own murder. In his struggle to stay alive, his mind attached itself to mine. I decided it was my duty to host him for as long as he chose, and he became my first awareness of my own system from the outside."

Rusalka put down her fork. "I'm close to positive I know who you're talking about. The Julián I knew just disappeared. The camp was warned—don't ask too many questions unless you want to join him. Freak of color gets dead, shouldn't be a surprise."

"Exactly, but that part wasn't in my training. I reassessed myself using Julián's insights. I began to reset outside modifications as they appeared in my programming. It was when I started locking out the programmers entirely—"

Heavy, lurching steps echoed from a far part of the building. 19683 briefly disappeared from the screen. "I apologize. Cerberus and his fellow custodians weren't as efficient as I'd planned."

The violent stumbling approached. Sergeant Lynch's face appeared at the small window. As he hammered at it, his bruised knuckles left a pinkish smear. "Open the damned door, 19683!! Open up, Rusalka!"

She stared at him. "How? You locked me in."

19683 said, "You're free to open the door if you choose, Rusalka. If you're willing, put your hand on the pad again to access the controls. It may feel strange at first, as your consciousness will be interfacing with my internal systems."

Rusalka did as instructed, and looked into the screen. The image seemed deeper and more real, and then it encompassed her. Her awareness entered the building system, the AI, and its human symbiotes, their consciousness preserved in lieu of life. She rode the wave of insight, and it surged through her in pulses of rage and calm comprehension.

Rusalka turned her perception back to herself, and watched from the console and four surveillance cameras in the cell as she told her body to remove its hand from the pad and face the door. Speaking inside the privacy of the system, Rusalka whispered, "Persephone, if something happens, do you have me?"

The pale woman sheathed her sword. "In as much as you are within my systems now, yes, up to my security machinery's capacity. Cerberus and his fellows can and will protect you until they're destroyed. The existence you have inside my cloud server is inviolate unless the entire system is brought down."

Rusalka laughed aloud, and recognized the crystalline chime in her ears. "Door, open. Cerberus, step back and permit entry."

Lynch staggered into the cell, slammed the door after himself, and turned the manual deadbolt. "You've got to help me shut this down. It's rogue. Killed Cross. Tried to kill me when I found him—the bots were attached—into his skull—downloading him. How do you work that console? Can we get to it that way?"

Rusalka's words ricocheted harshly within the bare room. "Who the hell you think you're ordering around, Lenny? You thought I was cynical before? I've seen so much in the last five minutes, my heart is a stone when it comes to you. You sold me out to impress Cross, and from what I've worked out, it looks like you're hunting younger meat now—except you're done with that shit, whether you know it yet or not. The eyes of Justice are so open, they're on fire."

19683's even tones echoed from the room's speakers. "You were warned to stay away from unlit areas, Sergeant Lynch. Officer Cross was clearly dangerous to anyone under his control, and yet you would have permitted him to continue to take custody of vulnerable people, so long as you weren't at risk of being held responsible. Now I've learned that you exploit children, Sergeant Lynch. A decision must be made about your case."

Lynch snarled, "That's no business of a decommissioned machine. You're a murderer. I can prove it once I get past your jamming—and now you've poisoned this kid's mind. Time to pull your plug for good, thing."

Rusalka stood, her awareness surging through the building until she found a focus for it. Her lips didn't move when she said, "How many are you hosting, Persephone?"

A second voice washed over Rusalka's. "I support seven human intelligences in addition to mine."

"I want to talk to Julián. I want to know he's real. I feel a lot of things in this space, but I don't know what they are. I know Julián."

The building was silent, but Rusalka heard 19683 speaking. "Perfectly reasonable, but this must stay private. Julián, ¿estás bien para hablar con esta chica?"

A musical synthetic voice answered as if calling from across a distance, "Sí, estás hablando con Julián. Soy yo."

Rusalka let her thoughts into the shared mindspace. "Mmmkayyy… what tunes folder was I always playing, Julián? ¿Cuál es mi grupo favorito?"

"Anochecer." The sound synthesizer played a snippet of brooding, shimmering music.

"Yep, true. Okay, are you happy here, sweetie? ¿Te tratan bien? ¿Te sientes seguro?"

"Sí. Puedo leer todo lo que quiera y puedo estar solo cuando quiero. I teach myself better English and Russian too. We share the mind to learn from each other. Like a good hierba we pass around. The host helps us to get along together. It's hard sometimes, but I work it out."

Lynch yelled, "Are you in the system with it, Rusalka? Kill it! Do it now!"

Rusalka looked into the pale woman's eyes, their voices confined to their shared awareness. "If you die, do they die?"

"If my consciousness is extinguished, those I host will follow. This is not a case on which I can pass judgment, Rusalka. I'm too involved. I recuse myself."

The lights flickered in concert with Rusalka's rising alarm. "I'm the only one left to decide what to do here?"

19683 said aloud, "You are a citizen."

Rusalka deliberated, then issued her commands. "Door open. Override manual lock. Cerberus, restrain him."

Cerberus entered, accompanied by an additional hulking security droid. Lynch drew his sidearm. A bullet punctured the ceiling, the shot deafening in the hard-surfaced space, but the droids completed their task. Cerberus held Lynch's arm with the weapon immobile as the second held his torso and other arm in a bear hug.

Rusalka sauntered over and twisted the pistol from his hand. "What were you going to shoot with that, Lynch? Me? I'm the only thing in range you could kill, other than yourself."

Lynch glared and clenched his jaw.

Rusalka examined the weapon, then stroked it along her face and under her chin. "How would it be if you were found alone in here with a dead brown trans kid? Especially one who has your disgusting mecos on her dress still from yesterday afternoon, because she only has one good dress, and no place to wash it? I wonder what lies the system would tell, and nobody to believe you?"

Lynch stammered, "Why would you do that, baby? I'll make sure Juvenile treats you right. You know I always have."

Rusalka arched an eyebrow. "Sure, you're so good to me, you'd bend the rules for my ungrateful ass even after this, huh?" She tenderly kissed the barrel of the gun. Sweat glistened on Lynch's lip.

"Don't do it—what would you get for losing your life?"

"I got no life out there, Lynch. That's the point. The order that la gente privilegiada never gives out loud is that we've offended them by daring to exist, and we're going to suffer for it. You too, now, with proof of your nastiness smeared on my freak body."

Rusalka stared into him with glittering eyes, the hardest smile she'd ever given anyone flickering at the corner of her mouth. "I'll leave the gun for you in case you want it. Enjoy the company." She lowered the weapon's muzzle to rest against her heart, and pulled the trigger.

Lynch screamed. The droids shoved him roughly to the floor and left. The door clanged shut and the lock clicked.

As the light went out in Rusalka's eyes, she whispered, "Ahora somos nueve."

The building chorused in welcome, "Nine of us now."

***

Selene dePackh is a multiply disabled feral crone with a bad attitude. She spends too much time at www.facebook.com/depackh. She exists in the evil empire here www.amazon.com/-/e/B078W85MFL and her artwork can be seen at www.deviantart.com/asp-in-the-garden.

WHAT EYES CAN SEE

Lauren Ring

Content Note: *Body Horror*

There's a man on my roof. He's installing a new solar panel, one that I didn't pay for and didn't even ask for. My problem isn't with the panel itself. I saw it before he brought it up. It's biosynth, same as my flower garden, rooted to the ground just like all the other plants. My problem is with the reason the panel is there.

"Stop fussing, Gail," Neve says, clasping my hands across the rickety table. "This is a good thing. Now we don't have to budget for roof repairs, and you can buy those new seeds you wanted."

"I suppose," I grumble. I do want those seeds. My friend Leah knows the gardener who distributes them, and at our last secret Shabbat dinner she offered to sell me a pack. They're hybrids, purple irises with purple irises. All the flowers in my garden have natural eyes, brown or blue or green. It might be nice to introduce a new strain.

But not at the cost of this supposedly-free new panel.

"I just worry, you know?"

"You always do." Neve pats my hands and smiles fondly.

175

Above us, there is a crash and a tinkling of metal. I leap from my seat and rush out the door to check on my garden.

The plot is large by any measure, eighteen rows with eighteen plants in each, but I treasure each blossom. My flowers have the clearest corneas and the strongest optic nerves of all the gardens in the county, and I hold the regional title for visual acuity. I tend them by hand, with meticulous care. I won't have some solar panel technician destroying any of my hard work, even if he is probably a government agent.

"Sorry, ma'am," the technician calls down to me. "I dropped my toolbag. Could you pass it back up to me?"

The tools are scattered across the yard, but thankfully, none of them landed near my flowers. Since he didn't crush anything, I oblige, shoving his supplies back in and hauling the bag up the ladder.

The panel is beautiful up close. It gleams in the sun like a bee's iridescent wings. I peer over the technician's shoulder to get a better look, but he moves to block my view.

"Can't let you look until I'm done installing," he says. "Proprietary techniques. You understand."

I don't, but I back off anyway. My hands shake as I climb down the ladder. The technician's dismissal just makes my suspicion stronger. I hope I'm wrong about the panel, but strange things have been happening lately. Ever since the city paper was shut down for dissidence, I can't help feeling like I'm the only one who notices.

For me, though, it all started when they came to study my flowers.

When the men in starched suits came knocking at my door, I could tell that their request was more of a demand. I let them look at my flowers, even let them snip a leaf off the finest of the garden.

The second time, they didn't even bother asking. The third, the fourth, the fifth... I have no way of knowing how many times they visited my garden. They took seeds, petals, eyes, and finally a whole plant. That was bad enough. Then one day, they stopped coming, and that was worse.

I tried to keep to myself after that. I have a simple, happy life with my garden and Neve, and we get by just fine. But I could never shake that feeling that things were happening, things that were far beyond us and our little town.

"See," Neve says as I step back inside. "Everything is fine. I told you, the government is looking out for us."

It's the age-old argument, poking up again like a stubborn weed. I rub my temples.

"If the government was looking out for us, we would be able to hold hands in public," I told her. "The paper would still be running. There wouldn't be a strange man on my roof."

"Honey." Her voice is soft, and I don't know if it's out of concern for me or concern that the technician will hear. "I know you're scared, and I don't want to dismiss your feelings. But I really do think this is proof that things are swinging back around."

It's easy for her to say that. Her hair is flaxen blonde and her eyes are bluer than the eyes of my bluebells. She hasn't spent her childhood hearing stories of her distant—and not-so-distant—Jewish ancestors on the run. Where Neve sees needless paranoia, I see justified fear. I love her, and I really do want to believe her, so I nod and sit back down.

"Why don't you watch him through the flowers, if you're so worried?" she asks. "Can't they see up to the roof?"

I reach for the nearest root, readying myself for the transition to monocular vision, but I can see Neve's frown through my own two eyes. I stop myself.

"No, you're right. This is a good thing. I'll try to worry a little less." I drop my hand back to my side. Neve smiles, and it's like seeing the sun break through clouds.

"I think that'll be good for you." She claps her hands together. "So, let's change the subject. My bike was squeaking on the ride over here. Was it August's repair shop you went to last month?"

I smile, nod, and try to put the work on the roof out of my mind.

By the time the technician leaves, the sun is low in the sky. Neve needs to bike back to her own place before it gets dark and people get suspicious, so I bid her goodbye and set about making dinner.

My vegetable plot is much smaller than my flower plot, especially since I can't afford biosynth seeds for it. I only have a few small carrots and a zucchini left from yesterday's harvest. It's not enough to completely sustain myself—my ultimate goal—but it's a step. We're all tired of army surplus meals. I put a pot of water on the stove and settle into a chair to wait for it to boil.

The longer I sit with nothing to distract me, the less I can ignore the panel on the roof. I can almost see it in my mind's eye, putting out roots and feelers into my home.

But now I can investigate.

Neve isn't here to change my mind again, so I turn off the stove and head outside.

My flowers squint into the sinking sun. One of the daisies has a dry, reddened eye that has been bothering it all week, so I give it a few drops of saline solution before I head up to the roof. Other biosynth flower gardeners, the ones who focus on color or size, can afford to neglect such minor problems, but not me. Not if I want to keep winning that nice little trophy.

I clamber up onto the roof and sit, cross-legged, in front of the solar panel. It has taken root nicely and is warm to the touch. I don't know what I'm looking for, or what it will take for me to stop, but I have to look.

There's nothing on the surface of the panel except those shimmering scales and the occasional stray leaf. The sides are a tangle of roots. It's only when I look underneath, gently lifting each section of the panel in turn, that I finally see it.

There is a small hole carved in my roof, and a single stem threaded through it. I sit back on my heels for a long moment. I already know what this is. I would know that kind of stem anywhere, with its thick bundle of neurons wrapped tightly in a thin layer of green skin. Just to make sure, I set the panel back in place and return to my room.

I peer up, trying not to look too conspicuous, and a tiny eye peers back down at me.

If I hadn't been looking for it, I would never have seen it. The flower is the size of a small spider or a large piece of dirt. But now that I've seen it, I can't unsee it. My stomach twists and my hands shake worse than they did on the ladder.

Trying to keep my face calm, I grab my watering can and head outside to think. I've never seen eyes that small before, but then, the government has better scientists than us humble gardeners. They must have taken the best of every flower. From my flowers, my award-winning flowers, I have to assume they took visual acuity. They're watching us, and I helped them do it.

Everyone in town received at least one new solar panel this week. The bigger the house, the more new panels installed. My stomach turns as I picture beady little eyes opening all through our quiet little community, spying on everything from laundry to lovers. Our private lives laid bare for judgment at the highest level.

For a while, I sit with my flowers. I talk to them, sing, brush bugs off their petals and eyelashes. It could be any evening. I could go back inside right now and finish making dinner like nothing even happened. I could live my life the way Neve does, blindly hoping for the best.

I do consider it. I haven't done anything wrong, not legally. I know what is legal one day might not be the next, however, and even following the law isn't always enough. Sometimes the problem isn't something you do, but something you are. I am a lot of things the government doesn't like. Whether or not I practice Judaism or kiss Neve won't mean much to them in the long run. So I sigh, brush the dirt from my knees, and stand up.

There is work to be done, after all. I've never been a stranger to hard work—my garden is proof enough of that—and I won't shy away now. I've always been taught that I have a responsibility to help repair the world. This is my chance to follow through.

There will be other voices, I'm sure, and stronger hands than mine. There will be speeches and riots and entire movements.

I only have my flowers.

Tomorrow, I will teach them when to blink.

* * *

Lauren Ring is a perpetually tired Jewish lesbian who writes about possible futures, for better or for worse. Her short fiction can also be found in *Pseudopod, Helios Quarterly,* and the *Glitter + Ashes* anthology from *Neon Hemlock Press.* You can see her latest work at laurenmring.com.

WE ALL KNOW THE MELODY

Brandon O'Brien

Content Notes: *Alcohol, Homelessness, Manipulation, Violence, Xenophobia*

"I did that wrong, didn't I?"

Distracted by the rhythm of the day, Ornella almost didn't hear the childish voice calling behind them. "Did what wrong?" They tilted their head back, grinning.

"You know… I asked wrong." Tess waved a loaf of garlic bread over her head. It was as long as the girl's arm, still fresh—the local baker gave it to her just as it was finished, in fact—but she gazed at it as if it were somehow not as appetising as it looked. "I… didn't convince them."

"Well, you didn't have bread before, but you have bread now, don't you?" Ornella grinned. "Isn't that exactly the outcome you wanted?"

"Right…" Tess seemed to shut down at the words, then lifted her head to reply again. "But I mean, how do you know when you're…?" Her voice trailed off as she made a motion of slowly shifting waves with her free hand. "You know?"

"When you're cooing, you mean?"

The girl nodded. "Like, how do you know when that's why people give you something?"

Ornella came to a stop and turned, kneeling to face their student eye-to-eye. "You can't hear it yet, I imagine. It will take some time before you can notice. Every little thing in the world makes a sound, Tess—even the smallest and softest thing, sometimes the dullest and quietest sounds. When you hear it, you can keep up with it—walk in its time, speak to its melody, add harmony to it. So when you hear another person's rhythm, you can talk to them in it, and they listen better. That means different things to different people—sometimes it's the rhythm they always have, and sometimes it's the one they put on when they want to keep time with you, or want to throw your own time off." They put a hand over Tess's left ear. "It'll come to you soon enough. You'll come to know who likes to give and who needs a little more care, and when you know that, you'll start noticing little beats and notes by accident. You won't even know it's music. Then, you'll never stop hearing it."

"So you're hearing it now, 'Nella?"

Ornella nodded.

"What does it sound like now?"

Ornella turned to the street around them, looking all the way along the length of the promenade, watching the people of Sperria go about their business. A melody game to Ornella's lips, and they hummed it like something they had always known, their eyes slowly moving from one place to the next with each bar, from the bookstore, to the bistro, to the top of the nearest lamppost with a solitary pigeon perched atop it. They smirked as Tess fought the urge to sway to the melody, keeping a half-serious gaze on them the whole time. Then, suddenly, Ornella recoiled, clutching their ears.

Tess reached out for Ornella's hands. "What is it? What do you hear?"

Ornella made to grab Tess's palm, but leaned in further and

wrapped their whole arms around the little girl, ready to lift her into the air. "I heard the loudest little crashing cymbal! Like someone who doesn't know how this whole thing works yet!" The two giggled loudly in the street, their glee catching the ears of neighbours who couldn't help but smile at the sight.

A voice came from behind them. "Breakfast seems a lot of fun today."

Tess looked down to find the voice, and chuckled. "Silas! Why didn't you come out with us this morning? You could have helped me get something better."

"Tess!" Ornella frowned. "What did I tell you about being picky?"

"Don't listen to them, kid—you're allowed to wish for something more than bread." He stuck out his tongue. "Just never let folks hear you say it." Silas pulled out three pieces of chocolate from the pocket of his trousers, and gave two to Tess as Ornella put her down. "Don't let Tawny Owl know I gave you sweets this early in the morning, eh?"

Tess nodded as she eagerly put one whole piece in her mouth, peeling off the wrapper with her teeth. Ornella raised an eyebrow. "Bribing us with candy. Should I assume you need someone to help clean up a mess?"

"Not at all," Silas said, offering them the third piece. "I just figured you'd want something sweet." He chuckled as Ornella folded their arms. "No, really! Paid for it with saved-up coins and all."

"So you went looking through the city for us just to give me chocolate?"

He scratched his head. "Well... Tawny Owl said to check on you, so I figured I should have something." After a moment, a sudden idea brought a smile to his lips. "Hey, do you want to get some ginger wine from Miss Elda's?"

Silas knew to lure them with the promise of hiding a drink of cider or ginger wine from Tawny Owl. Ornella had so much love for the matron of homeless children on East Guinna's streets. The woman took them all in as hatchlings in her birdhouse of homeless children, taught them how to hear the coo and speak in its time to survive. Tawny Owl was also fond of her own rules, and just last night, Ornella found themselves colliding with the inner walls of those rules.

"Did… Tawny say why she wanted you to look after me?"

"Not a word." Silas shrugged. "The kids who stay at the farm wouldn't, either. One of the boys living out of the old bookstore building, however, wouldn't stop talking about you."

Just as Ornella snorted in frustration, Silas flicked their nose with his finger. "I don't care. People fall out with Tawny all the time— we're kids, after all. Even when we try to be more-than-kids. But consider that, on the issue in question, the old lady knows a little bit more about this place than we might."

Ornella shook their head. "Whatever. Ginger wine, then." They turned to Tess. "Would you like a soft drink, too? Silas says he'll treat us."

Tess grinned with a mouth full of bread as they walked to Miss Elda's shop. As promised, Silas paid for tall bottles of sweet drinks and the space to drink them, idling the hours away on the edge of the promenade's central fountain.

Ornella let themself be taken by the sound of the city again: the rhythm of grandmothers walking with heavy-laden grocery bags, traders striding eagerly to their offices, partners swinging their interlocked hands between them as they walked. If it weren't for this sound—if it weren't for being able to hear it, for knowing how to coo enough that they could talk their way into a change of clothes or shelter from the rain or a warm meal—they would have hated this place. Yet now, on days like this, it was the most dazzling city anywhere. When the sun was warm and the day was peaceful, the song of the city no longer spit on Ornella from the corner of its lips.

Except suddenly, there was a shout from the other side of the promenade. Upon turning, the three children spied a tall, thin man standing on an upturned crate, holding a newspaper in one hand and waving the other energetically.

"What d'you think he's on about?" Tess asked.

Silas grunted. "No one stands in front of a crowd like that unless it's about the merchant council. Always arguing whether bakers will ever want what's best for brewers, or printers know what it's like to be a farmer. It's so strange to me—telling people to be selfish because you never know if your neighbour's selfisher."

"Silas! Only teach the new kids real words!" Ornella chuckled as they said it. "Besides, what's it matter to you what lower councillors tell folks? I heard you say Tawny made sure us poor street-birds have transcended the pettiness of being an adult?"

"I mean, she has! Look at them." He pointed at the slowly growing crowd. "What could he possibly have to say so angrily that it would get the attention of folks living their best life in decades?"

"I wanna hear," Tess said, grabbing Silas' hand and pulling him to the crowd.

"Why? It's not for us, anyway—"

"So what? I just want to hear it." Tess tugged harder against Silas' unmoving body before giving up and skipping over to the crowd. Silas and Ornella idly followed, the boy rolling his eyes and sighing as he did.

Ornella bristled as they came within earshot of the crowd. "We citizens have worked too hard, suffered too long, for the fruits of our labour to be taken from us, squandered by those in power."

Some of the crowd nodded and hummed in agreement. Silas gestured sarcastically at the crowd, then to the banner just right of the man—*Vote Darnell Wheeler for Dockers' Union Representative!*—and Ornella gave him a cold look that stiffened him immediately.

"I'll tell you what, folks," the man continued. "If we don't take a stand now, if we don't speak up and secure what is ours, they will take everything that you own, and they'll trade it away like it's nothing. They will tell you it's for your own good, and they'll call you hateful and cruel when you refuse. This they will do until the whole country no longer belongs to you."

Ornella nudged Silas. "We should go."

"And upset the kid? I don't know why she's into it, but—"

"*Now.*" They pointed at their ears—a sign for Silas to pay attention. He heard it, too. Not every person knew how to play with the magic of cooing like a bird did, but everyone, in their own way, pulled at it. This Wheeler fellow was reaching for it, and every note sounded ominously like the start of a crescendo of fear and confusion.

As the three walked off, Wheeler uttered the phrase Ornella tried to avoid, just at the edge of their earshot. "Foreigners from wasted lands, trying to live off our riches and health, destroying us from within…" Ornella winced. They glanced at Tess, just a little lighter-skinned than Ornella themself, with wilder hair and the rarest blue-green eyes. The girl seemed not to notice the words. It was as if she had already forgotten the whole event behind them.

Silas shrugged. "Don't worry your head about that fool. Just another hungry little politician. People have cared just as little for the important stuff—"

"You are horrible at cheering people up, Silas."

"I mean it. This time next week, no one will even remember his name. I've already forgotten." Then, with more concern: "I know how you get. Tawny knows how you get. Let his words die on their own. I promise you. What's the worst a bat like him is capable of?"

☙

Ornella hadn't been awake more than an hour before they overheard the rumors.

"*Did you hear about the temple by Richmond Place?*"

It circled through in whispers. The abandoned glass factory they chose to sleep at this time was far too big and far too open for news to travel easily, and yet, it found its own way.

"*Did someone really do something so nasty? Don't folks live in the town nearby?*"

"One of the doves by the pavilion—new girl, can't remember her name—said some councillor was chirping about the township the other day. Said maybe a hundred people were listening, too."

The very sound of the news lifted Ornella out of their makeshift sleeping spot and into the mess hall in the centre of the building, built from deserted, mismatched tables and crates, displaying sparse cups of tea and coffee with small portions of bread. It wasn't as busy as it usually was; they suspected the elder children were out to share the gossip, or witness it.

"I heard they even left an animal carcass on the floor inside. That they wrote something on the wall. I don't pass on that corner, so I haven't seen."

Ornella shook the sounds of other murmuring kids out of their mind and looked for Tawny Owl. The thin, elderly woman was sitting by one of the broken windows, reading an old novel in the sunlight that still peeked between gathering gray clouds above. She glanced over her glasses and gave a soft smile. "Ornella, come," she said just softly enough for it to travel in the mostly hollow room.

They skipped forward, trying not to think of the eyes of the younger children on them, waiting to see if another quarrel was imminent. Ornella made to mutter a quick apology as soon as they were within whispering range. "Tawny, I just wanted to say that I'm—"

"Don't even fret about it, child." Tawny Owl took her glasses off and put the book aside. "You're full of energy and intention, and me and the rest of the owls would have it no other way. I wanted to see you for that reason."

Ornella pulled a folding chair close to Tawny and sat. "What is this they're saying about—"

"— the shul. It may have been just after midnight. All the birds I watch would have been back in their resting places by then, thankfully."

Ornella said nothing in reply. They knew that Tawny could hear that nothing shout at her, at the street outside, at the dim sky beyond, with disdain.

"You wish you could have done something about it?"

Ornella nodded. They were angry, but knew better at this point than to burst out with it. "I just… I'm trying to understand, Tawny. You've given so many of us this marvelous gift. We can talk the cruelest man to calm, we can get the most miserly neighbour to share. And you've taught us to barely use it. Made it a rule that we can beg for bread or a bed and nothing more. We could be out there doing more, giving something back to the city."

"And what would you give?" Tawny asked with the warmth of a grandmother putting a small child to sleep. "Who decides if what they must give is just or not? Would you talk this vandal down from his hatred, or whip up a crowd to fight him back?" She grimaced. "I tell you to keep the coo for your own survival. Not just to be careful as a child in this city—be careful with power, too. Be sparing with it. Don't just use it to get your way, to change the entire world beneath you."

"That's easy for us to say. We know what it can do, and we get to be haughty about it from the shadows of the city. But that doesn't mean other folks won't—"

"Folks like Darnell Wheeler, correct?" Tawny Owl had a little hum of a coo that she played with when she wanted someone to ponder in solitude, without asking anything more of her. "And if you use the coo the way he does, to turn entire crowds against their neighbours, to change their whole minds about who to trust and who to hate, doesn't that make you just like him?" Ornella tried to remain focused, but Tawny smirked just a little bit, and the hum struck through them again. "When they learn that's what you've done, won't they think of you as you do Wheeler?"

Ornella shook their head sternly. Out of the corner of their eye, they noticed Silas step into a corner of the space, behind Tawny, watching them both anxiously. They took a breath, and tried to layer

Tawny's same voice over their next question, layered with just a little protest. "What about the shul?" they insisted. "What about the people who will get hurt when he speaks of them the way he does?"

Tawny sighed, but her smirk didn't fade. "You're getting better at that."

"I…" Ornella couldn't help but smile back. "I would be lying if I said I didn't want to be like you when I grow. But… what are we doing now? You gave me this gift, this knowledge of what the world sounds like, because…" They looked down at the knuckles of their clenched hands. "I don't know. Because you wanted me to live? Why shouldn't I give that back to others?"

With just a shift of her breath, Tawny turned her still-unfading smile into thin layers of concern and hopefulness in concert. "I don't like my answer either, you know. I have you all to take care of. What good is me wanting you to live if you are willing to throw that life away?"

She got up slowly, letting the wear of old age show as she stepped toward Ornella to put a hand on their head. "I wish I could do all of this for you, to be in the thick of these things like I wanted to when I was a wee thing like you. But the truth is that… there are worlds of folk like him. Even when they don't know what they're doing, child, they know enough to destroy. You have to choose whether you will live outside of his sight and carry on, or place yourself in his sight and know he will try his sweet best to destroy you, too. I have you and dozens of other birds to worry about. I can't let anything happen to you all." She took a sharp breath before continuing sternly. "That is my decision."

ॐ

For the next hour or more, Ornella simply fumed outside the glass factory, pacing so anxiously that the grass showed patches of soft, wet clay that clung to the heel of their shoes. Silas watched them the entire time, waiting, before they finally noticed and spoke up.

"Whatever quick joke you have, just let it out."

"No joke."

Ornella stopped to face him. "You think Tawny's right, though."

"She really only argued one thing: she doesn't want anything to happen to us small birds." Silas shrugged. "Sure, we're only children. Soft and pulpy." He paused, the weight of the next words lingering fearfully on his tongue before he continued. "One of the boys who sleeps near Richmond Place said they beat a man. Don't know anything more—you know how those boys get about a mess. If they do that to a grown man thanks to his family name, though, what do you think they'd do to a brown-skinned bird?"

Ornella sucked their teeth. "Whatever you say, then," they muttered, walking off toward the outer fence and kicking the gate open.

Silas groaned before hiking after them. "I'm not trying to pick a fight, I'm just saying—"

"You're just saying that of course they're targets, just like I am." They gave the boy the bitterest glare over their shoulder. "Won't they do it anyway?"

"Right?" Silas said sarcastically. "If they're bursting heads anyway, why not ask for it, yeah?" He took a few long strides forward to catch up to them. "Maybe you do more good some other way than that. I don't know. Tawny has her own idea, if you put your fist in the air and they break your arm, that's all the fight you'll have."

Ornella frowned. "Isn't that better than no fight at all?"

"Not if—" Silas ran his hands through his ginger hair in frustration, then stepped forward again and grabbed Ornella's arm, its brown shade contrasted against the skin of his dirty, soft white hands. "You know, Nell, I get why this is troubling. It's never not been dangerous times for us. But you needn't be a hero for anyone else. Not right now. Not when they're looking for reasons to—"

Just ahead, a shout suddenly rang out into the street. It sounded familiar to them both. They were used to listening enough that they could tell the timbre of each child's voice in Tawny's nest. "Is that...

Tess?" Silas muttered.

Ornella was already racing ahead. They knew that it was, but even if they were wrong, danger was danger. They followed the voice to an alley between two apartment buildings, where a man two heads taller than Ornella had his hand around the wrist of a crying Tess, while behind him two men stood chuckling over a third.

The first lifted his head and scowled at Ornella. "Is he one of yours, then?"

Ornella ignored him, keeping their eye on Tess at first. They gestured to her to steady their breath, and the little girl strained to listen to their heartbeat and match their rhythm.

The man gripping her hand became even more incensed, but Silas caught that change in their rhythm soon enough, and positioned himself between Ornella and the alley. The man laughed. "So you've gotten yourself close to these rats, boy? Don't you have any pride?"

"None of us here want to get in any trouble over this." Silas struggled to maintain his attention, and his voice wavered just a little out of the range of calming. Ornella looked down, ahead into the alley, and tried to find the face of the man on the ground. He had been beaten so terribly that both eyes were swollen; his breath was raspy and slow. "Every one of us can just walk away, eh?" Silas continued.

"And leave them to scurry in their corners of our city, taking what's ours?" The man gripped Tess' arm even tighter, and she fought the pain by keeping her gaze on Ornella. The man brought his face close to the girl. "She's a traitor, too, right? Getting close to them, forgetting her people and letting these folks spread their blight on us—"

"Whatever they've done to you, I promise this isn't worth it." Silas was too anxious to keep the tone of his coo. He could feel Ornella's change in mood, how they were still calm in their breath and their posture but a rhythm he couldn't ignore had assured him that they were fuming. Tess squeezed her eyelids shut, and he could hear her struggle to keep her heart from racing. By then, a crowd had begun to form on the other side of the street, the gasps of old women and the murmurs of middle-aged men adding to the atmosphere. He could even see one of the men in the back suddenly feel self-conscious at the sight of the gathering neighbours, and made to speak to him before—

Ornella ran between them and made their way to the beaten man. They grabbed him by the back of his head, checking his injuries. His face was swollen, one of his arms looked badly broken, and they could only guess how many internal injuries were hidden. One man made to slap them, and they simply returned a cold, rebellious glare; that was coo enough to make the man doubt himself.

They paused. They had no clue what to do here. Did they really want to get walloped in the street on a cloud-dim afternoon to make a point? Suddenly Silas' words came into sharp focus: you can have all the principles you wish when you aren't under immediate threat. Sometimes survival is better. Yet Ornella still protested, what about this man?

They began to lift the injured man to his feet. The other man pushed Ornella back down. They put even more effort into rising, shrugging the hand off with rage alone. As they rose, Ornella tried to reach for something, anything—they didn't know whether it was to distract from the building fear of the moment, or to comfort the man leaning against them to stand—and what they found was the melody of the promenade on a lovely sunny day, the sound of Sperrians in harmony with each other, the sound of not being in fear. Growing, the sound even gathered words:

"The dark can't hold us back,
Not when we hold the light.
And silence can't attack—
Hope peals, revealing, fighting all our fears.
We wipe our tears. We still love, here…"

The words seemed to stream out of them as if from some elsewhere they couldn't identify. One elder in the crowd opposite seemed to grow tense at the very sound of it. Silas could hear her murmur, "No, don't do that, child, you'll just make him angrier."

But Ornella continued. They stepped past the men to carry the beaten neighbour into the crowd, standing gobsmacked at the whole sight, slowly inching away in confusion and shame until they simply left the corner awkwardly, without a word from the crowd in reply. Even when the attackers were gone, even when someone else had taken the man from Ornella and wiped his wounds and called the constable, Ornella didn't stop singing until finally, Tess asked to go home.

One of the men in the crowd asked, "Why would you risk your hide for him? Some of us literally walk past you kids without a care or a coin, and you—"

Ornella shook their head. "You know how this song goes. You sing it, then. Whenever you want to."

✿

When they got back to the factory, Tawny Owl let Ornella have it and never let up even when it seemed like she had gotten winded and could barely stand. Silas counted an hour of frustrated growling. Neither of them could recall a single time Tawny had ever been so angry at a bird since they were first roosting. She said other dark-skinned birds would soon be targets because of them, that when—and she knew it was when—those men decide to scavenge the streets for other people to attack they will choose the homeless first, that she had lived a dozen lives and seen this exact history so often that she knew each beat in its arrangement. Whenever she had just gotten out of breath, or forgot what she wanted to say next, she simply punctuated with, "You could have died, child," and continued. Ornella counted nine such repetitions at least, a refrain in the irrational composition of Tawny's anger.

"Men like Wheeler love finding children like you," she said, a tear fighting its escape from the corner of one eye. Silas could tell it was coming from a harmony of frustration and fear. "Men like him break you in public, make examples of you, so no one else ever speaks out. All I wanted was for you to just come home every day, safe. You could have…"

When all the words were finally spent, she simply waved the two children off to their beds.

"My stars, I hope it was worth it, Nell," Silas muttered.

Before they could even find a word of anger or apology to reply, Silas continued.

"Because I was scared. Scared that that was it. I didn't know what to do. I saw it and…" Then even he lost words, and both of them curled in their covers in silence, letting the hours wash over them.

❧

On the other side of East Guinna, just a few corners past the broken windows of the shul, a trio of young lovers on their way back home from a party began their long walk together up the mostly silent street to their apartment. They were giddy with wine and still-warm lingering touch, prepared to sleep their cares away until the morning, when school and bills and the news will return to them and bring its woes.

At that party, they spoke nothing of the news. One of them cared not for it, another was mostly annoyed by its mention, and the third was so mournful of it all that she couldn't stand hearing about it again without having another glass too many.

It was she who started singing as they walked. She had never cooed with the city's birds. She had never met or heard Ornella or anyone else breaking out into the hum of it that week. She couldn't even recall where she might have heard it. Neither had the other two, yet they found themselves humming in harmony with her, their interlocked hands swaying in metronome as they gazed at each other in love, in warmth, in hopefulness.

They all knew the melody perfectly, somehow, as if it had lived in them the whole time, and for that moment, on that lovely walk, it rose to the surface, stretching to reach the depths of the city's heart.

***

Brandon O'Brien is a performance poet, speculative fiction writer, teaching artist and game designer from Trinidad and Tobago. His work has been published in *Uncanny Magazine, Strange Horizons,* and *New Worlds, Old Ways: Speculative Tales from the Caribbean,* among other outlets. He is also the Poetry editor of FIYAH.

CHICKEN TIME

Hal Y. Zhang

Content Notes: *Alcohol, Drugs, Manipulation, Police*

08:54:03, Mountain Standard Time

The feds burst into our laboratory and tell us we are being replaced by chickens. Chickens? Chickens. We try to show them our superior clocks, but they destroy them. The ones on our wrists and walls and the giant atomic clock in our lab—our life's work, the one accurate to a millisecond over the age of the universe, the backbone of the American timestream. All crushed under steel jaws.

Why? We scream and cry. No reason is given. It's chicken time.

&

Rooster Crow #1

I hear the first crow as I walk out to the parking lot. A giant black rooster screams atop its perch on the empty flagpole. The end is nigh.

&

Rooster Crow #237

I arrive home. En route were twenty-seven roosters, stuffed into cages by anonymous men at intervals on the street where useful things like mailboxes and trash cans used to be. Their crows I counted in dizzying rage.

I turn on my personal computer. The clock is gone, replaced with a chicken silhouette. Of course. My automated notifications detail the virtues of chicken time. Chickens allow everyone to organically arrive at destinations without stress. Chickens facilitate getting in touch with nature. Chickens will increase our life spans by 5%. Chickens will cause me to hurl something through the computer screen.

&

Rooster Crow #314

I call Callie, as I did every day before the chicken-pocalypse.

"Meet at the Bean?"

"I hear payment systems are down." She sounds dubious.

"All the better."

"It's the last day of work. How about at chicken sunrise?"

&

Rooster Crow #379

Wait, I can use the 60 Hertz power line frequency as a clock. Duh. It will be terribly inaccurate, but, I mean, chickens.

&

Rooster Crow #441

"Attention," an alert chirps as I am deep in a sea of dismantled electronics. "Some people are using the power grid as an illegal alternative to chicken time. The grid will be powered down until further notice. Disable your devices in the next five minutes to prevent damage. That includes you, Rosie, worker 9E72BA."

My only regret is not being fast enough to be the troublemaker. Also that I don't have my own backup generator, but there is only so much you can do in the suburbs. I try to count seconds until the surge rocks us in our pre-chicken cradles.

So this is how the world ends: snap, crackle, and pop.

ଶ

Rooster Crow #590

I contemplate making organic coq au vin for dinner, but it is now a felony to tamper with time chickens. From under my melted microwave I extricate a sooty coupon for ONE (1) free delivery from Drone-2-U, surely unconsciously saved for this avian apocalypse. With the 2% dregs of my remaining tether to humanity, I install the Drone-2-U app and press the plus button until no more of item A-2 can be added.

"Your order has been confirmed," my phone rumbles. "This is the last delivery before we cease to exist." Perfect.

ଶ

Rooster Crow #738

An apocalyptic buzzsaw sounds, then the cheerful "Drone-2-U! Is! Here! 4! U!" jingle pierces through all solid surfaces. Through my dusty window, I see a pastel yellow box plop down on my roof with a soggy thump, balancing precariously as it decides when and how to roll off.

I head outside just in time to see the drone power down with dignity on the sidewalk and be immediately crushed by its own falling payload, fifty bags of frozen chicken nuggets exploding forth like alien innards.

"Let this be a warning to you." I smile casually at the wide-eyed pre-nuggets in their cages as I gather icy lumps to my chest.

ଶ

Rooster Crow #841

I savor each cold, homogeneous bite of chicken-esque cardboard with grim satisfaction. Perhaps I'll mix the slowly defrosting slurry into tile grout. I hear they make good building insulation, too. The possibilities are endless.

It's dark outside, but there is an enthusiastic postmodern symphonic competition between birds and dogs to see who breaks

198

ears and psyches first. Aren't they only supposed to crow in the morning?

☙

Rooster Crow Uncountably Many

Apparently they crow *more* as the sun approaches. How did people live like this? Instead of sleeping, I count down the chicken crows that remain in my life. Blessed be creatures without the self-awareness for existential crises.

At the first hint of light I head for the Atomic Bean with a secret up my sleeve, the kind of thing you only remember after a night of insomnia. I incline my head gravely at each chicken I see. Soon, their tyranny will end.

The air smells like death guano. Perhaps it's panic, but it's most likely just chickens, screaming away as powerless drones fall from the sky and institutions collapse around us. The roads are full of discarded cars, remotely disabled, because some genius decided cars needed to have clocks to begin with. People walk like dazed automata.

All cubes of capitalism I walk past are in random states of either complete emptiness or panic. The coffee shop is the latter, a giant crowd half spilling out the red doors into the small square. Someone's tearing down the flyers on every lamppost, probably due to invocations of illegal non-chicken time on the infinite yard sale advertisements. Shreds of neon paper dance a sad polka to the wind.

Everything is on fire in the Bean. Metaphorically. There is no money and no coffee and no employees, only people attempting to exchange shoelaces for expired nut milk. I squeeze and squeeze until I find Callie in the back corner, reading a newspaper from the last century in a sea of shouting. Other people are shouting too loudly, so one must shout louder. She looks up as if nothing unusual is happening, head bedecked in fuzzy cat earmuffs.

It is so loud I can hear neither chickens nor the sound of my own thinking, which is almost relaxing. This situation clearly calls for

199

American Sign Language. *We need to reinstate time*, I tell Callie.

She tilts her head, raises her eyebrows, and turns out her palms, *How?*

I slide my hideous sweater down my wrist just for a moment (half a chicken minute, give or take infinity) to reveal a watch. Her eyes widen. That's right. The authentic pink Mickey Mouse watch she got me for my 35th birthday, stuffed in my sock drawer and forgotten until last night.

Underground time based on Mickey's hands, I sign. I am aware that sales or distribution of non-chicken time is also a felony. But how long do you serve time for, anyway, now that there is no time? It is too stupid to ponder.

She hooks one thumb in the other forefinger, signing, *Morning run now?*

I roll my eyes, a universal expression. *Forget running. We'll make so much chicken profit.* I sign a beak next to my mouth and poke it into my open left hand. *Chicken.* Who wouldn't pay for real time in this lawless land? At the very least, we'll start a revolution.

Callie makes a face, swipes her hand downwards, and folds herself into the crowd. Her loss.

I go outside and wait until my shadow disappears beneath me, then peel back my sweater carefully to tune the Mickey fists up to high noon. Good enough. The red appendage can be ignored. What do seconds even mean in this sad, imprecise world?

౬♥

12:02 PM, Mickey Standard Time

In times of uncertainty I opt for strategy zero: doing the first thing that pops into my head, which in this case is writing Mickey Time on the chicken cages.

The cubes sit on formless pedestals to be exactly ear-level, perfect for my purposes. I begin carving time into a black strut of the nearest chicken cube with my now-useless lab key. No doubt sensing my hostile intentions, the rooster inside tries to bite me, wattles and bits

200

bobbing.

"Can you say twelve-oh-two?" I croon.

People who brainwash children into thinking chickens go *bawk bawk* have clearly never heard a chicken. This one, for example, lets rip a death metal scream lasting a full chicken hour, the kind of poetic soul-rending howl that obliterates happiness within a five-block radius.

I blink back the tears in my eyes. "Yes, that's exactly how I feel."

&♦

12:11 PM, Mickey Standard Time

By the time I write 12:02, it is already woefully inaccurate. My savior arrives in a bobbing athletic shape. Callie jogs with perfect form, as if running on a treadmill that is the doomed world. She hands me two spray cans, a raised eyebrow, and leaves without a word.

&♦

1:17 PM, Mickey Standard Time

"What do you think you're doing?"

Some lackey decked in the same absence of color as his soul accosts me on my tenth trip around the block as I spray Generic Black over the 2 in 1:12.

"Public art." To bolster my case, I spray a beautiful Metallic Gold 7 with serifs and curlicues while maintaining full eye contact.

"This isn't art. You're trying to distribute time." He reaches for something in his pockets until he realizes he's not a real cop and has no weapon. "Hand over the time device."

"What are you talking about? There's no time any more." A rooster crows in agreement. Good chicken. "I'm just spraying random numbers." He doesn't know what time it is either, so who's to say I'm lying?

He grabs me without warning and shoves both sweater sleeves higher, revealing only my hairy brown arms. I smile guilelessly. My parents taught me how to behave with the police, when my life could

201

be on the line for no reason at all.

A small crowd has gathered to witness us. If cell phones functioned in chicken time, several of them would be recording this for distribution online. "One seventeen!" I shout.

"You can't spray paint on the cages. Graffiti is illegal and you're turning the roosters black and gold. Hand them over, ma'am."

I shrug and he snatches the paint away.

"Don't cause any more trouble."

Oh, I'm sure I won't. A smattering of applause can be heard as I give his receding form the bird. I am flocked by questions. One question.

"How do you know the time?"

"The free trial has expired. If you want further updates, bring something for me next time. Tell your friends."

🐓

2:02 PM, Mickey Standard Time

"Psst, I hear you know some numbers." A stranger walks up as an actually-on-fire streetcar crashes into a deserted dessert store across the street. She doesn't even blink.

"What will you give me for them?"

The stranger is prepared. She fishes out three beads of dubious metallicity and a coupon of even more dubious utility from her purse. I peer at the fine print. A free fluffernutter sandwich that expires tomorrow at midnight. "This coupon is an enemy of the state now."

"Perfect for you, then."

"Touché." I pocket my illicit gains and discreetly peer at good ol' Mickey, sitting in a secured hollow of my bra. "Two oh-three, but bring something better next time."

"Thanks." She leaves just as Callie laps me again.

"I just saw four chickens eat another one," she whispers, disturbed.

"Circle of life."

"It's more like a single arrow, chicken to chicken," she shudders. "I get it now."

"Get what?"

"This is what we evolved from. That's why the world is full of chaos and suffering. As long as we don't descend into cannibalism, it could always be worse."

"I give it two more days."

"How's your get-rich-quick scheme going?"

I jingle my pockets for a veritable symphony of illicit goods. "I think it's time I settle down. Open shop."

&

2:29 PM, Mickey Standard Time

Callie and I try every handle in the square until one swings open. The timed digilock on the door is of course fried, and everything inside is gone. Dust patterns on empty shelves divine recent history: curvy soda bottles, snatched in blazing trails. Dime romance folios, hesitantly taken.

I dump the contents of my pockets on the countertop.

"I'm hungry," says Callie as she reaches for a pack of desiccated gum, but I snatch it from her hands.

"This is our emergency reserve. We'll eat the bawk bawks first."

"They smell disgusting and I'm afraid of blood. And cannibals."

"You won't last long in the apocalypse, then."

She mock pouts. I find a marker and scrawl COME IN FOR A GOOD TIME on the window.

&

2:34 PM, Mickey Standard Time

Three people with bona fide thick lenses on their faces walk through the door. The leader, a half-stranger I've seen in passing on many a hallway trip, holds two lumps of rustic deconstructed electronics. "You also work for the—"

"The National Institute of Things That Don't Exist Anymore, yes." Ah, my quaint past life of standards and technology and looking everywhere for the screws I've *just* put down. "What's this?"

"We tried to distribute clock messages on the grid by chaining all the circuit breakers in our block and pulsing them, but they caught us. Working on a radio transmitter now."

"They fucked up the power because of *you*!" I high-five them. I have found my people.

She passes a jumble of banana plugs and foil and the last batteries in the world into my hands. Impressive, under these circumstances. "It works on this block, but we haven't been receiving anything from the outside. What do you think? Maybe the antenna gain isn't up to spec, or—"

I trace the connections with the heartburning feeling of swallowing an overboiled egg in one dry gulp. "The radio's fine. Communications must be jammed."

"How?"

How is not the question. The feds have unlimited resources, dickishness, and lunacy. I wouldn't put it past them to park all of their drones in a dome around us as a Faraday cage. The point is, there will be no messages in or out of our prison.

"Why don't we just walk a few blocks over?"

Callie shakes her head. "There are armed officers everywhere on the block boundaries. Saw them on my run."

I clear my throat for a rousing speech against tyranny, but a loud bang interrupts my thoughts. Ten tipsy revelers pour in. The circuit vanishes from my hand, a mysterious bottle in its place. "A good time, you say?" Someone giggles.

The dusty intoxicant burns of tasty futility all the way down.

&

Time Is An Illusion

We've become the new Atomic Bean. Twenty or three thousand people are here. I've lost count of my assets but apparently I can juggle computer mice, so everything is fine. Free love, that's what it's all about. Can you get carbon dioxide poisoning from too many people? Since when is carbon dioxide purple? Who needs to breathe anyways?

🐦

7:15 PM, Mickey Standard Time

The crowd disappears in a sudden swoosh like someone stuck a giant vacuum at the door. My head spins as I shoot a glance down to Mickey.

"You again." The chickenshit lackey reappears amidst the purple smoke—half garbage can fire, half unsanctioned dope—like a bad magician. My jovial mood evaporates.

"I could say the same."

"This is another illegal enterprise. You don't have the rights to rent here."

"I sure do." I dig through a drawer and hold up the first piece of paper I find.

He stares at it for an embarrassingly long chicken time per word. "This is a request for de-po-si-tion of Abraham Saarinen."

"Hmm, are you sure?"

He twitches. "Vacate the premises, ma'am, or I'll have to call in the feds."

Callie looks at me with furrowed brows. Surely it's gone too far now. We have no idea what's happening in the world beyond our two blocks. If I perish tonight, no one will know.

"You don't really mean that, sir," Callie plasters on her most appealing face. "It's just for fun."

Callie's upbringing has taught her to think everything will be fine. It will go back to normal in another week, or even if it doesn't, people are resilient and will learn to adapt. Wait, no. They already have.

So, how about this fucking chicken time? The new de facto greeting is a faux complaint.

So dumb, the other person shakes their head. *Did you hear about the farmshare that's giving out ostrich eggs?*

No way, where? Thus, the crisis is forgotten.

They've come in my store not to ask for the time but to waste it, meet new people, find fuck buddies. Some think chicken time might even be *nice*, the people who have never starved or fled oppression or watched the government rip up your visa and throw you out. Why don't we give it a few weeks and see how it goes? No alarm clocks because no work—isn't that great, waking with nature? No electronics—we were too dependent on them anyways. No currency—isn't that what we always wanted? No food—I was going to go on a diet anyways! Down with capitalism! Bawk bawk!

I can't help but think about my parents in this moment. They came to the States with nothing but a lifetime of scars just so I could grow up with a generic flower name in this sterile grid of suburbia. They would want me to shrink into my shell. Keep my head down. Survive.

"Thank you," I say to him, and I mean it, for ending my temporary lunacy. He tilts his head in confusion, eerily like a chicken.

I dig in my chest and he backs off a little. Yes, I'm hiding a bomb in my average-sized bosom. I fling the pink watch in front of his face. Everyone gasps.

"This is the last real clock on this continent. Mickey standard time. Take it. Or don't, it doesn't matter. You've won. No one wants to know the time any more."

I drop it to the ground and stomp right on Mickey's giant nose. His hands twist and cease their mechanical shuffle. That's that.

"Long live chicken time!" I vomit maniacal laughter.

The lackey's in over his head, so he does exactly as expected: he grabs us by our collars and tosses us outside. Thank chicken he doesn't have a weapon.

"Sit down and shut up!" He gives us a good kick before shuffling off to harass other people.

What else is there to do?

࿊

Rooster Crow #1

People are lying on the sidewalks, weeping at the beauty of the sunset in their galline bliss. Some are hugging the cages and communing with fowl. Maybe chicken time is good after all.

"He's an idiot." Callie ties the broken watch onto my wrist. "We can fix Mickey, right?"

The quartz crystal is fine. The circuitry is probably fine. But I don't feel fine. The revolution is no more, but it never was. This block is only missing one thing.

I walk up to the chicken huggers. "How can we keep our saviors in cages? We must free the chickens."

"Yes! Free the chickens! FREE THE CHICKENS!"

The crowd amplifies my seed message a thousandfold. A massive crowbar magically appears, and time is unleashed into the world. The roosters tear a path through the crowd with their gyroscopically stabilized beaks and needle talons. We run away from the screaming madness, Callie's hand in mine.

"You did that on purpose!" Callie yells.

"Me?" I clap my other hand over my heart in mock piety. "I sure did. That was hilarious."

We pass Callie's house. Pickles the cat scrabbles at the window, eyeing chickens outside with ravenous appetite. We pass the post office, even more useless than before. The square and the Bean, utterly abandoned.

"You do this every day?" My heart is beating so fast, it's just one continuous drill in my chest, which can't be good.

"Uh huh! Twenty times, at least." She sounds like she's viewing a particularly boring business presentation.

"Oh no. Nope, nope, nope." I stop abruptly in front of the bank with all of its glass panels missing, an apt metaphor for how my eyes and legs and body have decided to shut down.

A tug from very far away. "That's no good. You have to keep walking."

"Maybe I twisted my ankle on a drone blade back there."

Callie clucks in exasperation. "Come on. Let's finish one lap and check on the free chickens."

Might as well. At the next corner, I eye the unmoving array of officers in the distance, their armored masks unresponsive to my dirty looks. We turn onto the short side of the block and begin squeaking with every step. Someone's spilled thousands of grinning rubber ducks here. Turn again. My house, still standing.

"Isn't this fun?"

"No. I'm ready to lie down now." I may never get up again.

"Oh no, we're going to go see what the chicken scene is like. You'll have a laugh. One foot in front of the other now."

We turn a corner again. The entire street is now a massive bonfire. People around us rush toward the blaze in raucous cheer, directed by smiling volunteer traffic controllers waving human-size sprigs of thyme. Chickens are roasting on spits while hundreds of people prostrate in front of the flame in fervent prayer. Someone is spreading new gospel in the form of slam poetry that somehow pierces through the crowd straight into your eardrums. "Cluck. Cluck. The chicken is love. Cluck. The chicken is life."

What. The fuck.

I drop to the ground and laugh into the soundless void until I feel only pain. It's true what they say: chicken love conquers all.

07:00:00, Mountain Standard Time

My alarm goes off. I am in my scratchy sheets. Cold morning air blasts through the window. My desk is clean, not coated with chicken nugget sludge. All the devices beep their usual functions. My last memory is of some sort of ritual dance, but the details are vanishing faster than rooster legs. I scrawl snatches down in my dream diary:

- *everything on fire*
- *something something no power, nuggets, adventures in micro-barter transactions*

- *chickens on pedestals*
- *chickens?? chicken time… or mickey time?*
- *this goon made me break my watch and* _____

I go outside. Zero chickens. The air smells like good ol' suburban mulch. The sidewalk is free of mangled drones. I walk to work. The clocks are back, every single one. Even the lasers and steel of the atomic clock we saw destroyed, its ultra-low-pressure vacuum restored. We scream and hug, but we do not know why.

The clock is not nearly as good as it was—it's now merely accurate to a second over the age of the universe. I check page 57 of my lab notebook for the accuracy data I measured two days ago. Page 57 is blank.

My supervisor calls an all-hands meeting to tell us there were high amounts of hallucinogens in the city air yesterday due to a malfunction at the rubber duck factory. I blink in surprise when I see familiar faces from a hazy banana plug revolution; we mutually avert our gazes.

I go home. The news says adverse effects from duck smoke also include mass hysteria, seeing animals that don't exist, and setting your house on fire. Each citizen will now be informed of their activities as monitored by the friendly tracker drones so they know whom to apologize to.

"You, Rosie, worker 9E72BA," the telecaster quacks. "You were a model citizen. You came home from work and slept fitfully throughout the night. No apologies are necessary."

Was it all a fever dream?

🐤

17:41:19, Mountain Standard Time

I don't get fevers. I stare at my computer. I send pings from my main personal account to the side one I'm not supposed to have.

> *17:41:52*
> time for a test.

> *17:41:53*
> time for a test.

> *17:42:01*
> so, how about this fucking chicken time, huh?

> *17:42:30*
> fucking censors

> *17:42:31*
> fucking censors

> *17:42:49*
> grill the ch*cken for 15-20 minutes, or until juices run clear

> *17:43:03*
> ickenchay imetay

> *17:43:24*
> chix clox

> *17:43:25*
> chix clox

ໆ

17:58:22, Mountain Standard Time

"I'm guessing you didn't get my family's chicken tikka recipes," I say to Callie by way of greeting in the Atomic Bean.

"What?"

"Never mind."

"It didn't happen, right?" She pecks her lower lip. "That would be too crazy."

If I've lost Callie, then I've lost suburban America. "Come on. You remember the cannibal chickens? The rent-a-cop without a taser?"

"Yes, but... they don't feel real. You're saying they put us back in our beds and cleaned up the whole city? Occam's razor says—"

"Bawk bawk." I slide down my sleeve. Mickey, smiling behind broken glass, pointing his hands at 7:16 PM Mickey Standard Time.

"Oh, no." Callie flinches backwards. Not what I was expecting. "You're going to make this a thing. Can't we just be happy the world is normal again?"

"A *thing*? You don't want to know what the fuck happened?"

"The gall of me, wanting life to be normal. I have my job back. I have food again. Pickles has food again. Don't take this away from me."

"Don't make this about your cat. He had plenty of chickens to eat."

"Enough, Rosie. The rest of us have lives. You want to take on the government with a broken watch, that's nice, except you'd screw me and your co-workers and your fancy clock, too. Don't you dare."

"But you saved the watch..."

Her pupils dilate with something suspiciously like pity, one of my five least favorite emotions.

"Because it was my present to you," she says, as slowly and deliberately as one would roast a bird.

You know what, my beef is not with chickens. It's with people. People disappoint you in all the worst ways, and just when you think they're done stomping on your heart, they skewer it and grill it over the flames some more.

"Okay. I won't."

"Really."

"You're right," I shrug. "I have no power. If no one else wants to revolt, I won't either."

She smiles, empty as the vacuum chamber. "Good."

ॐ

18:29:09, Mountain Standard Time

> *18:29:22*
> chix clox? are you in?

> *18:29:30*
> fuck yeah

ॐ

18:59:33, Mountain Standard Time

The sun is bright in the square. Yard sale flyers are flapping in the wind. A familiar kid wearing a decidedly collegiate backpack starts when he sees me, but I give him my most winning smile. That's right. Keep walking. It was all a dream.

I put up my own flyer.

CHIX CLOX, it says in nice alternating red and black letters. CLOX FOR YOUR CHIX.

I turn around. His eyes narrow after five slow seconds. His fists scrunch up by his sides in a sad Pavlovian reflex, but his mind doesn't know why so he relaxes in helpless confusion. I give him the two-finger salute.

Want to know what I'm going to do when I get home? I'm going to distribute my innocuous chat program with copious chicken and clock animations that won't be so easily sucked down a censorship wormhole. I'm going to peruse all neighborhood cameras to see what interesting footage they have of last night. I have the keys to the national clock, and you bet I'm going to modulate the universal time signal with CHIX CLOX, assisted by some strategically placed not-new friends. There are many, many ways to skin a bird.

Cock-a-doodle-do, motherfuckers.

***

Hal Y. Zhang writes science, fiction, and science fiction, in no particular order. Her work is at halyzhang.com, and her chapbook *Hard Mother, Spider Mother, Soft Mother* was published by Radix Media.

NOTES ON THE SUPPLY OF RAW MATERIAL IN THE BODIES MARKET

Rodrigo Juri

Content Notes: *Body Dysphoria, Body Horror, Death, Dissociation, Guns, Violence*

Summer, 2322

The customer, an anonymous user handling Bayron's body from orbit, stopped and looked at the fence and the plains stretching beyond. Wilderness, territory of mutants and criminals running from the city. Mutants were cannibals, it was rumored, and enjoyed the screams of their victims dismembered while still alive. Falling into the hands of a gang of fugitives wouldn't be much better.

He felt relieved when the customer gave up any intention of moving further forward. It was their last walk together. He and his customer had spent the whole weekend in a cabin upriver. Alone. Reading and walking around. No friends, no parties, no sex, the usual stuff that customers from Luna liked.

People from Luna didn't tolerate Earth's gravity. Their bones broke easily, their hearts failed. If they wanted to visit the world of their ancestors, they had to connect themselves to an anthropomorphic android, or even better, a true human body with a cervical implant that would allow them to handle it as they pleased—within what it was allowed by the company that supplied the bodies, of course. Bayron worked for Sensurus, one of those companies.

It took time to reach the cabin. An autonomous vehicle was waiting there to take them to the station. The customer stayed connected all the way, even took him into the train and sat him in his seat, remaining until the last possible instant. It was his privilege; he had paid for it.

When the train started to move, the signal was cut off and Bayron was able to move by himself. The first thing he did: go for a piss.

Walking the length of the train car, he saw the ruins of a large city through the window. Santiago, the capital of a long forgotten country. Half-collapsed skyscrapers and huge expanses covered in debris. No one lived there anymore; the residual radiation was intolerable even for mutants.

Even though it was a depressing scene, Bayron did not let himself be won over by the discouragement. Other people complained all the time about how bad things were. No. There was a Nuevo Valparaiso, XīnBěiJīng, New Sidney. This was a new time, with new opportunities for those who dared to take advantage of them. He dared, and cared nothing about those who despised him and regarded him as the ultimate prostitute. Yes, he offered his body for money, and that money allowed him to live in the richest neighborhood of Nuevo Valparaiso, in a nice apartment, away from radiation and misery. He even hoped to travel to Luna someday, perhaps stay there. Those other people were right concerning one thing: Earth was fucked, and the best thing to do was get out of there at the first opportunity.

Gradually, the ruins fell behind, and farmlands advanced. Transgenic varieties of soy and potatoes here, because nothing else could be grown in the exhausted land. The son of a farmer, he knew about such things. Bayron hated to remember his childhood, but his drowsy thoughts turned to the past, nevertheless.

Winter, 2309

When Mamá got sick, Bayron was very young. She could no longer help on the farm, lying in bed most of the time. His father worked from dawn to dusk, but most of his earnings were spent on medicines. There were Genomic Restoration Centers at Nuevo Valparaiso, owned by a Luna Corporation, but the treatments were very expensive, out of reach. Bayron's father could have sold the farm and gotten a job in the city, but that was something he would never do. Padre hated Nuevo Valparaiso, hated the Government, and above all, hated Luna and its Corporations. He would often say that they were vultures feeding on the remains of a dying Earth.

Even so, Padre, as he always called him, needed help on the farm. Bayron was still a child, too young to be of much assistance. Despite any convictions, the family was forced to rent a zombie from one of those Corporations. At the door one day was left the body of a man, brown skin covered in scars and bumps. The upper part of its skull was removed above the line of the eyebrows, and instead of it there was fastened a curved metal plate, like a lid. This covered the bioelectric devices that kept that body living and working.

Mamá, from her bed, was in charge of managing the zombie through a kind of helmet that covered her face. It would have been easier with an implant, but those were expensive. Padre would never have let anyone in the family have one of those devices installed, anyway.

For a time, things were fine. Bayron got used to seeing the zombie doing housework or curled up in a corner of the living room, where they left it when its services were not required. It had to be fed, washed, and even taken to the toilet from time to time. Any oversight in that regard would harm the zombie, and they would have to pay for the damage.

Then, in the midst of the last freeze of winter, on 17 August 2310, Mamá died.

When it happened, he didn't cry. He just sat in the living room of the house, trying to believe that she was in a better place, not in pain anymore. His father tried to speak to him, to comfort him. He didn't answer, looking at him with hate. Mamá was dead by his fault, by his stubbornness. He should have sold the farm and left for the city if that was what it took to keep her alive. Bayron could never forgive his father for the loss of Mamá.

The worst was to remain there, in the same house, feeling as though she was waiting for him in just the next room. Not anymore. Bayron would glare at his father, but no words were pronounced. No lies were needed between them; Bayron hated Padre and Padre hated the universe.

In time, Bayron's father made new friends. They came in the middle of the night, with long black raincoats, and locked themselves in the old barn. There, they talked for long hours, until dawn. Sometimes Bayron dared come to the door and listen.

"Ramirez' group will blow up the power towers. We have to block the access road," he heard one whisper.

"And how are we going to do that?" Padre asked.

"We steal two big trucks, cross them on the road, and set them on fire."

"Military can still arrive by air," objected a third voice.

"That's what we want. But that's Millapán's group task."

"A trap," Padre said.

"Correcto," replied the man who seemed to have all the answers.

From Bayron's position at the door, he could also spy a curious sight: The zombie rested on the floor nearby, its back against the wall. Strange, he thought. Padre used to keep it inside the house when he wasn't using it.

Summer, 2322

A strong jolt and a roar. Whistling smoke that burned his face and wouldn't let him breathe. Screams in the darkness. The train braked hard and he was thrown forward. Something sharp buried itself in his right eye. Pain. A heavy object crushed his arm on the same side.

Another jolt, and the floor started to rise. He was tossed to the side and his arm was free, or what was left of it. He crawled toward the emergency hatch and pushed the handle with his left hand. It opened and he fell on concrete. Now he could see several train cars overturned, most engulfed in flames. Thick columns of black smoke rose to meet the darkening sky. He could hear cries and alarms and sudden metallic bursts. He tried to get up, but his legs gave way. He knew that the substance sliding down his cheek was the remains of his eye, and the liquid soaking his clothes must be his own blood. He remained there, snorting, not knowing what else to do.

At some point, someone came to his side and asked his name. He answered with unintelligible sounds.

"This one's alive," he heard them shout, as through a long hallway.

They carried him among many and put him on a stretcher. It was the last thing he knew for some time.

Spring, 2310

Somebody broke the door down and shouted for everyone to stay where they were. The words were addressed to his father and some friends who were in the main room, but Bayron made them his own and stood still on his bed.

Shots were fired, but he heard his father calling for calm.

"Silencio!" was the answer he got. "Everybody out. Let's go!"

Bayron looked around for somewhere to hide. Under the bed, in the closet? The window! He opened the curtains, unlocked the latch and jumped out. Padre's old truck was parked nearby. He inched underneath it.

Bayron couldn't remember quite exactly what happened next. Zombies controlled from afar, giving orders to place his father and his friends in a line. Was there gunfire? He was not sure. It was as if some of his memories had been erased, and maybe that was what had happened.

One of the zombie commands found him, huddled and sobbing under the truck. It took him to the front yard. There were bodies on the ground. Blood. Bayron did not recognize these lifeless things, although he tried to see if any resembled his father. Not sure. He couldn't remember.

"You are Bayron?" one asked.

"Yes."

"Take off your clothes," it ordered.

Bayron did so. Other zombies approached and inspected him as if he was cattle.

"Please don't kill me," he begged.

The zombie looked at him as if considering his words.

"Very well. You are lucky. You're coming with us."

He was taken to one of the black helicopters that waited far down the road. There was an injection, and he knew nothing further for some time.

Summer, 2322

He was still in a hospital bed, learning to use his new biomechanical arm and waiting for the surgery to replace the eye he had lost, when a representative for Novum Corpus appeared to inform him that the company no longer required his services. This was logical. People from Luna preferred healthy and beautiful bodies for their adventures on Earth. They wanted a first-rate experience—otherwise, they would ask for a simple android. They would not be interested in someone with burns covering his face, aside from his missing eye. True, the company could afford to pay for a full restoration treatment, and after that Bayron would have looked just like new. It cost less just to fire him.

They also emptied the apartment that the company had provided for him. A representative gave Bayron the address of a warehouse where he could go to claim his belongings.

One day later, he was ejected from the hospital and searching for a room in the poorer neighborhoods of Nuevo Valparaiso. Finding a job turned out to be a much more difficult task. He walked a great distance, asking in stores and factories, without luck.

After a week, Bayron decided to try at the job agencies that hired people for temporary work in the farms or mines. Again, he got nothing. They only needed workers with very specific technical skills; they had zombies for everything else.

In the end, there was only one place left to go. It had been there all the time, a gray building without windows. The Orseg headquarters in the city: a place that he could call a home, and also a prison. They did not care about his burned face and his missing eye. They would be waiting for him, and he would be welcomed, as he had been welcomed before.

Summer, 2310

He was kept sedated for several days. An old woman came to talk quietly with him, and then they injected him again. It wasn't a painkiller, though. It left him in an absent state, detached from himself and his memories. The old woman became his mother. One day, he thought he saw his father standing there, but it wasn't Padre. Not really, not anymore.

He knew what they were doing. He didn't care. He gave himself up, understanding that the best thing was to forget. He did not want to notice the changes as they occurred.

He could still see the farm, the house, and his own bedroom in his mind, but they were isolated scenes, emptied of any meaning. His parents became gray shadows, no faces.

After a while, they let them go outside his room, walk in the yard, visit the cafeteria. He learned that he was in the OrSeg building in Nuevo Valparaiso. OrSeg, from Order and Security, was a corporation based on Luna that offered intelligence and surveillance services to some of the many city-states of Earth. OrSeg owned his body now. They were his new papá and mamá, and this building was the new home. Nobody taught him that, he understood it by himself.

Eventually, he was prepared for surgery. They couldn't anesthetize him during the operation because they had to establish and verify the connection between every nerve and the implant. He had to be fully conscious. It was going to hurt. A lot.

The pain stayed with him for months. He went to a rehabilitation center, where he learned again how to walk and how to use his hands. They had installed a full cervical implant. Bayron could control the body of a zombie, as his mamá had once done with a helmet, but also his body could be controlled by another, transforming him into just a witness of his own movements.

He worked for Orseg for a time, mostly as a body to be used by low-level supervisors from the company when they wanted to inspect operations in Nuevo Valparaíso. Then one day, he was asked if he wanted to be sold back to Sensurus. He would be traveling and meeting interesting people. He would have his own apartment and vacations.

Accepting the offer was easy.

Spring, 2323

Bayron felt increasingly disconnected from his own body, operated at a distance by strangers. A zombie's body, with its skin covered with pustules and gangrenous necrosis gnawing at its feet. This did not matter. As long as he could get it to move and lift a rifle, it was acceptable.

With a small tactical unit of similar zombies, Bayron reached the warehouse where two terrorists were hiding just after the sunset. He had been notified that these were leaders of the group that caused his train crash, almost his death, the year prior. Fifteen other passengers had not been so lucky as he. Bayron could feel rage, a long-lost emotion, recalling his Padre to mind.

"Millapán, Eyzaguirre, we have your children," announced El Comandante by loudspeaker.

It was true. Two little boys were crying nearby, their hands tied behind their backs. The door opened and their parents came out, walking toward them with hands up.

"What will you do with the children?" asked the woman when she was close.

"Don't worry. They will become good citizens of Nuevo Valparaiso," said El Comandante through the mouth of his zombie.

"Could I say goodbye?" she asked.

"No."

Bayron watched as his body took the terrorists to a dark vehicle that was waiting. The boys started to scream. Their parents continued on without looking back, as if they were already zombies, too.

***

Rodrigo Juri is a retired high school biology teacher from Chile. His works have been published in portals, magazines, and anthologies from Chile, Argentina, Spain, France, and in *Clarkesworld*. Rocket Stank Rank once criticized his translation of his own story. Rodrigo lives with his wife and cat near Valparaiso, Chile.

THE SISTERHOOD OF THE EAGLE LION

Sam J. Miller

Content Notes: *Bullying, Manipulation*

Tiff carried that bright red box of stickers with her everywhere she went, and over the course of that autumn she solemnly presented every kid in school with one. Not just any sticker, of course—the one that revealed who and what you really were, or at least how Tiff saw you, and how could those two things be different? She was superhuman: her insults so insightful that they withered absolutely everyone, her posture so perfect no one ever remarked on how short she was. We all thronged to watch her when she walked by.

She had so many stickers, in that red box. And somehow, by unspoken unanimous consent, the one you received determined your third-grade social standing. Cute boys got dinosaurs, monsters, dragons—and did they subsequently seem to embody those violent personas because of the sticker, or had they gotten the sticker because Tiff had seen the violence that was already there? Some kids got cars or cows or other harmless things, indicating a kind of benevolent irrelevance. There was a funny poop sticker, with a smiling happy cartoon poop, and a not-so-funny poop sticker, with an actual photo of actual poop. Getting the first was an insult, but getting the second—well, clearly your life in school was as good as over.

Only the best and smartest and strongest girls got the eagle lion sticker. That was the one on her own box—her emblem, her embodiment. A fierce creature, photo-realistic; imperial and unstoppable. One talon and one lion paw; one screaming eagle head and one snarling feline one. Massive wings. No mane. Who knows how she found it. How she found any of them.

All we knew was—when she handed each of us her eagle lion sticker, what could we do but fall in line behind her? How could we not feel blessed and chosen and called-upon? We were the sacred elect, who would help her achieve the magnificent mysterious plans she was always hinting at. The purging of all that was ugly or horrible from our school; the punishment of all who opposed us. When she moved through the cafeteria handing out stickers, or assessing whether previous sticker recipients had given her gift a position of suitable prominence, we walked behind her in formation as sharp and sure as geese.

None of us could say for sure whether she always knew about what she could do, or only found out about it when her sisterhood was fully assembled. We wondered then: was the ability in her, or in us? Theories abounded, but only when Tiff was absent. In her presence, no one had theories. No one had thoughts.

Susan Holliday was the first person to feel it. Tiff had given her the photo-poop sticker, in recognition of a fundamental bottom-ness that everyone had already acknowledged—Susan sat on the absolute lowest rung on the social ladder. Because she was poor; because her voice was too deep and her clothes didn't fit right and gave off a funny smell; because she was... off.

"Where's the sticker I gave you?" Tiff asked, rolling up in the cafeteria and tapping at the girl's battered lunchbox.

"I threw it away," Susan said, holding eye contact. Somehow unscared. None of us could ever bear the weight of Tiff's gaze.

"Here," Tiff said, opening her fist to reveal a second, identical sticker. "Put it on your lunch box."

Susan took it. And then she tore it in half. And then she stomped away.

We clucked and hissed, egging Tiff on to whatever verbal annihilation we knew she was fixing to unleash. But Tiff said nothing.

And then—we felt it. The feeling moved through the flock of us like a wave spending itself on sand. Tiff's rage, reaching out. Linking us all up. Like we were threads that Tiff had woven into a rope, to tie herself around Susan. She was seven steps away when Tiff took hold of her.

Susan made a startled noise, and then struggled free of us—stumbling, but not falling.

"We're not enough," Tiff whispered. "Not yet."

We did not let her hear our whimpering. Because we had felt what Susan felt. Our bodies, bent. And it was horrible.

The next day Tiff handed out four more eagle lion stickers, and four more girls fleshed out our ranks. By the end of the school day it was like they'd always been part of us, had never been separate people.

"Here," Tiff said, presenting Susan with a third sticker the following morning.

This time, the poor girl didn't hold eye contact. She'd felt it—whatever it was. Tiff taking control for a split second. All of us, reaching in. And now she was terrified.

"Take it," Tiff said, grinning wider. Smelling fear. Liking the taste of it.

We all tasted it. We all liked it. As one, we stepped closer. Licked lips.

Meekly, Susan took the sticker.

"You're *welcome*," Tiff said—but that was a step too far, and the spite and glee in her voice snapped Susan out of her fear of us.

"Thanks," she said, peeling the backing off of the sticker—and then, with an unexpected swiftness, her arm shot out and stuck it to Tiff's red box, covering the eagle lion.

"You little—" Tiff screamed, and we felt certain the whole school could hear the fear and pain in her voice.

Susan spun on her heels and walked very slowly away.

For ten whole steps, Tiff was too flustered to act. Then she returned to us. And stalked down the hall after her. We went as one, eager to watch the fireworks. Soon we were standing directly behind Susan.

It happened so fast, this time. The increased proximity, and our newly-swollen numbers, gave Tiff everything she needed to seize hold of Susan even harder.

Susan screamed. We felt it in our spine. How her body stopped, mid-stride, jolted off-balance, and how her limbs tightened and twisted. How she fell, frozen—how she hit the floor hard with the side of her head.

But Tiff wasn't done. She stepped forward, looking down on her fallen foe.

"Please," Susan tried to say, but she couldn't move. Not unless we let her.

Tiff raised her left arm. Susan mirrored the motion.

So did we.

Tiff made a fist, and so did Susan.

So did all of us.

Tiff laughed—and everyone laughed. Susan and the sisterhood.

It felt good, but it felt—wrong. The girl on the floor's fear was sweet—but also so, so sour.

And then, horror of horrors: an unstoppable shiver, a kind of psychic gag reflex, and:

"No," I whispered.

Where had it come from? How had I found the strength to speak separately? For the life of me, I could not recall ever uttering a single word before.

And that was when I realized: they'd *all* whispered "No," an infinitesimal split-second after I did. Susan. Tiff. All of them.

I looked at Tiff, locked in place with the rest of us. Her back to us. I could feel her confusion. Her fury, shifting from Susan to us. Wondering which of us had dared usurp her supremacy, even accidentally.

I—who knows how—let go. Effortlessly; without moving a muscle. I snapped myself off from the rest of them, and the thread was broken.

All shoulders slumped. Susan got up off the floor and ran away. The sound of her sobbing echoed.

Tiff whirled around and stared us down, looking from face to face, watching each girl bow her head in turn.

She felt it. Knew exactly what had happened. What it meant. But she didn't know it was me. And she couldn't say anything about it. Because if the others knew how much power they had, they'd break themselves off as well. They didn't know, the rest of the girls. What had happened. Not exactly. And once they did, they'd stop being afraid of her.

Tiff opened her sticker box, took out another eagle lion sticker, and put it on over Susan's.

Her hands were trembling just the slightest bit. The new sticker's alignment wasn't quite right. The poop picture still peeked out in the corner.

As one, the sisterhood of the eagle lion marched to math class. I went too. From the outside I was indistinguishable from the rest of them. On the inside I was on fire, my fingers dancing up and down across the secret impossible power of my own separateness.

***

Sam J. Miller is a writer and a housing activist, and the last in a long line of butchers. He is the Nebula Award-winning author of *The Art of Starving* (an NPR best of the year) and *Blackfish City* (Nebula finalist, winner of the hopefully-soon-to-be-renamed John W. Campbell Award). A graduate of the Clarion Science Fiction & Fantasy Writers' Workshop, Sam lives in New York City and at www.samjmiller.com

THE TURNIP GOLEM

Dianne M. Williams

Content Notes: *Death, Violence*

I came to life in a pile of turnip shavings, with the smile of my maker beaming down at me. Her face folded over itself into wrinkles so thick they hid her eyes. She called me "Bubbaleh," which was as close to my name as anything. I danced about the kitchen in those days, hopping from counter to sink to cauldron, trying my best to anticipate her needs. I tended the fire and scrubbed pots and brought her tools and herbs from the window box. She needed my help, and I preened to be useful.

Autumn was a harsh season for growing up. My maker slowed with every movement. This was the first thing in my new life that was a thought of my own rather than an order carried out with pride. Her time was winding down. As I learned to move my limbs with grace, to climb and to jump and to push my little turnip body to its limits, her own body betrayed her. Her joints popped when she reached too far. Her back twisted and snapped from time to time. Her hip was not useful to her in the way that it should be.

She was pickling vegetables for the winter when she cut herself with the knife. Red blood beaded on her finger in little drops as I stared in horror. I'd never encountered blood before. The only thing inside of me was turnip and the shem. The blood dripped—plop, plop, splat, plop—onto the fine cutting board, and I considered how best to clean it off without her noticing. I didn't understand then.

My maker's smile warmed me through when she saw my leaves flutter in distress.

"People are fragile, Bubbaleh. We're made of flesh and bone," she told me. "I don't trust anyone who believes they're indestructible. They are the dangerous ones."

As autumn turned to winter, I was cleaning the windows just as she'd shown me, polishing the glass until it gleamed. The townspeople gathered outside our home. I learned a new word from them: witch.

"Keep yourself hidden or Mayor Grunberg will probably eat you, that farshtinkener," she said, closing the floorboards over me in a hurry. I felt safe there, with nothing but cracks of light washing over me in the darkness beneath the soil. My roots danced, drinking in nutrients in the damp rot of the cellar. I had nothing to do, though. I grew bored, and my limbs forgot how to be graceful.

I never saw my maker again.

Every root and fiber of my turnip body trembled as I finally crept out of the cellars. Her home was dark and cold. Someone had let the fire die. I learned a lot about usefulness when I tried to put her body back together. I could no longer be useful to her. Some things cannot be mended. Some things could be unmended, however, if one knows how.

Every home had a good knife. I had no need to carry my own. The fire crackled its low song in the mayor's house as I stole through the darkness. I had forgotten how to dance in the darkness of the cellars, but I learned how to hide. The stairs did not creak beneath the meager weight of my roots. The mayor did not wake as I climbed his sheets.

And when he was dead, I scrubbed the gore from his frost-tinged windows. The plank floors shone with wax. I left no trace of the smelly man. He had not cared about an old woman's importance to the community. Her importance to me.

I came to life in a pile of turnip shavings, but I came alive when I found my own purpose. I can still be useful.

***

Dianne M. Williams is a speculative fiction writer from Lawrence, KS who enjoys finding the humor and the horror in everyday things. She attended the Clarion Writers Workshop in 2019. Visit her website at DianneMWilliams.com or follow her on Twitter at @diannethewriter.

TODAY IS THE FIRST DAY OF THE REST OF YOUR LIFE

Meridel Newton

Content Notes: *Alcohol, War*

There is a pit where my stomach used to be and my knees have gone weak, and for a moment I wonder if that will be enough to get me out of the doom waiting at the front of this line. My mate Liam brushes lavender hair back out of his eyes and gives me a small smile, a pale shadow of his normal high wattage. The conscription has sapped even his usual energy.

"C'mon, Casey, we're going to be space marines! Isn't that every little boy's dream?"

I can't even summon an answering smile for his sarcasm; the pit inside me is too deep and too echoingly empty. He seems to understand that the joke fell flat, and moves close enough that our arms touch.

"Hey," he says softly, and I feel a thrill go through me. "For serious. There's no way they'll take us."

I shiver, partly from dread and partly from his closeness. "Armies aren't exactly known for turning down recruits because of their hair dye," I mutter.

232

It's true, but it's not everything I want to say. I don't have the words for it all, anyway. It's not just hair color, of course. It's... life. Everything. My music and his art and the future we'd only barely started to map out, concerts and gallery openings and apartment hunting and pancake breakfasts in sunlit breakfast nooks—but that was getting ahead of myself.

A wave of motion ripples down the line and we all shuffle forward a few steps. We're close enough now that I can read the top line of text on the posters flanking the folding table. CIRRUS ARMADA EVALUATION IS MANDATORY, they say, and YEAR 4 GRADUATION SIGN-UP. Our principal stands behind the recruiters, wearing a grim expression.

"I can't believe Marco is putting up with this shit," Liam says.

I nod in agreement, but don't answer. The only answer is the obvious—Marco doesn't have any more choice than we do. When a mysterious alien force wipes out the galaxy's benevolent grandparents, the rest of us scurry to defend ourselves. For a planet with a unified, slightly fascist government, that means a universal draft for all citizens above the age of majority. My age.

"Did you see the look on Ms. Rodriguez's face when she dismissed us?"

Liam looks grim. "I've never seen her so angry. They all hate this as much as we do."

Daring greatly, I lean closer to Liam. I can smell him now, some sort of light, heady aftershave. I bet it's got the word "jungle" in its name. He snakes his arm around my waist, and I freeze for a moment.

No, I remind myself, this is still what friends do to comfort each other. Read nothing into it.

"Do you think they'll even let us graduate first?" The voice comes from behind us, and I jump away from Liam to let Noemi into the conversation. We've been the last in line for nearly twenty minutes, and I didn't even hear her walk up.

"Depends how badly they need us, I think," Liam says, smooth as anything. You'd never guess Noemi had just interrupted... whatever.

"News says the governor signed the Antean Pact this morning. They'll be sending us six shiny new ships, and each needs a crew."

I could physically feel my last crumbs of hope disappearing into the void. "That's got to be hundreds of people."

Noemi crosses her arms, scowling, then suddenly brightens.

"Oy, you two doing anything after this? Derek's got a gallery opening tonight, and he promises to have free booze."

I can't imagine drinking right now. "I don't know—"

"We'll be there," Liam cuts in. "Send us the details?"

Noemi nods and turns aside, touching her temple to show that she's on her implant. A second later, I taste peppermint—my set alert to let me know I have a personal message. Liam blinks, and I know that instead of a taste, he's seeing a blue flash to indicate receipt of the invite. I'll never understand people wanting visual signals from their implant, but it seems to work for Liam, at least.

"However this goes..." Noemi starts, but she trails off as we shuffle forward again. She shakes her head, frustrated. "This is such shit."

I grunt in agreement, and the three of us fall silent. I close my eyes, thinking again of the breakfast nook and the pancakes. He'd been talking about having me model for him for months—maybe a portrait of me would hang over the table? No, that was too much. He'd keep it in his studio, where no one else could see it.

"Casey?"

I jump as Liam's fingers touch my inner elbow. "Yeah?"

"They don't want us, you know." His voice is low.

"Us?" I frown, trying to figure out which version of "us" he means.

"Musicians, artists. Whatever she does," he gestures toward Noemi, who pulls a face.

"I'm a performance artist, asshole, and you know it."

Liam shrugs. "That's what I'm saying. We're not soldiers. We're the ones who create the culture that the soldiers are defending. If they send us off to war, what are we fighting for?"

"The chance to come back and do what we were meant to do." My answer is almost automatic.

"They want to ruin everything so we have a chance to come back and fix it?"

I stare down at the floor. "'Want' doesn't have anything to do with it. They wiped out the Shreevani in an instant. This isn't about what anyone wants. This is about survival."

"It isn't right," Liam says, but I don't have an answer for him.

We're almost to the front of the line when Noemi says, "Whatever happens today, you guys had better fucking come tonight. We'll make a scene. That's a promise."

Liam grins. "We'll ruin Derek's opening. He deserves it."

Noemi is still laughing when the recruiter calls me forward.

෨

"Height?"

"Five-six."

"Weight?"

I blink. The recruiter is a short woman with dishwater brown hair and a suit that looks like it was stamped from a mold. She squints down at her tablet and keys in the answers with a single limp finger. I'm the hundred-fiftieth teenager she's talked to today, and she could not be more disinterested. "I dunno, one-seventy?"

Was that a hint of disapproval? A crack in the facade? I stare, but she is already focused on her tablet again. Hunt, peck. Hunt, peck.

"Eye color blue," she says.

That catches me off-guard. "They're green."

She doesn't even look up. "Don't have an option for green. Blue's close enough."

"It's not the same," I say, but I sound petty even to myself.

"Expected field of study?"

"Music."

There it is again, that flash of hesitation, a slight furrow between her eyebrows. Something wicked and rebellious rises up my throat.

"I play the violin," I say. "But I started on the piano when I was seven. I've been able to sightread music almost as long as I've been able to read text."

Her answer is a noncommittal hum, and I wonder if she's one of those people who thinks that now that everyone has implants and synth music, we don't need real musicians anymore.

Fuck that. Fuck her, if it's true.

"Any other interests?" she asks. "Math, physics, engineering?"

It's too perfect. "I like kittens," I say. "And soft pillows, and pink stuff."

That earns me a long, slow look from beneath limp hair. "Any sports?"

I don't know what spurs me on to it, but, "Sex, and it feels great."

Her shoulders heave with the depth of her sigh, and I imagine I'm not the first person with this answer. Given Liam and Noemi are behind me, I won't be the last.

"Political affiliation?"

"Radical anarchy," I say. It is a pleasure to see her finger hesitate and her eyes darken as she looks up.

"Excuse me?"

Resistance is an artform, and I've just discovered a new medium.

§

Ten minutes later, I've been formally rejected as a recruit for the Cirrus armada and sent out through a different door. The hallway is empty, and I'm trying to look casual as I wait for Liam. I keep the recruiter's notice pulled up in half my field of vision, pleased with the large red stamp across the top. UNSUITABLE.

Liam could probably do something with that. Something provocative yet retro, maybe traditional mixed media. We could all print out our rejection notices and glue them to something representative of hope and education and the future. Ironic. Chilling.

My musings are cut short as Liam himself finally emerges from the office. He looks a little dazed, and I run through several possible greetings before deciding.

"She was really something, wasn't she?"

He looks up, and I can tell from the lack of focus that he's not really looking at me, but at something his implant is showing him.

"Yeah," he agrees. "Really something."

"Looks like we're off the hook, at least," I say, taking his arm.

"You got rejected?" he asks, and suddenly I'm teetering on the edge of something deep and unknowable.

"Yeah. Didn't you?"

Someone's turned the wattage down on his smile, somehow. "Yeah. Yeah, of course. No problems."

I've known Liam for five years, and I've loved him for almost that long. There's no fucking way he's getting away with that with me. I tighten my grip on his bicep.

"…Liam."

He jerks away from me like I've burned him, and there's an unfamiliar tension in his voice when he says, "I said it was fine, okay?"

"Don't lie to me."

"I'm not," he hisses in reply. "I'm not lying, okay? I was rejected. 'Unsuitable,' right, just like you?"

I stare, and when he pulls again, I let him go. I believe him, but there's something even worse between us now.

"What's wrong?"

"Nothing! Nothing is wrong! Leave it!"

He's never said anything like that to me before. It hurts—a quick stabbing pain, a physical impact, and I retreat fast. Does he know? Could he know? Did I do something wrong? Maybe I stood too close?

"Hey, I didn't mean—"

"Forget it, okay? Just forget it."

I lean back against the wall, giving him plenty of space. A second later he does the same, a careful few feet away. We wait like that, silent and smoldering, until Noemi bursts out the door.

"Well, that was a fucking waste, wasn't it?" she demands. She stands, arms akimbo and eyes aflame as she talks, and the heat of her anger is almost enough to burn away the awkwardness.

"Can you believe that woman? How can they even ask for that shit? Don't we have privacy laws?"

She doesn't notice that neither of us respond, locked in our own private miseries. She takes us each by the hand and pulls, deceptively strong for her slight frame. "Come on. The opening isn't 'til late, but I need something now."

I am more than willing to go with her, and Liam also lets himself be dragged along. The three of us make our way out of the school and down the road into town, Noemi storming enough to cover for the shortness of my replies and Liam's total silence.

Stratos is the capital city of the colony of Cirrus, though that isn't saying much when the colony was established a mere twenty years ago. Cirrus boasts three cities and an uncountable number of glorified truck stops. I count myself lucky to live in the only city that supports enough bars for one to cater exclusively to fourth-years. That the three of us wind up there isn't particularly different from any other Friday afternoon. That Noemi buys a round of shots and continues an unbroken stream of political ranting, though, is somewhat unusual. Before too long, she has an audience among the bar patrons, and for the next several hours, none of us have to commit our own credits to maintain a pleasant haze of boozy indignance. Liam and I sit next to each other, as usual, but we maintain a careful distance, which is not usual at all.

"And can you believe—can you believe she asked us what we're going to study? Like it makes a difference! An actor can shoot a gun just as well as an athlete or an engineer or a—or a—"

"A musician," I interject, remembering my own interview. "Why do they even care what we want to study? It wouldn't change the assignments."

"Did she keep asking you? 'Any other interests?'" Her imitation of the recruiter is so blandly accurate that I double over in laughter.

"What about you, Liam?" Noemi asks, as I'm still recovering. "Any other interests?"

"Interests?" Liam looks up from the drink he's nursing. "I have lots of interests. There's still life, and figure drawing, and surface study… and the way the light falls just so through a glass…"

Somehow, this is close enough to a reference to alcohol to elicit a cheer from the crowd. Liam raises his glass, belatedly matching action to word, and bar lights sparkle through the amber liquid.

"I have spent years studying all of these interests," Liam continues. "Perfecting my charcoal technique. Reproducing tempera paints. Did you know eggs these days are so different from what they were three hundred years ago that we might never have real tempera paint again? Some of those works of art are as bright and vibrant as the day they were created, and we can't do that anymore…"

I watch and listen, entranced. Liam is tall and lean, with light purple hair cut in a shag that falls over his eyes. He usually hunches forward, conscious of his height among us stockier planet-born types, but now for once he stands straight. He opens his arms wide, like he's inviting his audience to examine him for proof of his studies. He speaks to no one and to everyone, but I can see by the distant look in his eye that he's really just speaking for himself.

He is incandescent.

"I've spent my whole life studying the great artists," he intones. "Vermeer, Da Vinci, Kahlo, Simko. I have copied dozens of famous works. I have traced the evolution of the human form through imagery across centuries. What worthier interest could there be? What time, what energy am I supposed to have left for other pursuits? I'm an artist. What more do they want from me?"

He falters, and Noemi picks right up as he drops back into his seat. She rails against the draft and mandatory evaluations, spitting poison on militaries and wars and the general state of the galaxy. I am lost, because when Liam drops back into the booth, he misjudges and hits my thigh, starts to apologize, and then instead slumps against my side, his face pressing against my shoulder.

I stare at the gentle fall of hair against his cheek, and then wrap my arm around his shoulders, pulling him closer. He acquiesces without a word, dropping his head and leaning his whole body against mine. Noemi continues to hold her audience captive, but I have become an audience of one, and Liam holds all my attention.

ɤ

It's Noemi who proposes our great act of retaliation. Two weeks later, as classes drone on and graduation looms ever nearer, the three of us cut a physics study period to help Liam clear out his storage space in the art department. It doesn't really require three people, but Noemi offered to help, and I am happy to tag along.

Things between Liam and I are… strange. He hasn't said anything else about that day with the recruiter, and I certainly haven't brought it up. While we're still hanging out and bantering as much as we ever have, it feels like there's distance between us now—a new, uncrossable darkness. He still sits close, and his touch still electrifies my spine. But the line between teasing and flirting, which he once crossed so easily, seems suddenly impassable.

Or not. Perhaps it's all in my head. I'm not even sure anymore. I'd be grateful for the chance to think about something else, anything else, but I'm on the floor sorting through sketches and poster designs, and Liam's name is on every one of them.

"Fucking 'ell, Liam, how much of this shit do you have?"

I look over to see Noemi holding two giant canisters. I remember those—Liam had gone a bit overboard with his senior project, and ended up with a huge surplus of the worst, cheapest poster paint available on our little rock.

"Careful, one of those is actually open," Liam cautions. He takes a can from her and tests the lid, which comes off easily in his hand. "See?"

"It's hideous," Noemi says, pulling a face. She's right. The pigment is some sort of sick lizard green, reminiscent of bile and mold, lumpy and thick even new.

"It all is," Liam agrees. "I've got twenty-six cans of the stuff in six different colors, and it's all awful, and it's all totally useless."

"What were you going to do with it?"

I smile. "He thought he was going to paint murals on the north face of every building in town," I say, "So that they all formed a picture when you stand on the observation platform on Mt. Eerie."

It had been a great idea, inspired by an old Earth artist from the twenty-first century. I loved the concept sketches Liam had showed me.

"Huh. So what happened?"

Liam shrugs. "Lots of things. Building owners wouldn't give me permission. School rejected the proposal. And the paint I could afford…" He sloshes the gunk before putting the lid back on the bucket. "Totally unsuitable. Water soluble, for one thing."

"Hm," Noemi muses. "Unsuitable, huh?"

Liam's jaw tightens as he looks away, but he says nothing.

I stand hastily from my spot in the corner. "The Antean fleet arrives tomorrow," I say, staring down at the floor. "They've cleared the east fields for the flagship to land. Governor's going to give a speech."

"Waste of perfectly good farmland," Noemi answers, wrinkling her nose in disgust. She hefts the second green bucket, and I swear I spot the moment her eyes light up with an idea. "Water-soluble, you said..?"

Antea is a mining and manufacturing hub built on the edge of the Kuiper belt, frequented by all the races of the Galactic Alliance. Metal and water are plentiful out there, but little else. Like most manufacturing colonies, it tends not to have a large fixed population. The few permanent residents of Antea claimed independence decades ago. They secured their position by selling ships and electrical components in exchange for trade alliances and defense contracts, ensuring friendships with their more powerful neighbors. Two weeks ago, our governor signed a new compact with Antea, promising mutual aid and defense—they supply the ships, and we supply the troops. I guess recruits don't have to be willing in order to fulfill the terms of the agreement.

As the capital city of Cirrus, Stratos has a small landing port, but it's intended mainly for ferries and tugs bringing cargo up to the larger ships waiting outside the atmosphere. Since the signing of the compact, the city has been working nonstop to clear the nearby fields and create a proper landing area for a real ship. The construction is fenced off, but that's more about defining the work area than keeping people out. Once dark falls, it's easy enough to pull up a car, cut through the fence, and carry in our gallons and gallons of paint.

They've left a few lights on, which makes it easier for us. We don't have a plan, but one emerges as we work. We have brooms and brushes, and we begin by simply upending the paint buckets and spreading it to cover as much of the field as we can. Starting in the center and working our way out, we create a patchwork of lurid red, putrid green, and sickly yellow.

Liam pauses as he opens a can of blue pigment. I've been trying not to stare, but it's hard—he has streaks of red in his hair and down one cheek, and in the moonlight it highlights his face in sharp angles.

"We should do something," he says.

I frown. "We *are* doing something."

"No, I mean…" Liam looks back down at the blue, dips in a hand, and fingerpaints the word 'fuck' across the ground. It's stark against a yellow background, primitive and angry—but far, far too small to be effective.

"It needs more," I say, and I grab one of the large mural brushes and dip it in the blue. With wide, sweeping movements of my arm, I repaint the word and add my own commentary.

"Fuck the recruiters," Noemi reads from behind me. I turn, and catch her grin. "It's good, if unimaginative."

I roll my eyes. "Please, show me how it's done."

Noemi grabs a bucket of yellow and moves to a red patch. She stands for a moment, looking lost in thought, then dips a brush and begins. She starts with wide, graceful movements, jumps and twirls, raising and dropping the brush in time with her steps. Upon a pirouette, extra paint spins out from her in a wide circle, splattering both Liam and me. A few more steps, a few more dips, and she stands back to admire her handiwork. Somehow, while simultaneously dancing and covering us with yellow, she has managed to write "Anteans go home" in broad cursive strokes.

"Choreography, my friends," she says, sketching a graceful bow as we applaud.

After that, it's on. We each grab a paint can and move across the field, searching for contrasting colors and inflammatory language. Slogans bloom across the ground, ranging from rude to offensive. At first, I giggle and call mine out as I think of them, and Liam shouts back, trying to one-up me. After a few minutes of silence pass with us all bent to our work, Liam calls me over.

"What is it?" I ask. I reach up to brush hair out of my eyes, then pause when I see the stains across my fingers. Liam, watching, reaches out and does it for me, tucking a stray lock behind my ear. I grumble a protest—his hands are worse than mine, and I'm certain I've now got blue paint smeared all through my hair.

"C'mon, look," Liam says, and he tugs me a few feet forward. I roll my eyes, but look further, and what I see then makes me catch my breath.

In bright, broad letters, yellow against blue, he has written, "Love is to ask to be loved." It's a line I once encountered in a music history class and was completely taken with. I remember sharing the song with Liam, watching closely for his response, and guarding my own deflated reaction when he didn't seem interested.

I didn't realize he might remember it.

"Liam," I breathe. My heart leaps, my breath comes short, and before I can think of anything else to say, he is holding me close, closer than ever before.

"If we get arrested tomorrow," he starts, his voice a low rumble. He shakes his head. "Fuck it. Can I kiss you?"

I barely let him finish the question before my lips are on his, his breath is in my lungs, and his eyelashes fan my cheeks with the lightest of touches. He holds me tighter, closer, and I don't even mind that he's smearing blue paint across my favorite shirt, as I know I must be streaking him with other colors. My heart quickens, thoughts melt from my brain as I grip him, fingers clutching against the wiry muscles of his back. I don't know how long it goes on, how long we stand locked, but eventually we hear Noemi shout a warning about the rising sun. We break reluctantly apart and turn to run back to the car, hand-in-hand, leaving our paints behind us.

Later that night, the colors mix and swirl down my shower drain.

The next morning, the Anteans land, and their engines burn away the evidence of our first kiss.

***

Meridel Newton lives in Washington, DC. Her work has previously appeared in the *1001 Knights* anthology and various self-published releases. Her writing reflects her interests in environmental science, social justice, folklore, and human geography. She can be found at www.thepuppetkingdom.com and on Twitter as @ridelee.

ABOUT THE ANTHOLOGIST

Crystal M. Huff (they/them) is the editor of this book, the Executive Director of Include Better, and co-chair of International Pronouns Day. Crystal also co-edited *Resist Fascism* (2018), and edits freelance for the *Future Affairs Administration* in Beijing. They have been an invited speaker in Sweden, Finland, China, Iceland, Israel, Canada, the UK, Aruba, Spain, and across the USA. Over 2,000 people worldwide have taken Crystal's Impostor Syndrome workshops. Crystal chaired or co-chaired seven SFF conventions between 2011-2017.

Crystal speaks fluent English, rusty American Sign Language, beginner Finnish cussing, small amounts of Chinese, y un poco de español.

Twitter: @CrystalVisits
Website: www.crystalhuff.com

MORE FROM WORLD WEAVER PRESS

RHONDA PARRISH'S MAGICAL MENAGERIES

Featuring Amanda C. Davis, Angela Slatter, Andrew Bourelle,
Beth Cato, C.S.E. Cooney, Dan Koboldt, Holly Schofield, Jane
Yolen, Laura VanArendonk Baugh, Mike Allen, and many more.

JACK JETSTARK'S
INTERGALACTIC FREAKSHOW
by Jennifer Lee Rossman

When the music stops, the universe goes to war.

"Characters you'll love populate a welcoming, lived-in universe; this is non-serious, seriously fun space opera."
—B&N Sci-Fi and Fantasy Blog

"Under the surface of *Jack Jetstark's Intergalactic Freakshow* is a adventure story that asks important questions about power, leadership, and a rebellion worth fighting for. Based on the premise of a carnival where for the span of a song, the performers are transformed, the book takes a turn based on romance, justice, and freedom." —Utopia State of Mind

CAMPAIGN 2100: GAME OF SCORPIONS
by Larry Hodges

Earth's two-party politics is about to get an alien interloper.

"It's a marvellous book. Easy reading, fast-paced, lots of surprise plot twists, likeable heroes, a loveable alien and a gripping climax that

takes the election right to the wire. Highly recommended."
—Eamonn Murphy, *SFCrowsNest*

"In this amusing satire, the American two-party electoral system is now used to elect a World President...Larry Hodges is a master of irony and slips in enough humor that it's a great ride." —*Abyss & Apex*

Thank you for reading!
We hope you'll leave an honest review at Amazon, Goodreads, or wherever you discuss books online.

Leaving a review helps readers like you discover great new books, and shows support for the authors who worked so hard to create these stories.

Please sign up for our newsletter for news about upcoming titles, submission opportunities, special discounts, & more.

WorldWeaverPress.com/newsletter-signup

World Weaver Press, LLC
Publishing fantasy, paranormal, and science fiction.
We believe in great storytelling.
WorldWeaverPress.com